THE BLANK WHITE PAGE
A JOURNEY OF SELF DISCOVERY

ALI SPOONER

<u>ALSO BY ALI SPOONER</u>

Single Books

From the Cradle to the Stone

Holy Water and Whiskey Scars

The Ghost of East Texas

The Trophy Wives Club

The Bee Charmer

Forever Home

Ruined

Back in the Saddle

Open Your Heart

South of Heaven

Shotgun Rider

The Settlement

Love's Playlist

Cowgirl Up

Twisted Lives

The Epitaph

Terminal Event

Bailey's Run

Erotica

The Wolf and The Unicorn

Series

The Island Series

Neptune's Ring

Venus Rising

The Hunter Series

The Devil's Tree

Bound

Sasha Thibodaux Series

Sugarland

Bayou Justice

Line of Sight

Strong Southern Women Series

Diamond Dreams

Gator Girlz

True North

Footprints

Cast Iron Farm Series

The Mountain Whispers

The Star Child

Soul on Fire

The Sky People

Turn the Page

Songwriters Series
Six Strings and a Dream
Midnight in Nashville
Out and Loud

Co-authored with Annette Mori

Heart Strings Attached

Free to Love

Trouble in Paradise

Co-Authored with K.L. Gallagher

Hat Trick

THE BLANK WHITE PAGE

A JOURNEY OF SELF DISCOVERY

ALI SPOONER

Affinity
Rainbow Publications

2024

The Blank White Page
© 2024 by Ali Spooner

Affinity E-Book Press NZ LTD
Canterbury, New Zealand

1st Edition

ISBN:
ISBN: 978-1-99-104069-5 (paperback)

Editor: Angela Koenig
Proof Editor: Lisa M
Cover Design: Irish Dragon Design
Production Design: Affinity Publication Services

ACKNOWLEDGMENTS

I thank my fans for following my stories and providing great feedback and encouragement. Writing would not be so much fun without you. Thanks to Affinity, Irish Dragon, for the cover art and the team of editors, readers, and publishers who continue to help me grow as a writer.

DEDICATION

I dedicate this story to Laura, my older sister, who is battling through medical issues. You are strong and resilient and the leader of our pack. Never forget, I love you MOST.

TABLE OF CONTENTS

CHAPTER ONE

I stared down at the memorandum on company letterhead in disbelief. I secretly hoped I was having a nightmare, refusing to wake up to my everyday reality. My father, Charles Chastain, Sr., had set a meeting for my younger brother, Charlie, and me to discuss his "Sundown Plan," as he called it. Charlie had always been a daddy's boy, being the only male child, and naturally assumed that once Father retired, he would automatically step into the company's chief executive officer role. Charlie was four years younger than me and held the position of chief financial officer. He had skated through college, passed his CPA certification, and was a shoo-in for the position a few years after joining the firm. Charlie excelled at his subordinates maintaining the workload and was strictly a numbers person.

I completed an MBA at a prestigious Ivy League school and was at the top of my class. A complete opposite of

Charlie, I was a people person and the closer on the majority of our most significant real estate transactions. He could work the numbers, but he couldn't work the people. As the chief operating officer, I kept the business growing, and established the relationships and groundwork for repeat customers. Chastain International was one of the fastest-growing brokerages in the United States and several European countries.

I looked at Charlie, and it was apparent that our father's plan details were just as shocking to Charlie. His face blanched white at the first competition Father arranged for us. I reread the first statement and looked up at my father. It stated, "The first task I place before you is a test of your resilience and creativity." I was comfortable with that statement and continued to read.

"My children, you have served the organization well and brought exceptional skills to the company. It has become difficult to select my successor based on your performance in the office. You both excel in your areas of expertise. I have decided to look outside the box and challenge you to a competition that will allow you to demonstrate the skills necessary to take Chastain International to the next level as a corporation."

"What the fuck?" I heard Charlie mumble. "You want us to do what?" Charlie asked for clarification.

"My instructions should be relatively straightforward. Each of you will be delivered to a primitive location, Tatum in Alaska, and you in Canada, to survive for six months. You will be supplied with the bare necessities to survive and are expected to use your skills to find creative ways to thrive in this environment. I will continue paying your salaries during your absence, but you will have little access to those funds where you will be living."

"Six months, really, Dad?" Charlie complained. "This isn't like sending us off to summer camp."

Fortunately, I remained quiet and allowed Charlie to dig his hole a bit deeper.

"This test will be the farthest thing you could imagine from a summer camp. You will have staple food supplies, protection, transportation equipment, and a satellite phone only for emergencies or to order supply drops. Or to call me if you want to tap out," he said, glaring at Charlie. "If you can't survive six months with nothing but your instincts and creativity, you surely won't thrive in running this company."

I continued reading while Charlie continued moaning.

"We will leave in thirty days?" I asked.

"That's correct. That should allow you time to get your affairs in order here and to prepare for life in the wilderness. I will provide more detailed information about your living arrangements and basic supplies tomorrow after this has more time to sink in. You will be within a day's travel of a small town or village that can be utilized to resupply your needs. However, this must be done by land or water before winter arrives. Afterward, supplies are only delivered by bush plane once a month. You will be expected to hunt, fish, and forage for your food."

"At least you won't leave a fiancée behind," Charlie growled at me.

"I'm sure Carol can survive without you for six months," I said.

"Tatum's right. You shouldn't marry her if she can't support you through this adventure."

"If we choose not to participate?" Charlie asked.

"I am prepared to cast a search net for someone suitable to run the company after I retire," Charles stated.

I nearly laughed when I saw Charlie's face go from white to green. I hadn't realized how whiny he was when challenged. He must have noticed the smirk on my face. "This is right up your dyke alley. Was this your idea?"

"I am as surprised as you."

"I've been thinking about this for months. If you have a suitable challenge to test your fortitude, I will entertain it, Charlie, but your clock is ticking."

All Charlie could do was shake his head.

"I suggest you learn how to survive during these next thirty days. You have much to discover about living in primitive conditions through the winter."

I nodded to him. "Is there anything else you want to share with us today?"

Charles chuckled and shook his head. "No, I believe I have shocked you enough for one day."

"It certainly wasn't the meeting I was expecting," I said with a smile.

"We will meet tomorrow morning again," Charles said and left.

"What the fuck," Charlie growled, and stormed from the conference room.

†

I returned to my office and poured coffee before going to my desk. "You have certainly rocked the boat on this one, Dad."

My fingers flew across the keyboard as I searched for books and manuals for surviving winter in Alaska. I had done primitive camping with an ex, but I suspected this would be far more challenging than I had ever experienced. I printed off lists of gear and supplies I would need to compare to the list Dad would provide. This should give me an idea of what I needed to transport and what to purchase once arriving in Alaska. Bills were already arranged for auto payment, so that wouldn't be an issue.

"Alaska," I said as I rocked back in my chair. Dad had come up with a great test, but I wasn't sure either of us would complete the challenge. "All I can do is give it my best."

I had been an athlete in high school and college and had received the nickname Tate. It was the one thing Dad hated worse than Mom giving me the name Tatum. He had pushed for Charleen, but Mom had insisted on her maiden name. He managed to call me Tatum, but Tate would never pass his lips. I smiled at the thought of him realizing his daughter might end up showing more balls than his namesake. I could imagine Charlie grumbling to Carol about how unfairly Dad treated him.

While I loved my brother, I didn't approve of his taking the reins from Dad. He was excellent in finance but lacked Dad's leadership in running the company. I worried some top staff would jump ship if Charlie was appointed CEO. I took a sip of coffee and stared at the screen. A video of Alaska in the winter was playing across my screen. It was beautiful, but I knew there would be all kinds of hidden dangers to overcome. *Could I do this?*

†

I stopped for Chinese take-out on my way home and continued my research. I scanned the list of supplies I had printed earlier and knew that clothing would not be provided. My search started with footwear, and I researched several waterproof boots. Thick wool socks would also be a must. Jeans and thermal underwear made it to my list, with a half-dozen flannel shirts and several pairs of insulated coveralls. Outerwear would need to be rated for below-zero conditions, so I checked the equipment closely to ensure I chose the right weight and fit.

It was late into the night when my eyes started to cross from reading the computer screen, and I decided to call it a night. Tomorrow was Friday, so I could spend the entire weekend researching once I found what region I was heading into. As I lay in bed, my mind whirled with ideas. I probably should have felt terrified, but a part of me was excited about this adventure. Life in the city had become routine, and time in the secluded wilderness would allow me to contemplate where my life was going. I enjoyed and excelled in my career, but my heart longed for more. The problem was in not knowing what that "more" entailed. Twelve to fourteen hours a day and being at the company's whim made a stable relationship impossible. Also, traveling to Europe on short notice wasn't uncommon, sometimes for extended periods. Six months might seem an eternity, but I wasn't sure it would be long enough to sort out my future.

CHAPTER TWO

I was anxious for the meeting with Dad. Before the session, I consumed several cups of coffee, so my system was utterly caffeinated. When I entered the conference room, Dad was alone.

"I knew you would be the first to arrive," he said. "You see this as an important test, don't you?"

"Yes," I replied. "I can see a great value to this adventure."

Dad frowned. "I hardly think your brother feels the same." He pushed a large envelope toward me. "Looking at that place makes me wish I was younger," he said. "More so than Canada," he added as Charlie entered the room. He passed Charlie a similar envelope.

"Should we open these now?" I asked.

"I think you two should take the rest of the day off to review the information inside and be prepared to ask questions on Monday morning."

"You are set on us going through this, aren't you?" Charlie asked.

Dad nodded. "My mind is made up and you haven't presented an alternative challenge."

"Thank you, Dad." I stood to leave the room and gather my keys for the ride home. I could hear Charlie pleading with Dad as I exited the room. *Suck it up, buttercup.* I grinned and kept walking. I grabbed my bag and headed to the elevator, eager to get home and review the information packet.

†

I placed my bag and envelope on the table and made a pot of coffee. *Lord, I hope I can have coffee.* I didn't think I would survive without my morning liquid incentive. Coffee, for sure, but gourmet flavors and creamer would not be an option in the bush. In the bush. *Now, where did that thought come from?* I opened the envelope and spread the contents across my kitchen table.

My eyes gazed across a landscape that was as immense as it was foreign. Mountains were in several photographs, and their snow-covered peaks looked like they kissed the sky. I unfolded a map of the area and found a large red circle near the Copper River with GPS coordinates. Glennallen looked to be the closest town to the location, but it wasn't exactly close. I pulled the map up on the laptop and couldn't find any roads leading into the area. The river was the only access, by boat or floatplane. I shouldn't have hoped for an accessible route. Dad did say we would be stationed remotely.

My heart sank when I saw the cabin and a few outbuildings. I wasn't expecting luxury accommodations, but the place looked like it could be condemned by city standards. At least the inside of the cabin looked livable. One significant area served as sleeping and cooking quarters. Well, if you could call a two-burner stovetop cooking. There at least had to be some electricity to the building. A solid-looking woodstove also had a cooking surface and a separate door that might conceal an oven. A small table served as the dining area. The cabin rested on a small hill about a hundred yards from the river, which made me worry about flooding. Then I remembered I would be long gone in time for the spring ice break-up when flooding threats would be the highest. I had to admit, the view from the front door was excellent.

The smaller buildings appeared newer, and I sighed with relief when I saw a sauna and a toilet area. It was not precisely the indoor plumbing I was used to, but it was better than an outhouse and a river to bathe in. The remaining building held some form of a fuel tank, a pile of split wood, an ATV, and some small tools. A small solar panel system bordered the other side of the cabin. It wasn't huge, but it was a power source. There were several photographs of the surrounding area capturing beautiful mountain scenery. No noise or light pollution, at least. There was one final building, but I had no idea what it was until I returned to the notes about the property to find it was a smokehouse.

I googled the area for fishing and game, and it appeared I'd hit the jackpot for fish. Several species of salmon were common in the Copper River. *That might explain the smokehouse*, I thought. I made a note to find some instructions on smoking fish and to determine if there were other means of preservation.

The list of supplies included a fly rod, gill net, and cast net. I'd used a fly rod before, but using nets to catch fish was not in my repertoire. Add that to my list of educational videos. Fowl seemed to be ample in the area, from waterfowl to grouse and ptarmigan. More training on how to hunt and process birds.

There was a nice firepit area with a grill and two Adirondack chairs. If the weather was accommodating, I could easily bet this would be a favorite spot.

Returning to the pictures of the inside of the cabin, I found a queen-sized bed. The supply list included two sheet sets, four blankets, and a down comforter. *I'll be adding my own flannel sheets to my supplies.* A dozen Bic lighters, pots, pans, dishes, cups, and other kitchen necessities would be helpful. *Yes, there is a coffee pot. Not electric, but I can cope with that.*

The food list wasn't surprising. It contained bags of dried beans, rice, cornmeal, grits, canned items, and large quantities of other staples such as salt, sugar, coffee, and flour. I smiled and jotted down, two cases of quart-size mason jars and a pressure cooker. *Note to self, learn how to can.*

A twelve-gauge shotgun, a twenty-two rifle, and a .308 rifle with cases of ammunition were listed, as well as a nine-millimeter handgun and shoulder rig with several boxes of shells. A Bowie knife and scabbard rounded out the protection and hunting equipment.

I remembered seeing a photo in Dad's office of him holding a large salmon. I wondered if he was in Alaska and if I could get his fishing advice. Nothing appeared to prohibit asking anyone for assistance before we arrived at our destinations. I read back through the information and could not find anything, so I decided to pay Dad a visit the next day.

There was a reservation for me at Copper River Bed and Breakfast for two nights once I arrived. I would have a full day to obtain my supplies before being transported to my new home by boat. My essential goods would be prearranged and purchased for me at the Trading Post in Glennallen. Again, there didn't appear to be anything that would prevent me from adding to those supplies.

"Resilience and creativity," I reminded myself.

I made a note to contact the bed and breakfast to discover if I could have items shipped there and to inquire about the storage cost. Then, I returned to the laptop to pull up the website for the Trading Post to survey the supplies I could purchase there. The clothing and boots were even better quality than I had found on other sites. Buying as much there as possible would make sense as the locals would understand what was needed. I was relieved to find propane tanks. I had decided to purchase a small Blackstone griddle for cooking, and full-size propane tanks would last longer and could be refilled versus the smaller disposable gas canisters. My list also included a six-hundred-watt solar generator that would add electric connectivity to the cabin as long as the sun could charge the batteries. I knew a small single-cup coffee maker would be a luxury, but it would be more convenient than waiting for the coffee to be perked the old fashion way on the stovetop or firepit. There would be no internet connectivity, but an iPad Pro would be much more convenient than notebooks and writing implements, and make it easier to journal my adventure. I added a small backpack to my Trading Post list and took a meal break, ordering two of my favorite calzones for delivery. That would allow me to work through lunch and dinner without leaving the house.

The more I researched supplies and equipment, the more my excitement grew. The challenge, while shocking at first, was beginning to sound like something I needed in my life. I watched several videos on how to process salmon for smoking and canning. It didn't look complicated, but I was sure there would be a learning curve. I wasn't sure I could hunt large game such as moose or caribou, but I knew the fish and fowl would provide the needed protein in my diet. I needed a resource guide on edible plants for the area as I would not arrive in time to plant a garden for vegetables. I would buy potatoes and other vegetables with a long shelf life if possible. Eggs would be important, too, if I could safely transport them.

That thought made me look back at the notes for transportation equipment. A skiff with a gasoline motor, a new ATV, and snowshoes. I had experience driving a boat, so that shouldn't be too difficult, and the ATV sounded like fun and would be a challenge to learn. Snowshoes would be a new experience, but apparently highly useful for getting around in the winter months. I also noticed a small sled in the photos that looked like it could be pulled manually or by the ATV.

Collecting firewood would be as critical, or possibly more so than food, for cooking, heating, and bathing. My research showed that alder wood was plentiful for smoking, and several spruce and birch species were available for heating. My eyes searched the photos for the size of the woodpile, and I feared it was nowhere near what I would need to survive the winter. I would need to spend time each day working on firewood and food. I presumed a gill net setting would allow me to work on other projects while the net worked magic. After watching several videos, I thought I had the gist of setting a net. Finding the correct spots in the river for fish might take considerable time, so trial and error would be critical.

"I wonder," I spoke aloud as I walked to the computer.

After entering the address, I pulled up Google Earth images for the GPS coordinates of the cabin. The satellite image made me aware of the enormity of the area and how secluded it was. Even after scanning outward as far as possible, there was no evidence of a town or other dwellings. I would indeed be alone. I shook off my trepidation and returned to the original mission. My heart pounded when the image scanned a grove of standing dead spruce that didn't look like a horrible distance from the cabin. That would be my woodlot.

I'm unfamiliar with alder, so I must study that one. What am I thinking? I also need to learn how to use a chainsaw so I don't cut one of my limbs off. Much to discover in the next thirty days. Suitable work gloves, check.

My head was swirling with ideas by the time the food arrived. I placed the boxes on the table and grabbed silverware and a drink from the refrigerator. The notepad beside me had rapidly filled with lists of supplies and areas to learn. It was overwhelming initially, but I was determined I could do this.

The aroma of the calzones filled the room when I opened the lid, and my mouth began to water. *I'd better eat my fill of these before I go. Red meat, too; oh, how I will miss a good steak.* While I ate, I contemplated the videos on preserving salmon, and decided smoking and canning were the two I would use. The smoker could be used with other meats, which was a plus. Tasting the delicious flavors of the sausage made me wonder if I could buy links of sausage or other dried meats that would add some variety to my diet. Visions of sausage strings and cured hams wrapped in cloth made me smile. Beef or bison jerky would also help until I could harvest fresh fish and game.

The availability was present at the Trading Post, but the prices were extravagant, and I decided if I had a place to ship and store, these products would be good choices to purchase elsewhere.

I remembered channel surfing one night and watching a show where chaga fungus was dried and ground into a product to make tea, which helped boost the immune system. That reminded me that I needed to purchase a guide on what plants could be used for medicinal purposes. I would use a satellite phone for emergencies, but getting proper medical attention in a timely manner could be problematic. I made a note to pack a first-aid kit.

After storing my leftovers in the refrigerator, I walked out on my balcony. The hustle and bustle of people rushing to their destinations filled the air with a cacophony of sounds and smells. I was so accustomed to living in the city. Would the serenity of the wilderness be welcome, or would it drive me insane?

Returning inside, I resumed planning and texted Dad to let him know I would stop by tomorrow.

Will you and Mom be home in the morning?
Yes, will you join us for brunch? Around ten?
Sounds great. I'll see you then.
Goodnight, Tatum.
Goodnight, Dad.

I flipped through the photos again while the calzone heated in the oven then retired to the living room to eat and enjoy some television.

†

"Well, this is perfect timing," I said as the television started on a channel featuring homestead life in Alaska. Picking up the remote, I clicked on the record series button. I knew some activities were enhanced for entertainment purposes, but I felt it might potentially be educational.

My eyes were glued to the television as the family used a gill net to catch salmon. *Damn, they were colossal fish, and a single fish could probably provide several meals for me.* Calculations filled my head, and I thought maybe sixty of these fish would help feed me through the winter if they were smoked or canned. I paid particular attention to the number of fish they caught. That could be a full-time job for me for weeks if I hit a run, but it would be time well spent. I could set a net, cut and haul some firewood, and check the net between deliveries.

I would arrive in Alaska during moderate temperatures and days of up to eighteen hours of sunlight. They would be long days, but I could catch up on sleep once food and firewood were in ample supply. I needed to learn to pace myself and learn to work economically so I wasn't wasting time or energy. After several episodes, I felt drowsy and called it a day. There was so much to do quickly, but I thought I had made a good start and was proud of my accomplishments.

†

The warm water was relaxing as it flowed down my body. It had been a long week, capped off by the biggest challenge of my career, but I felt invigorated by all the possibilities. I would prove to my father that I exhibited all the skills needed to take over the company, especially resilience and creativity. I wondered if Charlie across town was as confident in his abilities.

As I stretched out beneath the sheets, my mind relaxed. If, by chance, the position was given to Charlie, I knew my days at the company would be limited. I would still have a job, but I was positive he would make life as difficult as possible. Charlie would see me as a constant threat to his company leadership, but the thought of that didn't concern me. It might provide the impetus I needed to make a career change I was reluctant to make alone. *Only time will tell*, I thought as I turned out the light.

†

My flat was only a few blocks from my parents' home. I would be doing a lot of walking during my adventure, so I decided that this day was as good as any to start walking more. The morning was temperate, but the temps would rise to nearly ninety degrees by noon. I wouldn't miss the heat waves that overtook the city for weeks. There were still many communities where homes were not equipped with air conditioning, resulting in numerous deaths each summer. The residents tried everything possible to stay comfortable, and the fire departments in those areas often opened fire hydrants for the children to play in and cool off. I wiped a bead of sweat from my forehead. No, I wouldn't miss the heat at all.

Mom greeted me at the door and ushered me into the dining room. "Your father is just about finished cooking."

"I love his breakfasts," I replied.

"The one meal he really enjoys cooking. How are you?"

"I'm good, Mom. I wanted to see if I could pick Dad's brain. I know he's been salmon fishing, and I'd like his advice."

"For your wilderness challenge? At first, I thought it was a horrible idea until I realized the merit of the competition." She leaned in closer to whisper. "I don't think he expects either of you to remain for six months, but he's eager to see who can thrive in adversity."

"Ah, good morning, Tatum," Charles said, carrying large platters of food.

"Here, let me help," I offered and placed a platter on the table. "This looks and smells delicious."

"Pour a cup of coffee and join us," he instructed.

Mom had begun serving plates while I was retrieving coffee. She handed me a plate mounded with food.

"Do I look like I'm starving?" I teased.

"You are thinner than the last time I saw you, and you need to enjoy your father's great breakfast while you can."

"That's true. I haven't had eggs Benedict in ages."

"Eat your fill, and then you can tell me what's on your mind. I hope you aren't deciding to forego the challenge." Charles frowned.

"Quite the opposite," I replied after swallowing. "I want some advice."

"Fair enough. Let's eat, and then we can get down to business."

†

After helping Mom clear the table, I poured a fresh cup of coffee and joined Dad in the living room.

"What's on your mind, Tatum?"

"I've reviewed your proposal several times and did not see anything that prohibited us from seeking advice."

"No, not at all. That's why I wanted to give you time this weekend to determine your questions."

I nodded. "The area you have chosen for me looks beautiful and appears to be a location for plentiful opportunities to fish for salmon. I remembered seeing a photo of you holding a large salmon, and I wanted to solicit your advice on fishing. I've fly-fished for trout years ago but have never caught something the size of a salmon."

Charles smiled. "I caught that fish at the very spot you will be living," he replied. "I've owned that camp for twenty years."

"What? How come I never knew that?"

"It was my spot to visit when I needed time to decompress and recharge," Charles answered. "The cabin isn't beautiful, but it is functional. It will keep you warm and safe during your time there."

"The list included gill nets and cast nets. Did you ever use them?"

"No, my visits were pretty short-lived, so I didn't have the need to harvest fish for survival. I would recommend visiting some educational sites on that method of fishing. The fly gear is weighted to capture fish the size of salmon, and I'll provide you with a list of lures and flies I found most beneficial. Those were some of the best-tasting fish I have ever eaten."

"If my calculations are close, I must harvest and process at least sixty fish."

Charles considered my assumption for a moment. "I think that is a real number if you plan to hunt birds to provide variety. You won't be able to catch that many with a fly rod, so I think the best option would be the gill net. Try the fly rod if you have time while waiting to check your nets. There is nothing like hooking one of those beasts."

"I don't think I will be able to harvest large game such as a moose or caribou, so can I survive on fish and fowl?"

"The Indigenous populations have done so for years."

"That's true. I know you will have the basics on order from the Trading Post, but can I supplement the order with the clothing and other gear I'll need to have? The quality of goods from a local vendor would more closely match the needs for the environment than I could find here."

"There's nothing to prevent that. That was a creative idea, and you wouldn't need to travel with a dozen bags."

"Do the solar panels there adequately supply the cabin?"

"It will power the stovetop, a lamp, and maybe a few other items."

"Would it be prudent to use a portable solar inverter to supplement the solar system?"

Charles smiled. "You have been doing your homework. I think that's an excellent idea."

"I want to take an iPad to document my adventure. I know there will not be phone or internet service, but it would prove more compact than writing supplies."

"That would be interesting to read," he replied. "The longest I've ever stayed is two weeks. Maybe once I retire, I'll spend more time there."

"By yourself," Mom replied. "I enjoy my conveniences."

"Understood, my love." He turned back to me. "I'm proud that you are planning well for this adventure."

"I know it won't be easy, and there will be hard times, but I am excited to see if I can accomplish this task."

Charles sighed. "I wish your brother shared your enthusiasm."

I shrugged. "I don't know what to say to get Charlie motivated."

"And that's not your responsibility. I would never put either of you in harm's way without protection or an escape route."

"I don't plan to survive eating rice and beans the entire time," I told him.

"I have a feeling you will do well. You appear to be planning well and learning new skills already. I'm proud of you for that."

"Thanks, Dad."

"I anticipate you traveling to Glennallen at least once for supplies and setting up a delivery by bush plan once the river freezes. The boat and ATV have been checked out mechanically, and you will begin with twenty-five gallons of gasoline. I suggest you refill empty containers when traveling to town and order plenty when you get resupplied."

"Will I be able to pay for items with a credit card, or do I need to plan to carry cash?"

"You will be able to use both in Glennallen. Call ahead to order supplies so they will be ready when you arrive. If you don't believe you can make the trip in one day safely, spend the night at a hotel and start out early the next morning. You might consider staying over for a hot meal and a shower. The sauna is adequate for bathing, but you must change out the water and keep the fire going all day before you bathe."

"I think gathering firewood and food are my first two priorities when I arrive."

Charles nodded. "The firewood will be the most time-consuming chore and necessary to help you survive winter. If you are successful with the gill net, you should get a good supply of fish quickly if you choose good sites. You can fly fish for a fresh meal while the others smoke."

"I plan to take the pistol and the shotgun with me when I cut wood. If I'm lucky, I can hunt game birds or small game."

"That's a good plan. Always have protection. It is a remote site, so other predators may be there."

"I'm sure I'll have hundreds of other questions, but I'll make a list to ensure I cover everything."

"That sounds like a good plan. I wish I was younger and could join you on this adventure."

"Thanks for a great meal. I'll see you Monday."

"Have a great weekend, and make sure we see you several times before you leave town," Mom said.

"I will, Mom. See you soon."

"Goodbye, honey," Charles replied.

†

I returned home and called the Copper River Bed and Breakfast, and they assured me they had room to store packages for me at a minimal cost. They did caution, however, to order early to get items delivered due to delays coming into Alaska. I wrote down the complete shipping address and went to work ordering my supplies.

A call to the Trading Post assured me that they had all the clothing and other needs on my list, and I paid for the goods that would be packed and added to the order my father had already purchased.

I sighed when those two significant tasks were done. A computer search led me to scheduled hunting seasons. Moose season was limited to very short periods, and caribou were by permit only. Elk, deer, and goat ran from August to December. A deer or possibly elk would be the largest game animal I could hope to obtain. Even that was a question in my mind. I wasn't sure I could shoot Bambi. I guessed that depended on how hungry I was.

Returning to the computer after a coffee break, I ordered three sets of clothing, some boots for travel, and a light jacket. Satisfied I had made significant progress, I decided to take a break. I called for an Uber and drove to a nearby outdoor sports store, where I spent hours perusing the aisles and making a list of items to consider for purchase. Surprisingly, a thing I hadn't considered previously was a sleeping bag. The store had a vast selection, and I found several options for my list. When I returned home, I would check to see if the Trading Post had the needed items. If not, I would place an order with the store for shipping. I checked the time and laughed. My Apple watch would be of little use. When I returned home, I would shop for a kinetic watch that didn't rely on batteries.

After ordering a spinach salad, I arrived home, ate a late lunch, and finished ordering the additional supplies. I relaxed on the couch and watched a few episodes of the homesteading shows I had recorded. It wouldn't be a glamorous life, but I felt more confident each day.

†

The night before I would fly to Alaska was spent with my parents. Charlie had been invited but opted to spend his last night with Carol.

"He's still stewing over this competition, isn't he?" I asked Dad.

"He's done nothing but whine about it for a month. I will be surprised if he lasts more than a few weeks. I don't believe he's prepared as thoroughly as you. Let me offer one more piece of advice."

"What's that?"

"Find a cedar sapling and chip it into small bits. You will need to drop some in the toilet to help reduce odors. Saw dust helps, too." He grinned. "You must bury the contents away from the cabin at least every few weeks, if not sooner."

"That is important information to know." I returned Dad's grin. "You really wish you could be on this adventure, don't you?"

"If I were a younger man, yes. If the transition goes well, I will try for a month next spring or summer."

"I think I'll go to a tropical island somewhere while he's gone," Mom teased.

"That sounds fair." I smiled and hugged Mom. "I will see you when I return."

Mom had tears in her eyes. "Stay safe and try to enjoy yourself."

"I will. Thank you for offering to water my plants. They will probably thrive for you."

"Are you sure you don't need me to take you to the airport in the morning?" Dad asked.

"I've already got arrangements made, but thank you."

†

The walk home had gotten much less taxing as my endurance increased. I imagined I would be walking quite a bit in my temporary home. My bags were placed at the front door, and I walked into my bedroom to shower and relax for the night. I couldn't resist sending Charlie a text.

Good luck, Charlie. See you in six months.

I didn't expect an answer, so I wasn't disappointed when one didn't arrive. I rinsed off in the shower. My alarm was set, and I would have a long day of travel tomorrow, so I turned off my light and willed sleep to arrive.

CHAPTER THREE

The car service was right on time, and with a final look at my home, I climbed into the car to start my adventure. It would take several hours by jet and small plane to reach Glennallen, where a vehicle from the bed and breakfast would meet me. I took advantage of every Starbucks available to enjoy the richness of the brewed coffee. I looked out the window as the jet departed O'Hare and wondered how long it would be before I returned home. After a short stop in Seattle, I went to Anchorage, where I would connect with a small plane service. As I pulled my carry-on bag across the tarmac, the small plane was dwarfed by jets. Better than a very long bus ride, I imagined. My checked bags were loaded, and I handed over my carry-on for storage.

"First time in a small plane?" the pilot asked. "I'm Tom, by the way."

"Yes," I replied with a nod.

"I make this flight several times a week and could probably do it in my sleep, but I promise to keep my eyes open today."

"Thanks. I would appreciate that." I grinned and climbed the steps he was pointing to.

After I was buckled in, he turned to me and another passenger. "All set?"

I nodded, took in the area as we taxied, and then took off for Glennallen. The landscape was even more beautiful than I had imagined. The dense forests were a vibrant green, and the water in rivers and lakes looked crystal clear. I assumed that some were fed by melting glacial ice, which added to the water's hue.

"We are coming up on the Copper River," the pilot announced.

The water was beautiful, and I could only imagine the schools of fish that would migrate up the river. It felt like no sooner than we had leveled out we began to descend, and the small town of Glennallen came into view. The landing strip looked like it had seen better days, but the pilot landed smoothly and taxied to the building I assumed was the airport terminal or the main office. A battered Ford pickup sat beside the building and looked twenty years older than the driver. A young man approached me as I deplaned.

"Are you Miss Chastain?" he asked.

"Yes, Tatum," I replied, offering my hand.

"I'm Troy, and Ma sent me to fetch you today and bring you to the hotel. Are those your bags?"

"Yes, they are, Troy."

"Sit tight, and I'll have you loaded in no time," he replied and jogged across to the plane.

After loading the last bag, Troy opened the door for me.

"Thanks." I smiled. "Is it always this beautiful?"

"Until winter fully arrives in January," he answered. "It's tolerable until then."

He pulled up to the front door when we arrived at the bed and breakfast. "Go in and get checked in, and I'll bring your bags."

I reached into my pocket, intending to tip Troy.

"This is all part of the services you've paid for. I'll load your bags and boxes on Tuesday and take you to the port."

"Thanks, Troy." I walked inside and was welcomed by a middle-aged woman I presumed was Troy's mom.

"Good afternoon. You must be Miss Chastain. You favor your father," she added. "I'm Elizabeth, and you've met Troy already. You have many boxes that have arrived. I have them stored in my office."

"Thank you. Please add the storage fee to my bill."

Elizabeth shook her head. "Charles has already made payment for everything."

"That's perfect. Could I convince you to lend Troy and his truck to me for a little while? I'd like to check with the Trading Post to ensure all my supplies are ready. I'd also like to grab something to eat."

"The diner is a great spot, but don't eat a heavy meal. I have a welcome feast for you if you join Troy and me."

"I'd love that. Thank you. Is there anything I can provide?"

"If you're a fan of ice cream, you might want to pick up a half gallon for dessert. It will be your last opportunity until you return."

"Duly noted. Do you have any preference?"

"No, but I'm sure Troy will convince you to get some Rocky Road." She smiled.

"That's not a bad choice at all. I'll see if we can get some variety," I told Elizabeth.

She turned to her son. "Once you've helped Ms. Chastain store her bags in the room, she wants you to take her a few places."

"Alright," Troy answered, taking the larger bags down the hallway.

I looked at my watch. "Is it really three o'clock here?"

"Yes, it is. That's why I recommend you eat lightly. Dinner will be at seven. Make sure Troy introduces you to Erica. She and Troy will take you to the cabin on Tuesday after you've rested well and gotten all your arrangements made."

"Thank you. Will Erica be at the Trading Post?"

Elizabeth laughed. "She's the owner's daughter and bookkeeper, so she'll be there. Troy says she's excited to help you get moved in. Any day outside is a good day for her."

"I can relate to that. The four walls of an office can become so depressing sometimes. Even when you've got a great view."

Troy rushed back. "I'll take this last bag and then hang out here until you are ready to tour the metropolis of Glennallen," he teased. "That won't take long." He laughed.

"I won't be long," I told him as he left my room. "The diner first, though, so I can knock out some hunger pangs."

"No problem. I'll see you soon."

The room was beautiful and decorated with what I presumed was local artwork and handicrafts. I relieved my bladder and placed my small bag on the end of the bed. I tucked my wallet into my shoulder bag and searched for my exuberant tour guide. As promised, he was sitting beside his mom in the office. My eyes landed on a large stack of boxes.

"Are all those mine?"

"Yes, ma'am. Between this stack and what Erica has packed for you, you are well-stocked to begin your journey."

I probably overthought a few things, but I prefer to be over-prepared if possible.

"No matter how well you think you've planned, there will always be something you wish you had. You have time to make those assessments and travel here a few times before the river begins to ice over. Tom, the pilot that brought you in today, makes the supply deliveries once the ice is safe."

"How long will it take to make the trip by boat?"

"A good five hours, maybe six, with a heavy load. That's why it's crucial to get an early start on Tuesday so Troy and Erica can make it back safely. Even though there will be sunlight late into the day, the diminished light can hide obstructions in the river, causing safety hazards."

"It will also allow you time to get settled in and unpacked before all the hard work begins," Troy said.

"That makes perfect sense, and I'm usually an early riser, so it shouldn't be a problem."

"Let's roll then and get some food in your belly," Troy replied.

"I'm right behind you," I answered. "We'll see you later," I told Elizabeth.

"You're in good hands," Elizabeth called out to me.

"Diner, here we come," Troy said, opening the door.

"What do you recommend?"

"The bison burger is off the chain," he replied. "A little pricier than a regular burger, but well worth it."

"Will you have one with me?"

Troy smiled. "I'm a growing boy, so I never turn down food."

"Thanks. It's no fun eating alone if you don't have to."

Troy pulled into a parking spot, and we entered the diner. When the waitress came for the order, he told her, "Two bison burgers with the works and fries."

"To drink?"

"Do you have coke?" I asked

"Which flavor? We have it in regular diet and cherry vanilla."

"Cherry vanilla for me," I replied.

"Sounds good," Troy answered.

"I'll get these going and bring your drinks out." She smiled warmly at Troy.

"Seems to really like you," I teased. I watched the blush rise to Troy's cheeks.

"We dated for a while this last school year. "I'm going to university soon, so I didn't want to start anything serious even though Lisa did."

"Smart young man. What do you want to study?"

"Either business or environmental conservation. Maybe both."

"Those are both fantastic goals and would serve you well here."

"My thoughts exactly. I could help Mom with the business and work to protect our environment."

"Are you and your mom alone? If you don't mind me being nosy."

"Dad was swept off a crab fishing boat when I was ten. His body was never recovered, but Mom and I are doing well."

"I'm sorry, Troy. I shouldn't have asked."

"It's no problem, Ms. Chastain. Mom used part of the insurance money to move back here and buy the bed and breakfast, and she put the rest in a trust for my education."

"Do you have other family members here?"

"Yeah, you'll meet them when we go to the Trading Post. My uncle and his daughter, Erica, own the business."

I smiled at him. "That's good to know."

"When I come to town to resupply, should I plan on spending the night to get a fresh start the following day?"

"Honestly, I would. You can get a hot shower and several hot meals."

"That's what I was thinking, too."

"Two bison burgers," Lisa said as she placed plates in front of us.

"Thanks, Lisa," Troy answered.

"I'll bring some refills on your drinks." She smiled. "Maybe we can get together before you go to university next month," Lisa hinted.

"I'll check my work schedule. Business is heating up."

"You know how to reach me," Lisa said and turned away to start back to the kitchen.

"She is definitely warm for your form," I teased.

"She's what?"

"Sorry, dating myself here. Lisa's very into hooking up with you. Better?"

"Gotcha." Troy chuckled. He leaned across the table. "I'm not interested in being a baby daddy yet."

"You have an education to obtain first," I replied.

"Exactly," he answered.

I took a bite of the burger. "Oh, my goodness. This is fantastic."

"Told ya."

"No way I'm eating all of this," I said, cutting it in half. "Can you eat another half?"

"We can't let it go to waste." He grinned and handed his plate to me.

"Thank you."

"No, thank you. I haven't had one of these for a while. Hey. If you don't return before I head off to school, would you mind if I visited to check on you? Maybe bring whatever supplies you order?"

"I would like that. I have a sat phone for ordering and emergencies. I'll call in an order with Erica and ask that you deliver. I'll pay extra for the delivery. When do you leave for school?"

"In the next month. I'm registered but have to attend an early orientation. I'll also be back to visit for scheduled breaks."

"I'll bet that once I get to the cabin, I'll discover I've forgotten a few things, maybe we can arrange for a delivery before you head to school."

"Perfect."

I looked at my watch. "How late is the Trading Post open?"

"Until eight, so we have plenty of time."

"Good, it will take a while to finish this meal. We need to stop at a grocery for ice cream before going home. I understand someone is partial to Rocky Road."

Troy smiled. "I am, but I can eat any ice cream."

I laughed. "We will get a variety."

"Cool with me," Troy replied.

†

I was in awe when we entered the Trading Post. "This place looks like outdoor heaven," I told Troy, who laughed.

"This place has anything and everything you need to survive in the bush."

"Agreed," I said as we walked toward the counter.

"Erica, this is Ms. Chastain," he introduced me.

I cocked my head. "Would you please call me Tate or Tatum? You make me feel old."

"Welcome, Tatum," Erica said. "Thank you for your business."

"I thought purchasing locally would make more sense since you know the environment."

"That we do. I have to say you did a great job of research."

"Is there anything I didn't plan for that you would recommend adding?"

"A few items, actually, and I added them to your order."

"That's perfect." I handed her a credit card to add the extra items.

"After all you've purchased, we can add a filet knife, a sharpening stick, and a magnesium fire stick. You'll need to keep that with you whenever you leave the cabin in case you need to start a fire for warmth or protection."

"That makes good sense. Will you keep the card on the account for when I resupply? Troy has offered to visit before he leaves for school."

"Sure, that's no problem. I have an encrypted file where I can store the data. Somewhere in your pile of boxes is a satellite phone. In case you need to order, I programmed the store number and my personal number."

Troy nodded. "You should probably add the bed and breakfast number if you will stay overnight on your town visits."

"I will, for sure."

"That's a good decision. Troy will be here at five on Tuesday morning to bring your goods and help us load your supplies. Will you be ready to leave by seven?"

"I'll ride with Troy. An extra set of hands will help to load faster."

"That's not necessary, but we never pass on help," Erica said.

"I want to make sure you two will be able to return safely," I replied.

"We should make it to your cabin around one, and it may take a few hours to unload. We can drive faster without a load, giving us plenty of time to make it home."

"Excellent. It's still hard to believe I'm doing this."

"Charles has every confidence in the world in you. He wouldn't send you here alone if he didn't."

"Is there anyone here that doesn't know my father?"

"He's been a great customer for years and has done much to support this community. The volunteer fire department is named for him since he purchased the building and all the equipment."

"That sounds like something he would do."

"He's been very generous to us."

"Understood." I looked at Troy. "Are you ready to give me the grand tour and stop for ice cream?"

"I was born ready."

"It was great to meet you, Tatum. I'll see you Tuesday morning, if not sooner."

"Thank you for all your assistance, Erica. You too, Troy. You've both been lifesavers."

"We want to help you succeed and fall in love with our homeland, too," Erica said.

I smiled at Erica. "I'm well on my way."

†

Troy was right. It didn't take long to tour the town. A fifteen-minute ride was all it took to see the highlights and arrive at the grocery store. I selected three half-gallons of ice cream and then made the mistake of walking down the candy aisle. When my eyes landed on Twizzler bites, I couldn't resist throwing six bags in the cart. Troy smiled at me.

"Yeah, I'm a junky. Those should last me a while. There is one more thing I need to add. Is there a small kitchen hardware section?"

"Two rows over," he replied.

I picked out two packages of heavy-duty cup hooks and saw his curious look. "To hang bags of onions, carrots, and potatoes," I replied. "I didn't see mention of any root cellar at the cabin."

"It's never been used for long-term stays, so one was never built. Your solution is a good idea and will save your pantry space. Just let me know what fresh vegetables you want, and I'll bring them out on my visit."

"One last purchase," I said. "I know this is a luxury, but I love my coffee. I bought a small Keurig and would like some K cups to use before I convert over to regular coffee."

"No problem," Troy said with a smile, leading me to the coffee aisle. I picked out four large boxes and added them to the cart.

We passed a table with green bananas, so I grabbed two bunches that should take days to ripen. "We better get out of here before I fill a cart and sink the boat with all my purchases."

"There's no worry of that. Erica's boat is built to haul a large amount of supplies."

"Does she make deliveries to people living on the river?"

"For some that don't have easy means to make it into town, but most people enjoy visiting with people when they come resupply. I imagine it becomes quite lonely out there."

"Dad said there is a small radio, so at least I can hear other voices."

"Saturday night is bush night, so people can send messages to their loved ones living remotely. Try to listen in from eight to ten."

"I will. Thanks. We better go get this ice cream in the freezer."

†

Elizabeth cooked a delicious steak dinner with a variety of vegetables. We managed to save room for ice cream, and then I began to yawn. I was surprised it was still light out.

Elizabeth saw me looking out the window. "You will adjust to the long daylight hours and enjoy sleeping late tomorrow if possible. It may be your last restful day for a while until you get set up."

"I'm definitely looking forward to a hot shower and bed."

"It's almost midnight where you came from. Your body will catch up, too. Let us know if you need anything."

"Thanks, Elizabeth. This was a wonderful meal, and your rooms are fantastic."

"Thank you. I'll cook some breakfast when you arrive in the morning. Troy will be gone early, helping Erica make a delivery to an elderly couple downriver. He'll be back in plenty of time for dinner. Does fried chicken and the works sound good to you?"

"Sounds perfect. Is there anything I can help with?"

"You can keep me company if you wish. Only one cook in my kitchen, though." She grinned. "I will have a pot of coffee brewed if you're interested."

"I'm always interested in coffee." I looked at Troy to find him grinning, but he didn't utter a word about my secret stash.

"I will see you in the morning. Troy, be safe tomorrow."

"Always." He smiled.

"I will have your lunch packed in the morning," Elizabeth told him.

†

After turning on the shower, I stripped off my clothes and stepped into the warm water. I never knew a shower could feel so good. I would shave as closely as possible tomorrow when I woke up. I had purchased a waterproof razor that could be recharged, so maybe I wouldn't look like Sasquatch when I came to town. I chuckled as I turned off the water and dried off.

The bed was calling my name, and I slipped into a long T-shirt and climbed beneath the covers after turning the lamp off. I barely remember laying my head on the pillow.

†

When I woke up the following day, I felt invigorated. I showered and shaved, then found Elizabeth in the kitchen.

She smiled and looked at her clock. "Is this your idea of sleeping in?" she teased.

"Well, it is almost nine in Chicago. I slept like a rock last night."

"The fresh air and hard work will help you sleep at night. A month out here would cure any insomniac." She chuckled. "I have fresh biscuits, gravy, and juice when you're ready."

My stomach growled at the mention of food. "That sounds wonderful."

"Pour some juice and coffee and then skedaddle from my kitchen," she teased.

"Yes, ma'am," I answered with a smile.

"I need to run to the grocery store this morning. Is there anything you need?"

"Would you mind if I ride with you? I can't remember Ziploc bags on my supply lists, and I think the gallon-sized will come in handy."

"Most definitely. Did you order a variety of seasonings and spices? Sometimes, a bit of garlic and cinnamon can make a pleasant addition to a meal."

"I'll pick out a selection. Thanks for the suggestion."

"My pleasure," Elizabeth replied as she placed a massive plate of food before me.

She must have seen my surprised look. "Work like a horse, eat like a horse. Whenever you can enjoy a large hot meal, take it. You'll be surprised how quickly you burn calories in the bush."

"I guess I'll know for sure after tomorrow."

"Excited?"

"Yes, and a bit terrified, to be honest. Life in the city has spoiled me. I'm used to calling for a delivery or a ride somewhere."

"You have a lot of your father in you. Have faith in yourself, and you will be fine. The path will have bumps, but you seem clever enough to overcome them."

"I hope you're right. I don't want to let my father or myself down." I bit into a biscuit covered in gravy. "This tastes great. Maybe I should reconsider and just come to work for you."

"Your face is always welcome at my door. I hope you will visit whenever you come to town."

"I most definitely will."

"I need to make my shopping list while you eat. Holler if you need something else."

"I'll try my best to finish this." I smiled.

After eating, I washed my dishes and left them in the drainboard to dry before returning to my room for my shoulder bag.

†

Elizabeth was in the kitchen checking her supplies. "Thanks for washing the dishes."

"No problem at all."

"If you're ready, we can head to the store."

Elizabeth filled her cart, and I added the Ziplocs and spices to my cart. There was a vast selection, so I focused on rubs and seasoning that would work well with fish and fowl since they would be my primary food sources. I also added several boxes of protein bars.

Elizabeth looked at my cart. "Good choices," she said, and we checked out.

The cashier looked at Elizabeth as she rang up her purchases. "Whose the *Cheechako*?"

Elizabeth turned to me. "This is Tatum Chastain. She'll be spending some time at her father's cabin."

"Welcome to Glennallen," the woman replied with a softer voice.

"Thank you," I answered. "I'm falling in love with this place already."

"Good luck and safe adventures," she said as she handed me my change.

As we walked to the car, I looked at Elizabeth. "*Cheechako?*"

"It means a newcomer. You may hear that often until people recognize your face. No offense intended."

"None was taken," I replied. "My last name seems recognizable here."

"Your father is a big supporter of our community. Has been for years since his first visit."

†

The day passed quickly, and Elizabeth was cooking dinner when Troy arrived home carrying an empty picnic basket. He kissed his mother on the cheek.

"Welcome home. How were Marge and Michael," she asked.

Troy shook his head. "Marge's health is failing quickly. I don't know how Michael will live without her."

"That's sad to hear. Marge and Michael have been married since they were teenagers. Maybe he will move to Anchorage to live with one of their children."

Troy shook his head. "I don't see him ever leaving their homestead."

"You're probably right," Elizabeth answered, turning the chicken in the pan. "Go wash up, and dinner will be ready soon."

"I will. Did you have a good day?" he asked me.

"Very relaxing, and your mom took me to the grocery store."

"Should I be worried about how much more you bought?"

"I actually did well, I think. Some storage bags, seasonings, and some protein bars."

"That was smart. You need to pack some snacks and water even if you don't intend to go far," Troy said. "You will burn more calories than you ever felt possible, harvesting wood or fishing. Hydration is key, too, for maintaining good health."

"Noted," I said with a smile.

"I won't be long," he said, leaving the kitchen.

"You have a fine young man."

"I'm very proud of him, but I'll admit I will miss him when he goes to school. It has been just the two of us for so long."

"I hope the time passes for you quickly. I know Troy's excited to graduate and return here."

"This will always be home for him."

"I can understand that."

†

After another fantastic meal, I excused myself for an early evening. I set my alarm for an early wake-up and stretched out in bed. My mind whirled with excitement and trepidation, but regardless, I would start my new adventure in the morning and take things as they came.

CHAPTER FOUR

The skies were light but overcast when Troy and I left for the Trading Post port the following morning. Elizabeth sent us off with a large thermos of coffee and a picnic basket filled with sandwiches and chips for the long ride ahead of us. Troy had already loaded my boxes from the bed and breakfast along with my bags before we ate a huge breakfast. I tossed my last bag in the back and climbed in beside Troy.

"All set?"

"As much as I can be," I answered.

"You will be great. Have faith."

I nodded and looked out the window to hide my emotions.

Erica was already loading my supplies with a crew when we arrived. Troy pulled out a dolly, and we loaded boxes from the bed and breakfast. He grinned. "I told you it was too big to sink. Your supplies will only fill up about half of the cargo space."

"It looked like more at the store." I grinned.

"Remind yourself of that once you start unpacking. We will unload you, but the rest is up to you."

"Task number one for my new life."

"Then the real fun begins. Fishing and harvesting wood."

"I will point out some areas you must look for when setting your nets. Don't get discouraged if you don't haul in a full net on your first few attempts. You have to time the runs just right. If you're getting a few fish, leave your nets set for a day or two before moving."

"Got it."

"You've got prime equipment, so let it do the job."

When they finished loading, Erica looked at us. "I'd like y'all to join me in the cabin until it warms up some."

"You'll get no argument from me," Troy replied and held the door open for me.

I took a seat and settled in for the ride.

"Excited?" Erica asked.

"And terrified. I'm going to give it my best shot."

"Relax. You will be fine. You've planned well and have food to keep you going if you don't catch a fish or shoot a bird."

"That's comforting to know, but I'm sure rice and beans will get old fast," I joked.

"That's very true, so start fishing as soon as possible. A run for coho or sockeye should start soon in your area."

"I'm looking forward to learning the skills. I've tried researching everything but know a lot will be trial and error."

"Just don't get frustrated. Use that flyrod if you're out on the water waiting to check your nets. I know your dad has caught a lot of fish with it. You should be able to catch dinner that way and use your netted fish for the smoker. After you set it for the first time, make sure you've cut plenty of alder to use in the smokehouse."

"Will do."

I was amazed to see a plethora of animals near the river's edge as we passed by. "Are the animals always this visible?"

"Once hunting season opens, they will go into hiding more, but until then, you should see quite a bit. Did you print out the schedules?" Troy asked.

"I did, but the largest game I could hope for would be a deer. Either the seasons are too short, or you need a permit for moose and caribou."

"I told you she did her homework," Erica teased Troy.

"Just checking." He grinned.

"I've found a suitable location of dead-standing spruce for firewood, so I hope to find some alder along the way."

"You shouldn't have a hard time with that," Troy replied. "If my memory serves me well, plenty are close by."

We settled into a comfortable conversation, and I was glad to see more of the sun peeking through. "Does the weather change quickly this time of year?"

"If it's not raining or spitting snow before you head out, I'd still pack your slicker. You really never know when it might come to a quick shower."

"Don't forget your magnesium fire starter. You may need to start a fire to warm you in an emergency. I've also got one more thing for you." Erica opened a drawer and pulled out a bush hat with the Trading Post logo. "Even though the clouds may be out, you can get sunburnt in the woods or on the river. This will help to keep you shaded from the sun and the glare."

"Thanks," I replied and immediately placed it on my head.

"My pleasure," Erica said. "Wear it often."

"I will," I promised.

†

The hours and miles passed quickly. Troy stood and reached for my hand. "Come, and I'll show you good spots in the river to fish."

"Are we getting close?"

"Maybe another hour. Erica has made good time on the water today."

"It's unusually calm today, but I don't mind," Erica answered.

Troy showed me how to look for darker water. "These will be deeper areas but good spots to set your net. Anything too shallow, you'll drag the bottom and catch debris. There's nothing more irritating than untangling limbs and brush from a net."

"What about areas like those where a creek empties into the river," I asked, pointing to an area ahead.

"You have done some research. Those are good spots as well, just not too shallow."

"I appreciate all the help and insight you have given me."

Troy smiled. "I love this place, and there's no place I'd rather be. Living in Anchorage for school will be torture, but hopefully, I can buckle down and finish early."

"Do they allow you to take online classes at home for summer breaks?"

"I'm not sure, but I will check those out."

†

When I started seeing mountains in the distance, I began to recognize the scenery from the photos. "We are close now, aren't we?"

"Ten minutes after we pass this next bend," Erica answered.

When we arrived, Erica pulled next to the small dock. "Here we are. Why don't you take the keys and open the cabin, and Troy and I will begin off-loading."

I picked up my shoulder bag and took out the keys. After climbing onto the dock, I walked up the stairs to the cabin and opened the door. The air was musty from being closed for a long time, so I placed my bag on the counter and opened the windows to air it out. When I returned outside, Troy had put the first boxes on the porch. I was thankful Dad had the cabin cleaned before I arrived, but I would give it another cleaning once settled.

He looked up at me. "I'll get them here if you begin carrying them inside. If any are too heavy, move them to the side, and I'll carry them in."

"No problem," I replied and picked up a box.

It took two hours to unload everything and place it inside the cabin. When we walked back to the boat, I hugged both of them. "Thank you both for everything and your mom for a great lunch."

Troy smiled. "I will. I put my cell number on the counter next to the bag for when you find the satellite phone."

"Thank you. I'll call in a few weeks before you are due to come out. Be safe going back."

"We will. We'll see you soon. Good luck," Erica said.

I watched them drive away and turned back to the cabin. I sat on the steps to take in the beauty of the day. I was truly alone for the first time in my life.

†

I started unpacking the boxes I had shipped to Elizabeth. The Jackery inverter was the first box opened, and I carried it outside and installed the solar panels so it could begin charging.

The next item was, thankfully, the Keurig coffee pot. I located the K cups I had purchased and got a cup of coffee brewing. The smell filled the cabin as it brewed, and I continued unpacking. The ham and sausage strings were hung on the cup holders I had bought at the store, and slowly, my new home began to take shape. I broke each of the boxes down and slid them under the bed. They could serve many uses, from a surface to process fish to a starter for fires in the stove and firepit. I sipped on the coffee as I unloaded box after box, and felt like I hadn't made a dent in them, but my pantry and shelves began filling.

Two hours later, I took a break and walked out to the firepit. A slight breeze felt good on my face as I gazed across the river to the mountains. My small boat was tethered to the dock, and I was excited to scout out an area to set my nets, but that would have to wait until tomorrow. I strolled over to the smokehouse and opened the door. A pile of wood was inside, but I knew it wasn't enough to smoke the fish I would catch. The woodpile was painfully small compared to what I would need. A large stump was present to use as a base to split the rounds. There were two sizes in the pile. The smallest, I assumed, was for the cabin stove, and the rest was for the sauna and fire pit. I entered the sauna/bathroom and walked inside. The sauna looked large enough to have a nice bath. I turned on the water and was thankful to see the water flowing. I wasn't thrilled about having to carry water to warm for bathing. The toilet was interesting, and I slowly lifted the lid to check for critters. None were present, and a roll of toilet paper was on the shelf, so I emptied my bladder. There was a small bucket beside the toilet, and I dropped a small scoop of sawdust into the toilet and sealed the lid.

I sighed and returned inside to resume unpacking. I placed as much clothing as possible into the dresser and hung the coats on the pegs beside the door. A large package of toilet paper was on the porch with a stack of towels and washcloths. I would take them out on my next visit. Spices were lined up on the counter next to the stovetop. I plugged in the satellite phone and headlamps to charge when I unpacked them. I smiled when I saw Troy's number and programmed his number into the phone. The linens and sleeping bag were placed on the bed. My investigation had revealed the nighttime temps would be in the forties. I opened the stove and smiled to see there was a fire already laid. I would light it before bed and carry a few armloads of wood to place on one of the cardboard boxes. I would put more of the smaller wood on the porch before stacking the fresh wood on the rack to begin seasoning. I started seeing progress and made my way to the small table. I set up the iPad and keyboard and vowed to spend an hour each night documenting my journey. There was ninety percent battery life, but I shut it down. There was time for that later in the day.

There were ten boxes left, which I vowed to empty. My stomach growled, so I opened a protein bar and took a bite. I opened the Blackstone and assembled the legs. The propane tanks were sitting by the end of the porch, so I temporarily stored the grill there and placed the cover snuggly over the body. I spotted a small table in the shed that would be a perfect cooking surface for the grill. If there was still light left, I would set up the grill near the front porch and begin seasoning it with some eggs and a few sausage links. I unpacked condiment squirt bottles and filled one with olive oil to use on the grill. I would add extras to eat for breakfast before starting on chores. I placed a stack of work and thermal gloves on a shelf by the door. I would attach the Bowie to my belt before leaving the house. I loaded the pistol, secured it in the shoulder rig, and fitted it snuggly before hanging it beside the coats. I left the rifle in the case but loaded an ammo belt with shotgun shells. I would take the shotgun on my trips out to the woodlot. With the final box broken down, I looked at my watch. It was eight o'clock but still light enough to cook a meal. I retrieved the table and placed the grill on top before I removed the cover and attached the gas. I returned inside for a plate, four links of sausage, and three eggs that had cracked during transport. A second trip was made to get a spatula, knife, and oil.

After turning on the gas, I hit the igniter, and the grill came to life. I poured oil across the surface and used the spatula to season the grill. I reduced the heat, cut the sausage in half, and placed them on the grill. They were fully smoked but would taste better warm. I gave them a head start before adding more oil and cracking the eggs. I carried the shells to the firepit and returned to the grill. I plated the food once cooked, turned off the gas, and walked inside to eat at the small table. After drawing a glass of water, I sat to feast. I was surprised when I took a drink at how cold and refreshing the water tasted. My first meal in my new home was fantastic. I wrapped two of the sausages and washed my dishes.

I rewarded myself with a second cup of coffee and walked to the firepit to enjoy the hot drink. Afterward, I walked to the dock and saw a plastic storage container labeled Gill Net. "Tomorrow, I will start breaking you in. I have faith that we will make a great team."

I then walked to the shed, pulled down Dad's flyrod, and carried it to the porch. I would attach a fresh fly to it tomorrow and store the rest in the tackle box on the boat.

"Dad promised you would bring me luck and big fish," I said as I placed the rod by the front door.

Darkness was beginning to enter the sky. I picked up the toilet paper and linens before walking to the bathroom. When I returned to the cabin, I booted up the iPad and began typing.

July 3rd - Day One – I arrived at my new home and stored all my supplies. I was sad to watch Erica and Troy leave, but I had much to do before retiring for the evening. My first meal was a great breakfast cooked on the Blackstone, and then I checked my supplies to try my hand at using the gill net. I am confident I will learn to fish this way, even if it takes several attempts. I plan to fly-fish briefly after setting my net before returning home to load supplies and head to the woodlot. I plan to down six trees, remove the limbs, and begin cutting rounds. During my next visit, I can bring the sled and start hauling the cut sections home. This should take several hours, which I feel will be adequate for my first attempt at woodcutting. My eyes are growing heavy, so I will stop here tonight.

I changed into my sleep clothes and thought it felt comfortable inside the cabin. I locked the door and placed a long-handled Bic lighter next to the stove in case I needed to light a fire during the night. After shutting all the windows, I climbed onto the bed and stretched out on the sleeping bag without closing it. It would be easy to reach if I got chilled during the night. The lamp was switched off, and I listened to the night around me. I could hear a faint chorus of insects and an owl hooting in the distance. This had to be the perfect definition of peacefulness.

CHAPTER FIVE

I woke the following morning, slightly disoriented in my new surroundings. The room was chilly but not uncomfortable as I dressed for the day. I brewed a coffee and ate the sausage as I packed my day bag. I remembered the advice to pack snacks, a water bottle, and a rain slicker. I slipped the shoulder rig on and then a light work shirt and jacket. My eyes landed on the magnesium fire starter, which I added to the bag, and threaded the Bowie knife onto my belt. I took a deep breath.

"I believe I'm ready."

The air was cool, but it was a beautiful morning. I checked my watch and was surprised it was only six. This would definitely take some getting used to. I carried the fly rod and climbed into the boat before untying the bow line. I allowed the motor to warm up for a few minutes before turning it into reverse and driving upstream. Proceeding slowly, I watched the water for a deep spot per Troy's instruction, and when I felt I had located an area, I killed the motor and dropped the anchor. I moved the storage container closer and opened the lid. I lowered the buoy and weight over the edge and began feeding the net into the water. I lifted the anchor and started the motor to idle in reverse as I fed more of the net into the water. I was pleased the net was tight and straight when the last anchor and buoy dropped into the water. I glanced at my watch.

"Wow, that didn't even take an hour."

I drove out into the middle of the river and cut off the engine to float slowly toward home. I picked up the flyrod and spit on the fly before I began making my casts. The fly had been on the surface for less than two minutes when a fish struck the line. I was so shocked I almost forgot to set the hook. When I landed the fish in the boat, I was amazed by the size of it. *Plenty for lunch and dinner,* I thought. *No need to catch another just yet.* I placed the fish on a line and tied it to the side of the boat as I drove home slowly. I tied the line to the dock to keep the fish fresh until I had time to process it later. After securing the bow line, I climbed from the boat with my day bag.

I walked to the shed and started the ATV, allowing it to warm as I checked the saw for fuel, bar, and chain oil. I placed extra supplies in the back rack and secured the saw with a bungee cord. The ATV shifted into gear smoothly, and I started down a path I hoped would bring me directly to the woodlot. Along the route, I found a small grove of alder, and dropped and limbed two trees. A small section of rope was in the console, so I was determined to drag the two trees back to the cabin on my trip home.

I was delighted when the woodlot came into view, and I parked a safe distance from the trees. I pulled my hat down and slipped into protective eyeglasses. I made a mental note to check the shed for ear protection and would add it to my list if none were found. Cutting the alders had been good practice, and when the third tree hit the ground, my confidence had grown about how to drop a tree in the desired direction. I cut three more trees and took a hydration break before starting to limb the trees. The dead limbs were easy to remove, and I rested when they were all detached. I looked at my watch. Not nearly as quickly as setting the net, but I could see progress. I lifted a protein bar to my mouth and was surprised by how shaky my arm was. Yeah, I would definitely feel the exertion tonight. It took longer than I planned to cut the logs into rounds, but I stayed on task to reach my daily goal, and I was glad to shut the saw off for the day. I thought my arms were tired before. Now they felt like they weighed fifty pounds after cutting the rounds.

I stopped at the alders and hooked them to the back of the ATV. I pulled them close to the smokehouse. If I successfully caught fish, I would cut the smaller alders into sections to add to the smokehouse. I parked the ATV in the shed and entered the cabin to refill my water bottle and open a pack of jerky to snack on before checking the net. After retrieving a couple of five-gallon buckets, I walked to the boat. My heart began thumping as I approached my net and could see movement. *It may only be one fish, but I'll be happy landing my first.* After turning off the motor, I began pulling up the net. It was more than one. I had caught seven fish on my first attempt. After resetting the line, I grinned at the buckets overflowing with fish. When I returned home, I set the buckets on the dock and walked inside for the fileting knife and a section of cardboard. After fileting all the fish and coating them with salt, I hung them in the smoker and carried my first catch into the house. I would soak the filets in a water brine until I could cook them. I had harvested eggs from several fish that I put in a jar. I had no idea of how to preserve them, but I felt I shouldn't waste any part of the fish. After rinsing the buckets, I placed them back in the boat. It was still early, so I thought I might return to the net before retiring. I started the fire in the smokehouse and walked inside. I felt silly for calling for assistance on my first full day, but I really had no idea how to store the eggs.

Swallowing my pride, I picked up the sat phone and called Troy.

"Hey, this is Tatum. I have a question for you."

"Great, how is your first day going?"

"It's terrific, but I've encountered something I do not know how to handle. I caught seven fish in the net, and several had eggs, but I have no idea how to store them."

"That's awesome. Hey, Erica, Tatum caught seven fish on her first try."

"Incredible. Congratulations," Erica yelled in the background.

"Hey, Erica, what's the best method for storing fish roe?"

Erica came on the line. "Cleaning and brining the eggs using kosher salt may be challenging without refrigeration. I would place them in some of your jars and submerge them in the sink under cold water to keep them safe. I would eat it within two days. Do you like caviar?"

"Not particularly," I answered. "I've never acquired a taste for it."

"For shame," Erica teased. "I would recommend you return them to the river then. Other fish will eat them, and depending on the age, some may develop."

"I feel bad for wasting them."

"They won't go to waste. Another animal will eat them. Don't feel bad."

"Thanks for your guidance."

"It sounds like you had a good first day."

"I did, and I won't have any trouble sleeping tonight. I still have to cut more wood for the smoker."

"Good job. Call whenever you need to."

"Thanks, Erica. Thank Troy for me, too."

"You're welcome," Troy called back. "Good luck, and stay safe."

I chuckled. "Talk soon," I said and ended the call.

†

After drinking a glass of water, I refilled my water bottle and walked to the shed for the chainsaw. I checked the fluids and then began cutting the logs into smaller sections. The closer to the bottom of the trunk, the broader the widths became, so I decided to split those into smaller pieces. I carried a few to the splitting stump and used the chainsaw to mark them into quarters. Then, I used the splitting ax to finish the quartering. That worked so well that I decided to employ the same method on the firewood. Using a high-heat method of smoking would allow me to can the salmon. I needed to add a small refrigerator/freezer to my supply list, along with a vacuum sealer. With the addition of the Jackery inverter, I could use the power from that on the smaller appliances, saving the solar energy to run the cooling unit. I had plenty of jars to can the smoked fish and would add more to my list. Once my cans were filled, I would hold off on fishing until better storage options were available. The last thing I needed was a bad case of food poisoning.

I added more small logs to the smokehouse and peeked at the salmon. They appeared to be cooking well, and the smell was delicious. I was surprised that I still had energy left to burn, so I retrieved the shotgun and, after hooking the sled to the ATV, I returned to the woodlot. The first tree filled the sled, so I carefully drove it home and unloaded it next to the chopping stump. *Maybe one more load*, I thought and returned to the woodlot. I felt a tightness in my back as I loaded the second tree. A nice hot bath would probably help sore and tired muscles. After dropping the load and storing the sled and ATV, I filled the sauna tub with water and lit a fire beneath it to warm it. I had no clue how long it would take to heat the water to a tolerable level, but I still had work to do.

I moved the small sections of firewood for the stove onto the porch and began scoring the rounds into quarters with the chainsaw. I split several wood rounds and piled them into the empty rack before I took a break. As I sat drinking water, I wondered if I should recheck the nets. Soon, I would need to can the first batch of fish, which would give me an idea of how many fish I could catch and preserve immediately. Deciding to check the nets, I found four more fish had been captured and took them home to process. I placed them on a separate rack from the first batch and checked the time. I relieved my bladder and checked the bathwater. I was pleased it was beginning to warm, but I had another task to complete. My stomach was grumbling with hunger. I walked into the cabin and removed the fish from the water, patting them dry and then covering them with seasonings. The container of maple syrup caught my eye, and I poured some of it into a squeeze bottle. *Now is as good a time to experiment as any*, I thought, as I carried the pan of filets, a plate, a spatula, and a fork to the porch. My water bottle was still on the steps.

When the surface temperature met what I wanted, I placed the four filets onto the grill skin side down. I added a drizzle of maple syrup to two of them after I turned them and closed the lid. The air filled with the aroma of cooking fish, and I could smell the syrup caramelizing in the enclosed heat. After another five minutes, I plated the filets and let them rest while I tended to the grill. I picked up the plate and water bottle before walking to the firepit. The salmon flaked when I touched it with my fork, and the moist fish assaulted my taste buds. Before I knew it, I had consumed all four filets, my favorite being the ones with maple syrup. The sugary concoction added a whole new level of flavor.

"Wow, I was hungrier than I thought." I chuckled as I kicked back in the chair to relax and let the fish settle.

After washing my dishes, I selected clean clothes and hygiene supplies to walk to the bathroom. The water wasn't steaming, but it was plenty comfortable for a soaking bath. Sinking into the tepid water, I washed my hair and stretched out to soak in the warm water. I thought some Epsom salts would be an excellent addition to my shopping list as I felt tight muscles slowly relax. I soaked until the water began to cool and then bathed quickly before climbing out and draining the tub.

I spotted the pile of wood as I walked back to the cabin, and I shook my head. No need to get sweaty after such a perfect bath. Returning to the small kitchen table, I started a new shopping list as I sipped on coffee. A fridge/freezer combination was at the top of the list. I added more jars, Epsom salts, and a vacuum sealer with rolls of bags. A couple of large coolers would be helpful to store food once the snow began to fly and would save room in the freezer, but those could wait.

†

I started the iPad and began my daily entry.

July 4th - Day Two
How ironic that my first day alone is Independence Day. No fireworks filled the air, but the blooming flowers' sweet smells were an excellent substitute. I had a productive day today. My first batches of fish are in the smoker, and I harvested several trees for firewood. My first attempt at cooking salmon on the Blackstone was remarkable, and I surprised myself by eating all four filets. The maple syrup was a great addition. A soaking bath was heavenly and left me rejuvenated and ready to do more, but I'm resisting overdoing chores. This is a work in progress; there will always be something to do. I plan to work on canning the fish tomorrow and cook some pancakes and sausage for a hearty breakfast while the jars seal. Then, I will return to the woodlot to haul more rounds and begin splitting in earnest.

I'm finding the Blackstone was an excellent addition to my equipment and will serve me well in the future. I decided to sit on the dock and see if I could add some fresh fish to the stringer for instant meals as needed. Two or three would work well and keep me in a good supply.

✝

I added a hoodie and picked up the flyrod before walking to the dock. The moon had risen, barely visible in the fading daylight. The river flowed by peacefully as I began my cast. It didn't take long to catch two fish and add them to the stringer tied to the dock. I sat on the dock until the night grew chilly, and I heard the owl hooting in the distance. I took that as my cue to prepare for bed. Today was a great day, and tomorrow held great promise.

✝

The following morning, I woke to the sound of tapping on the tin roof and looked out the window to find it sprinkling. I pulled on my shoes and walked to the porch to move the Blackstone to a more protected area near the firewood. I needed to add a tarp to cover the wood on the porch to keep it dry from rain and snow. Canning would take some time, so hopefully, the rain would pass through while I worked inside. I pulled on my slicker and picked up a pan before walking to the smoker to bring the fish inside. They had a beautiful glaze and threatened to fall apart as I placed them in the pan. After adding salt to a pot of water for a brine, I cut the fish into strips to fit inside the jars. The eleven fish filled almost an entire case of jars. I would definitely need more jars if a refrigerator was not an option soon. I would check my nets later in the morning and pull them if another dozen fish were caught. That would give me an excellent supply, but I might need to consider calling Troy for a delivery to avoid missing the fish runs. Once I poured the brine into the jars, I screwed down the lids and assembled my supplies for cooking breakfast. I used a jar to prepare pancake batter and cut two more sausage links. Walking to the porch to cook, I heard the audible pop as a jar was sealed. I smiled and opened the door, hoping to listen to a chorus of sealing lids.

The rain had slowed, but the sky remained overcast as I cooked my breakfast. I cooked two large pancakes as the sausage heated and returned inside to brew coffee. After cleaning up from the meal, I checked the nets first to be closer to home in case the rain returned. Another ten fish filled the buckets, and I pulled the net, storing it in the container as I removed the fish. I made a mental note of the location with plans to return soon to fish the productive spot. After processing the catch, I hung them in the smoker and added wood to the smoldering coals.

I refilled my water bottle and packed my daypack with snacks. Some boiled eggs would also make high-protein snacks and be easy to transport. I slung the shotgun over my back and walked out to hook the sled to the ATV to return to the woodlot.

After five loads, all of the rounds were delivered to the cabin. I smiled at the massive pile of wood that needed to be split. I scored twenty pieces and prepared to begin dividing the sections. I removed the slicker, draped it over the shotgun, and started the task. I worked for several hours before taking a hydration break. The sun had broken through and warmed the air. I could feel a light sweat trickle down my back, but I kept my shirt on for fear of getting chilled. The water quenched my thirst, but an ice-cold beer would taste good. Maybe I would add a case or two to my order. The days were cool enough to keep the beer chilled without taking up precious room in the refrigerator. I added smaller rounds to the stack for the stove and stacked the quarters on the pile for outdoor use. The fish in the smoker had cooked for several hours, so I decided it was time to try out the smoked fish. I returned inside for a plate and fork before walking to the smokehouse. I could place several sections in a Ziploc bag and squeeze out all the air to store filets for a day or two. I removed a fish and walked to the firepit to enjoy a meal.

The filet had a beautiful smoked glaze, and the meat fell apart as I filled my fork. The taste was light and flakey but differed from the fish grilled on the Blackstone. It would be a welcome change, but my tastebuds preferred the flavor from the grill. After removing the remaining filets, I prepped them for canning, dated, and stored the first jars before storing them in the pantry. I opened a canister of coffee and made a cup in the Keurig. It wasn't the glorious flavor of a K cup, but sugar cut the bitter taste. I would need to alternate brews to make my K cups last as long as possible.

After the jars were filled, I returned to splitting wood. I felt like I had made tremendous progress and needed to take an opportunity to do some exploring. I would take tomorrow off to do just that. I wanted to explore what other resources were available in the area. I would like to find some feeder streams and see if they were part of a lake system. I would also keep an eye out for grouse or other fowl to begin supplementing my diet. A grouse would make a good dish similar to chicken and rice. That would be a tasty option from the fish. They would also cook well on the Blackstone with fried rice as a side dish. My stomach was full, but the thought of food made my mouth water.

I split wood until the last round was cut and stacked. The rack looked better but would not be enough to survive the coming months. I decided to cut a ham steak to eat with some scrambled eggs. I also placed a small pot with three eggs on the grill to boil to pack for an easy snack the next day. I topped off the gas in the ATV and stored the container with the remaining gas on the back rack. After allowing the eggs to cool, I placed them in a small container and put them in my daypack with a package of jerky. I had no idea how long I would explore, but I needed to prepare for staying out longer than anticipated.

I called Erica and gave her my list of items, and she assured me that Troy could deliver them next week. The refrigerator was the only item she did not stock, but she would purchase one and add it to her account. I sat on the porch steps listening to the night until the hooting owl sent me to bed. He had turned into my alarm to get some rest, and I never hesitated to sleep well after hearing his call.

I was about to slip into bed when I realized I hadn't entered my journal notes for the day. I walked to the table and turned on the iPad to make a quick entry.

July 5ᵗʰ - Day 3

Today was a fantastic day. A second batch of smoked fish was canned, and the rest of the wood I had cut was split and stacked. I tried the smoked fish for the first time and learned I preferred the taste of fresh cooked on the Blackstone. Once I have a vacuum sealer and a means to store freshly caught fish in the refrigerator/freezer, I can concentrate on more gill netting. I've decided to take a break from chores and spend tomorrow exploring to give my body a rest break. I placed an order with Erica and am looking forward to seeing Troy when he makes the delivery next week. My daypack is loaded with supplies for an outing on the ATV, and I will keep an eye open for grouse or other fowl during my adventure.

I turned off the iPad and then plugged the device in to charge. It was another productive day, and I fell asleep, looking forward to a day of adventure.

CHAPTER SIX

The following day was glorious. I used the pancake batter from the day before to make breakfast, and after refreshing my water bottle and drinking a cup of coffee, I picked up the ammo belt and shotgun and walked out to the ATV.

I drove down the trail and passed the turnoff to the woodlot to continue to ride beside the river. When I found the first feeder creek, I turned into the woods and crept through the dense forest. After several minutes, I saw a path that led to a small lake that fed the feeder creek. It wasn't a large lake, but obvious game trails led down to the water's edge. I turned off the ATV and listened to the sounds of the forest as my eyes scanned the beauty of the lake.

I caught movement off to my left and spotted a grouse that had landed in a tree twenty yards away. Picking up the shotgun as quietly as possible, I took aim and shot. I placed the ejected shell in my pocket and retrieved the bird. The blast of the shot made the air grow silent so I sat under the tree and waited for the forest to return to life. I plucked the feathers and processed the bird before placing it in a bucket on the back of the ATV. Then I drove to the water's edge to put water in the bucket to keep the breast meat moist. Game tracks were everywhere, and one set was so massive it couldn't be anything other than a moose. I witnessed fish jumping and made a mental note to bring the flyrod to catch the trout or other fish present. One of my worries had been my ability to keep myself fed, but that feeling was abating with my success at harvesting fish and now a grouse. It was just the beginning, but I was confident in my growing skills.

As I continued around the lake, I found a small section of forest filled with mushrooms. I recognized them as porcini, which were safe to eat, and I harvested a few handfuls, placing them in the container I had put the boiled eggs in. Now was a good time to eat a snack, so I peeled and ate the eggs as I trimmed the mushrooms. They should be tasty in various meals, from omelets to fried rice, and cooked as a side for the grouse or salmon. I could now add another skill to my repertoire. I could forage. I grinned as I washed the last egg down with a drink of cold water.

I found my next prize when I reached a grove of birch trees. The chaga was low enough for me to harvest. I carefully broke several large clumps from the trees and placed them in the back of the ATV. To my delight and amazement, another grouse came into view and joined the first in my bucket. This spot had turned into a gold mine, and I would return here for more of the mushrooms and chaga if I successfully blended them into my diet. Both varieties could be dried and stored easily, adding to future meals.

I motored home slowly and took my bounty inside. I rinsed and diced the mushrooms and sliced the chaga into sections for drying. I found I could use some fishing line to dry them on the porch. It was midafternoon when I hung the chaga, and my body remained full of energy, so I decided to return to the woodlot to drop more trees. The more I could accomplish now, the better. I dropped two dozen trees, removed the limbs, and cut rounds until my arms quivered. It was time to stop so I loaded the saw and drove home. As I passed the bathhouse, I decided to start a stack of wood there to warm the bath water. I found a spot away from the drain area and mentally planned a new stack. I parked the ATV and looked at the distance between the two buildings. That might be a good area for wood storage. The two buildings could provide some shelter from the elements as the weather changes. I had picked up a small limb and placed it across the back of the ATV, not knowing why, but as I sat on the porch steps with the stick in my hands, an idea began to form. After chores were done during the day, I needed a hobby to work on, and I decided to use the small hand saw to cut the limb into smaller sections and try my hand at carving.

I started with six pieces and carved on the first piece until a form appeared. I hadn't planned an image to create, but I saw a salmon beginning to come to life in the wood. That was an easy shape to produce for my first attempt, and I was pleased to see it come to life. I used the knife to smooth rough edges and cut designs into soft wood. I would allow the piece to dry and then use some ash and clay to rub in some color. Yeah, that was a good plan.

When I began to feel hungry, I started the Blackstone and placed a pot of water to boil for the rice. I put some of the diced mushrooms into the water when I added the rice and grilled two grouse breasts. The oil and seasoning brought out a wonderful flavor in the meat, and I was pleased with the outcome. If I used oil on the stovetop, I was sure it would taste close to fried chicken. I planned to test that theory the next day with the leftover rice.

After cleaning up from dinner, I sat on the steps with another small piece of wood. This time, I had an image in mind, and slowly, the owl appeared in the wood. I had not spotted him yet, but I thought my representation would be close. On cue, he appeared in a tree near the cabin and hooted to remind me it was time to retire.

July 6th – Day Four

My day of exploration was fruitful. I harvested two birds and foraged for some mushrooms. The mushrooms added a nice texture and flavor to the rice. I was so energized by the success I decided to drop more trees for firewood. I also began a new hobby today, carving the animals that have been a part of my new life here. I was pleased with my first two attempts, which proved a relaxing way to pass the time. Until Troy arrives with my next delivery, I will focus on firewood to bring in as much as possible. I am proud of the new skills I am learning in the bush, but it's time to rest and recharge.

†

Breakfast the following morning was an omelet filled with ham bits and more diced mushrooms. A dash of hot sauce turned it into a fantastic meal. After cleaning the dishes, I re-packed my daypack, picked up the shotgun, and walked to the ATV. I topped off the gas tank and loaded my chainsaw and supplies before attaching the sled. It was barely seven in the morning, and I was surprised at how easy it had become to wake up eager to start the day. After filling a small thermos with coffee, I drove to the woodlot. I loaded the rounds I had cut the previous day and resumed cutting until the sled was full. After ten loads, I needed to refuel my body. In the cabin, I turned a burner on the stove and added some oil to a frying pan. I coated the two breasts in seasoned flour and placed them in the pan when the oil was hot. I opened a window to allow the heat from cooking to escape the small cabin and listened to the birds sing as my meal cooked. When the breasts were done, I poured the last of the rice from last night's meal into the pan to warm and soak up some of the rich gravy that had formed. *Damn, that was a great meal.* I ate every bite and went back to work.

It took six more loads to bring all the rounds home, and as I began scoring and splitting the wood, I tossed the sections back into the sled to move them between the two buildings to start a new woodpile. As I chopped the wood, I planned dinner and grilled another salmon with more syrup. I remembered it was Saturday night, so I turned the small radio on when I moved inside to eat at the small table. Country music played for several minutes before a voice came over the airways, reading messages to family and friends. I was surprised when I heard my name.

"Tatum, we hope you are having a great first week in the bush. See you soon. Troy."

That was delightful, and I smiled the rest of the night. I was proud of all I had accomplished and hoped to impress Troy when he visited in four days. I listened to more messages as I made my journal entry for the day.

July 7ᵗʰ – Day five.

Hauled all the wood to the yard and have a nice stack started between the outbuildings. I plan to continue increasing the firewood supply until my new equipment arrives and I can resume fishing. I received my first bush message from Troy, which made me smile. I hope he's as proud of me as I am. Not bad for a city girl and Cheechako. *I planned to begin fishing again in three days and hope to send some salmon filets and roe back with Troy. I need to call him to confirm the delivery and ask him to bring a cooler with ice to take some fish home.*

†

After splitting wood for hours, I had made a nice stack between the two outbuildings, and I decided tonight would be a good time for a bath. The temperature had risen during the day, and I pulled off my work shirt and was still coated with sweat. I was surprised by how well the daily exertion kept the muscle soreness at bay. As I was fileting the two fish I would eat for dinner, I heard wings fluttering and looked up to find a raven sitting on top of the smokehouse. He cocked his head at me, curious about what I was doing.

"Are you hungry?"

The bird shifted his feet and nodded toward me. I sliced a piece of salmon and tossed it to land on top of the smokehouse. He startled and flew to a nearby branch. I carried a carcass, placed it next to the meat, and returned to my fish. I pretended to ignore him, and he flitted back onto the smokehouse to tear at the flesh. I left the second carcass on the cardboard and walked inside to rinse and brine the filets.

I peeked out the window and saw he was still enjoying his feast. I decided to fish to replenish the fish on the stringer. As I sat on the dock fishing, the bird flew to a branch just above the boat and watched. The raven wasn't the only thing eager for a meal. Within a half hour, I had added four more fish to the stringer. As I placed the last fish on the line, I looked up at the curious bird.

"If you're going to stick around for handouts, you need a name. I shall call you Poe."

I laughed at myself for naming the bird, but if Tom Hanks could talk to a volleyball for years, I could speak to a bird. "So, Poe it will be." I placed the last carcass on top of the smokehouse and walked to the cabin to prepare the fish for cooking. A cool breeze had picked up, so I slipped into my work shirt as the Blackstone heated. I lit a fire under the tub and filled it with water for a bath. I knew it would take time to heat, so I returned to cook and eat my meal. While sitting on the steps, I sipped coffee and found the bird still atop the smokehouse.

"No leftovers tonight, my friend, but I promise to feed you again tomorrow if you're still here."

I picked up a section of wood and began to carve. With a live model, I wasn't surprised that the figure of a raven began to form. I would build a fire to burn some of the smaller limbs I had trimmed from the alder and scorch the raven figure to blacken the wood. I had kept the oil from frying the grouse and would use some to give him a shiny gloss.

After placing the carving on the table, I picked out clean clothes. Soon, I would need to bring the washpot to the firepit to do some laundry. The water was warm enough to bathe, so I slipped out of my clothes and sank into the water. I rested my head against the back of the tub and closed my eyes. I wondered how Charlie was faring on his adventure.

When the water began to cool, I bathed and dried off before slipping into clean clothes. It felt good to be clean again, and I was relaxed as I sat down to add to my journal.

July 8th – Day Six

After another day of hard work, I made a new friend. A beautiful raven perched atop the smokehouse, watching me process fish, and I offered him some scraps. I was surprised he stuck around after finishing a meal, so I gave him a name. He would be Poe, and as long as he chooses to stick around, I would try to feed him when possible. In the morning, before I resume working on firewood, I plan to enter a grove of live spruce to see if I can hunt spruce chickens. They should be larger than the grouse and are said to have a nutty taste to their meat. If I run across another patch, I will also take a basket to harvest more mushrooms. The Chaga appeared to be drying nicely, and in a few days, I will try grinding some for tea. The three small carvings sat on the table. They really weren't a bad first attempt. The owl hooted my signal it was time for bed.

I fell asleep quickly and dreamed of Poe.

†

Rain moved in during the night, and I woke to the constant tapping of raindrops on the roof. I climbed from the bed and walked to the front door to look outside. The clouds hung low with the weight of the rain, and it appeared at least the morning would be a washout. After making coffee, I sat at the table and looked around. The bag of carrots and onions hanging on hooks caught my attention. I could eat breakfast and then chop some vegetables for soup for when I could venture out for a spruce chicken. I had a few large, empty jars left, which should be ample to store some soup. I cut a ham steak to place in a pan to heat and began making pancakes and scrambled eggs. I reached for my coffee cup and heard a tapping on the front window. I turned to find Poe staring at me.

"Are you hungry?"

I picked up a pancake and carried it to the woodpile at the end of the porch. Poe had moved to the porch railing to watch, and when I returned to the door, he flew over to the pile. I left the door open behind me to bring in the fresh scent of the rain and the sound of water flowing off the roof. After serving my meal, I took my plate and coffee to the table and looked across the river, watching the raindrops form ripples in the water. So peaceful.

†

I chopped and diced carrots and potatoes for the soup and found a small container to place the scraps into for Poe. He was nowhere to be seen when I put the container on the wood pile. There wasn't a scrap of pancake left. *I'm glad he enjoys my cooking.*

The rain slacked off around noon, and I decided to risk going to the spruce stand to hunt. I wouldn't melt. I pulled on my rain slicker and hat to walk out to the ATV as the sun began to peek through the clouds. Greenery shined with water as I drove along the now familiar path, and the air smelled fresh and clean. I'd never scented air like this in Chicago.

I parked the ATV at the grove's edge and stalked quietly until I found the first bird. I was surprised at how much bigger the bird was than the other grouse I had harvested. It was in the same family, but this was almost the size of a domestic chicken. After bagging two more birds, I processed the meat and returned to the ATV. I would fry one and boil one each for soup and dumplings. It was time to break out the cornmeal and make some fry bread. The soup and dumplings would store well and make a hearty meal to warm quickly on cold winter days. I used both burners to boil the breasts while working on the woodpiles. I filled the sled twice with quarter rounds and stacked them near the bathhouse fire pit before returning inside to check the cooking meat.

I reduced the heat and removed the breasts to cut them into cubes. When I opened a drawer for a knife, I saw something I had previously overlooked. A Case pocketknife was tucked into a drawer. Probably it had been left by my father. It would be perfect for carving. I removed the knife and opened it to inspect the blade. It seemed a bit dull, but I could sharpen it for carving. When the first breast was chopped, I added the meat to the broth, surrounded it with vegetables and a healthy portion of rice, covered the pot, and started working on dumplings.

I smiled at my progress when I dropped dumplings into the soup and added flour to thicken the broth. The cabin smelled heavenly. I sharpened the pocketknife blade and walked to the porch to carve a spruce chicken. The piece wasn't as impressive as the first three, but I was pleased with the smaller knife's maneuverability versus the Bowie.

Poe dropped to the ground near the fire pit for a drink of water before hopping on a chair to watch me. I lifted the carving piece to show him.

"It's not as good as the one of you, but I'm still learning."

When I returned to the stove, I added a handful of mushroom pieces to each pot and pulled the remaining jars from the pantry. I stared out the window at the wood still on the ground needing to be split. I planned to place at least one load at the firepit. That was an area I had not taken full advantage of yet, but I would remedy it soon. The view of the river and mountains was too beautiful to not enjoy as long as possible. At night the temps were cooler, and a fire would adequately cut the chill. After stirring each pot, I reduced the heat to a simmer.

I chopped another portion of onions and potatoes to cook with the breasts on the grill, and would also cook the fry bread. After checking the pots, I turned off the burners to allow them to begin cooling, so I could transfer the contents into jars. After splitting and stacking the last of the wood, I returned to the kitchen to store the food. A portion of the dumplings would not fit, so I placed them in a bowl, added more seasoning, and let the pots soak in the sink while I tried them. My eyes grew wide when I took the first bite of the bird. It tasted like blueberries, which were obviously a part of the bird's diet, but it was a pleasant surprise. At the first opportunity, I would take my basket to see if I could find the blueberry patch or any other type of berry and search for more mushrooms.

Berries would be great to add to pancakes. I grinned. *Always thinking of new ways to spice up meals. Maybe tomorrow, after setting the nets again. I hope I haven't missed the run.* I really wanted to send some fish back with Troy. He would be here soon for delivery, and then I would press hard to harvest as many fish and other game for winter meals since I would have a reliable means of storage.

After cooking dinner, I cleaned the kitchen and sat on the steps when I looked up at the chaga. It looked to be drying well, so I removed a small section, cut it into small pieces, and then used a spoon to grind it to a powder. I opened the iPad while the tea brewed, and when I felt it had time to cook, I added a bit of sugar to a cup and filled it with the fragrant liquid. I was surprised at the taste, and within minutes I felt a sense of overwhelming calm. I felt a silly grin fill my face as I felt almost giddy and wondered if that was one of the effects of the tea. *Not unpleasant at all,* I thought as I fought back the urge to break into giggles.

July 9th – Day seven

I am still experiencing a feeling of euphoria as I try to enter my journal entry for the day. It is challenging to focus on forming words, so I'll keep it short. Another great day and chaga tea is the bomb. Two days before Troy arrives. Good night, Poe.

†

When I woke the following morning, my bladder ached for release, so I rushed across the yard to relieve myself. Poe called to me from the top of the smokehouse.

"I know. Breakfast soon."

There were two pieces of fry bread which I fed him on the wood pile. Then I cooked a large ham omelet. The chaga tea didn't leave me with a hangover or other ill side effects, but damn, I was hungry.

I was eager to set the net and would make filets for Troy to return to town to share. I had plenty of gallon-sized bags and hoped for a big catch. Once I returned, I hooked up the sled to the ATV and brought in some of the alder brush for the firepit before topping off the tank and searching for berries. I tossed two five-gallon buckets and a wicker basket. I passed the spruce grove, going deeper into the forest until I saw another small lake. Walking around the edge, I found patches of wild lettuce and picked some for the basket. It would be great as a salad or a garnish for fish or fowl.

Ha, I'm beginning to think like a bush chef. I heard the flutter of wings and shot another bird. So far, the morning had started off great. I drove until I found a large patch of early ripe blueberries. I exited the ATV and released the trigger guard on the pistol on my shoulder. The birds and I wouldn't be the only ones foraging for berries. Bears would be eating anything in sight to fatten up for the long winter hibernation, so I would need to keep my eyes and ears open. The pistol would do little for protection but might be loud enough to scare him away or give me time to escape to the ATV.

I picked quickly and filled a bucket full of the juicy berries. I contemplated a second bucket but decided to stick to one until I could store them properly. It would be bad juju to waste such a pleasant treat. I added mushrooms to the basket and returned home to drop off my bounty. I poured the berries into the sink to soak and rinse off any sand or debris, and spread the lettuce and mushrooms on the countertop. After adding salt to the water to brine the grouse breast, I refilled my water bottle and snacks before walking to the boat.

My heart was overjoyed when I lifted the first float on the net to feel the weight of fish caught. It was the most significant catch, pulling sixteen fish into the boat. As I drove back to the cabin, I had a brainstorm. As I was rummaging through the storage shed, I saw three plastic milk crates and several bungee cords, and an idea popped into my head. The water wasn't below freezing yet but was as cold or colder than a refrigerator. I decided to rinse the filets, store them in Ziploc bags, and then place them in the crates to attach to the dock to remain fresh.

I dropped the filets into a pan to return inside to rinse them and bag them. Several fish were stuffed with eggs, and I gently placed the sacks in the pan with filets. One sack broke in half, so I put it on the smokehouse for Poe. "You're going to get fat sticking around here." He looked at me and then began eating the rich eggs. When I carried the pan into the cabin, I drained the blueberries and filled the gallon bags with berries, leaving a bowl to use in cooking. I planned to use one of the milk cartons to store the berries. Damn, I was becoming a genius. Dad would be proud of my creativity and problem-solving.

I carried the full bags of berries and filets and placed them inside the crates I had hung off the dock. There was plenty of room for more, and the water was cold as a cooler. I used some of the berries in pancakes for dinner and placed the grouse breasts in my homemade cooler. I would cook them in anticipation of Troy's arrival.

I used the last two sections of wood at the firepit to carve more salmon, and I was establishing a collection along the windowsill in the kitchen. I picked up the raven and used two pieces of kindling to scorch the carving without burning. Once the piece cooled to the touch, I picked it up and rubbed off the ash. Holding it up for Poe to see.

"Does it look like you?"

Poe's head bobbed, and I smiled back at him.

When the fire died, I walked inside and rubbed some used oil into the wood. I was pleased with how the oil made the wood shine. It reminded me of the sun reflecting off Poe's feathers.

"Yeah, that's it," I said as I placed the carving on the windowsill.

July 10th – Day eight.

My creativity kicked into high gear today, and I found a way to keep items cold and fresh using the water from the river along with milk crates and bungee cords. I could store a dozen bags of salmon and two bags of roe to send back with Troy with room left in the containers. I picked a bucket full of blueberries, an excellent addition to pancakes for dinner. Poe had a wonderful meal of fish scraps and a small roe sack. I added to my collection of carvings and scorched the raven to look more like Poe. Troy will arrive at some point tomorrow, and I'll cook the grouse breasts on the grill with some seasoned rice so he'll have a hot meal. I will harvest more salmon tomorrow now that I can store them until the refrigerator cools down to keep them. Goodnight Poe. Tomorrow will be a great day.

CHAPTER SEVEN

I wrapped a split sausage link in leftover blueberry pancakes for breakfast. After finishing my coffee, I walked to the boat to check the net and was pleased with the morning haul. I took a bucket of fish scraps downstream to drop them in the water. Poe had plenty to feast on. Ten more bags of filets and two packages of roe were added to the crates to chill. I didn't know how long the blueberries would last, and I knew I had hours before Troy would arrive, so I took two buckets and filled them at the blueberry patch. I was rinsing and bagging the berries when I heard Poe alert in the yard. He wasn't hungry, so I walked outside to find Troy pulling up to the dock. I dried my hands on my pants and walked out to greet him. I could see a large load of supplies, much more than I had ordered, leaving me curious. Maybe he was making another delivery further up the river.

"Welcome back," I called out as he tossed me his bow line to secure the boat. "You made good time."

Troy beamed. "I was loaded and left by five. I have two special assignments to complete today."

"Which are?" I asked.

"Your father called me. He was pleased to hear you were doing well but concerned with two things."

"I'm listening."

"He's never been here in the winter, so he wasn't sure if the water lines would freeze. He asked me to build a stand and deliver a hundred-gallon tank for you to store water. Erica was on the call, too, and she made a perfect suggestion. Your father immediately jumped on board with it, but we have work to do on project number two."

"You've got my attention."

Troy pointed at two sheet metal storage boxes. "We will bury these on the south side of the cabin for food storage. You can package and freeze bags and use the cold in the ground as nature's refrigerator."

I laughed, and Troy cocked his head at me. I leaned over and pulled one of the milk crates from the water filled with packages of fish. "Not as ingenious, but it's working so far."

"That's brilliant," Troy replied.

"I've got filets and some roe for you to take back with you. I hope you remembered a cooler."

"I did. Mom and Erica will be tickled. We won't finish today in time for me to leave for home, so I'm sleeping on the boat tonight before heading home tomorrow."

"Will you be warm enough?"

"Yes, I've got a great sleeping bag, and the weather is warmer than expected."

"So, where do we start?"

"Let's get your refrigerator into the house, and you can unpackage it and get it cooling while I set up your water tank and start adding water."

"Are you hungry?"

"Not yet. I will be later when Mom's sandwiches burn off."

"Just let me know when you start getting hungry. I have grouse and fried rice to cook when you're ready."

"That sounds really good," Troy answered. "It will take us hours to dig out a base for the storage containers, especially if the ground below is still frozen. I brought us an ice wedge, pick axe, and shovels."

"Let's get the fridge inside, and I will help you unload the water tank and base and then unload the rest of the supplies once the fridge is hooked up."

Together, we manhandled the refrigerator onto the dock and used a dolly to pull it across the yard. Poe called to us from the smokehouse. I grinned at Troy. "Meet Poe. He's a great moocher."

Once the fridge was inside, we returned to the boat for the water tank. It was awkward due to its size, but it wasn't heavy. Troy and I quickly placed it next to the cabin.

"I'll grab the base and start filling while you set up the fridge and continue unloading supplies."

"On it," I replied and returned inside. After positioning the appliance, I removed the cardboard, plugged it in, and slipped the broken-down box under my bed. I used the dolly to deliver the rest of the boxes to the cabin, leaving the metal storage boxes onboard. When I placed the two cases of beer on the dolly, I decided to open a box and drop several beers into a crate to chill. Those would taste delicious after a day of hard labor. After storing the supplies, I returned outside to find Troy outlining the area we would need to dig out.

"Where do you want me to start?"

"Grab your gloves, and you can start breaking ground with the pickax. I'm using the roof's drip line as a back guide. The water penetrating the ground will freeze, helping the containers to remain cold."

"That's smart," I replied. "Do you want some water?"

"Yeah, that would be great," Troy replied.

I walked inside to grab two water bottles and my gloves.

"Come take a break," I called to Troy. I handed him a bottle, and he sat beside me on the steps. "Should I hook up the sled to move the dirt?"

"That's not a bad idea. You can make a pile in case you see some erosion beginning. Check the water tank as you go by, please."

I took another long drink and went after the ATV. The water tank was nearly half full. I removed my work shirt and shoulder rig and placed them on the seat.

"I'm glad to see you are carrying your protection. Any issues yet?"

"No, things have gone surprisingly well."

"I can tell you've been busy. That woodpile is impressive."

"I try to harvest a load or two every few days. I don't reckon I can afford to run out this winter."

Troy grinned.

"What?"

"Your father will be proud to hear how well you're doing and that you plan to stick it out per your agreement."

"I've never felt so free," I said, grabbing the pickax. "I wake up every day eager to get to work."

"Have you run across anything you have doubts about?"

"Chaga tea was an adventure. The euphoria I felt was extraordinary. I haven't run into a situation I haven't been able to work through to resolution. I even heard your message on the radio, which gave me a big smile."

"I was hoping you remembered to listen."

"I did. Hey, how far do we need to dig?"

"A good three feet," he answered.

"I better get busy then."

"Keep breaking ground, and when I finish outlining, I'll start digging."

†

I could feel the sweat running down my body. The deeper we dug, the more compact the ground became, making digging difficult. My arms began quivering from the exertion, and I looked at Troy.

"I need a break."

"I do, too," he admitted propping the shovel against the cabin. "I'll be honest, this is kicking my ass."

"Could you drink a cold beer?"

"I most certainly could," Troy answered.

"Check the water tank and meet me at the firepit. I'll be right back." I walked to the dock and pulled out two icy bottles of beer. *Oh, hell yeah, this is going to taste good.* I handed Troy a beer, twisted off the top, and took a drink. "Now that's what I'm talking about."

"I think that's the best beer I've had in a long time. The water tank is full, but I'll leave this ice wedge just in case you need to get water from the river. The stand is high enough to dig a small trench and build a low fire if you see that the water is freezing solid. I don't think you'll need to, but I can't be positive."

"Are you up for another hour of work? I'll cook a great meal for you while you relax."

"I won't complain. My sandwiches are long gone. We've made good progress today."

"Yes, we have. It's been good to spend time with you. I've enjoyed the solitude, but it's nice to hear another voice occasionally. Poe isn't much for conversation."

"A raven looking after you was sent from the creator," Troy said. "I've never heard of one bonding with a human like Poe seems to have bonded with you, but I think it's pretty cool. He will alert you to any danger or movement in the immediate area if he's concerned."

"He alerted me to your arrival before I saw you," I said. "He doesn't seem to mind my cooking either."

"That's a plus." Troy grinned. "I think we have one section deep enough. I'll keep digging if you'll start dinner."

"Works for me. Thanks for choosing the aluminum bottles. I can rinse them out and use them on excursions and other projects."

Troy stood and stretched. "That was a consideration. Glass out here is not good." He handed me his empty bottle.

I walked down to the dock and plucked a package of fish from the crate. As hard as we had worked since his arrival, one grouse would not be enough to feed us. Grouse, salmon, fried onions and potatoes, fried rice, and fry bread should work. After seasoning the meat, I gathered my supplies and cooked on the porch.

Troy peeked around the end of the cabin. "Whatever that is, it smells good."

"I'm making a smorgasbord. I had no idea how many calories we would burn, so I added a few dishes. It should be ready in about twenty minutes if you want to wash up and relax. Maybe grab another beer."

"Let me empty this load of dirt and put the ATV away for the night, and I'll be there."

Troy was my first guest in the cabin, so I cleared the table and set two places before removing the food from the grill and placing it on the table.

"Damn. This looks great," Troy said as he handed me a beer.

"Take a seat, and we can get started. Thanks for all your help today."

"It's been a pleasure working with you, and this meal is a bonus. I don't know what you've done with this meat, but the flavor is awesome."

"I've been exploring a bit. A honey and garlic glaze on the grouse and maple syrup on the salmon."

"Simple, yet so tasty," Troy said. "This is really good." He took another portion of salmon.

"Eat all you can. I'll cook more if necessary."

"I will sleep like a baby tonight with my belly full."

"How much longer do you think we have?"

"Maybe two hours tops."

"Good. I want to get you headed home before it gets late."

"The trip home is always faster."

"Are you all set to head to college?"

"Yeah, but it's hit me that I will leave Mom alone."

"Trust me. Your mom will be okay. She has a great support system surrounding her. You need to focus on finishing school to come back home."

"What about you? What will you do after your six months here?"

I cocked my head at Troy. "Honestly, I don't know. I haven't really given it much thought. If I outlast Charlie, I will take over the company, but I'm no longer sure I want that. This adventure will be an opportunity for me to figure that out. Go home and shrivel up in an ivory tower or try something else."

"Is staying here an option?"

I shrugged. "I don't know. This experience has allowed me to discover much about myself, but I'm unsure about making it permanent. Time will tell, I guess."

"I think you would do well here permanently, but it would be lonely without a partner."

"No partner at home either, so that's not huge."

Poe had kept his distance since Troy arrived, but I took a slice of fry bread and a small portion of fish out to the woodpile. Troy helped me pick up the kitchen and saw the carvings on the windowsill. "Did you do those?"

I nodded. "Yeah, I did. I needed to develop a hobby for the early evening after working all day. I find it relaxing, and I never know what's coming from the wood until the image starts showing itself."

"Have you had a chance to do much exploring?"

"I've found two small lakes that appear home to various animals. I've located a nice blueberry patch, wild lettuce, and mushrooms and have hunted birds in several spots. And, of course, the chaga."

"That tea is good for what ails ya or if you just need a feeling of calm. I notice you have some drying, but it wouldn't hurt to have more, especially for the colder months ahead. You can dry it and leave it hanging until you can use some. If you grind it and it sits too long, it loses its potency."

We drank a third beer together, and Troy began yawning. "I think I'll call it a night. See you in the morning."

"Pancakes and ham steaks good for breakfast?"

"Sounds wonderful. Have a great night."

"Goodnight, and thanks for everything today."

"My pleasure. Thanks for a great meal."

July 11^{*th*} *– Day nine.*

Troy arrived today, and I was surprised that Dad had called to suggest making two additions for water and storing food. They will help me to survive in the coming months. I think Dad senses I am enjoying the adventure. I was confident Troy would give him a favorable report on my progress. We accomplished a lot today, and sharing a cold beer with Troy was a highlight. I think Poe is jealous of Troy as he wasn't as present as usual. Hopefully, things will return to normal once Troy leaves tomorrow. After breakfast, I will check the net and help Troy continue digging. Maybe he will join me on the boat to see my success with fishing.

†

The smell of cooking food drew Troy from his sleeping bag. "Do you always start this early?" He stretched as he walked across the yard.

I looked at my watch and nodded. "Pretty much. I like to get the important chores out of the way early. Grab a cup of coffee and our plates. Breakfast is almost done."

Troy ate a stack of blueberry pancakes, two ham steaks, and some leftover potatoes. I left a pancake for Poe.

"If I don't stop eating, I won't get anything done today."

"Do you want to ride upstream with me to check my nets? I'd like to fill your cooler with fresh fish and roe. We can buckle down and finish digging when we return."

"I'll dig while you process the fish," Troy answered. "Mom will be so excited."

"Do you want to take some blueberries also? I have several bags, and there are plenty left to pick."

"I certainly won't turn them down. They are sweet and juicy."

†

My fear of pulling an empty net quickly abated when Troy pulled up the first float and started freeing fish from the net. He looked at me and grinned. "You have found a great spot."

"What can I say? I had a great teacher. I followed your suggestions, and I haven't been stumped yet."

"Twelve fish of this size is a good haul. You won't starve this winter but may get tired of fish."

"I wanted to concentrate on the fish until I had plenty. I wanted to take advantage of this run while I could."

"Keep fishing as long as you enjoy it. You can freeze some of the packages and bring them to town to barter."

Troy placed the buckets on the dock. "I'll grab the ATV and sled to start digging while you process these."

I nodded. "I'm going to make a cup of coffee before I start. Do you want one?"

"I'm good for now." Troy turned toward the shed while I continued into the cabin. The pancake was gone as I walked by. At least Poe got his breakfast."

I added eight more bags of filets and one more of roe to the milk crates before dropping all the scraps into a bucket. Poe would get some later, but I wanted to help Troy finish the project so he could get underway. As I was turning toward the cabin, Troy emerged around the side.

"Hang on, and you can help me carry the containers," he called out.

"Are you finished digging already?"

"Maybe not, but I think we're close. I want to slide a container in to see if we need to go deeper."

After placing both containers on the dock, we carried the first to the trench and put it inside. "That one looks perfect." Troy pressed the corners until the container was solidly in place. "Let's try the second."

Troy shook his head. "We still need to dig a few more inches."

After settling the second container in the ground, Troy snapped two carabiners on the lids to secure them. He looked up at me. "It won't keep a human out, but I've never known a bear to unfasten a carabiner."

"I wouldn't imagine so." I grinned. "Now what?"

"I would recommend freezing the fish and then placing them inside here. If you start out frozen, I don't think you will have any problem. Feel the metal. It's cold already."

The metal was cold to the touch. "It will only grow colder as the ground freezes, right?"

"That's correct. You now have a bush freezer system." He smiled.

"Thanks, Troy. I've got fish ready in the smoker if you are ready for lunch. Then we can get you loaded and on your way home."

"That works for me. I'll grab the cooler if you want to serve some fish."

I returned to the cabin for a baking pan and two forks. I opened the smoker, removed three of the largest smoked fish, placed them in the pan, and carried them to the firepit. I took a seat next to Troy and handed him a fork. "No fine china for this meal."

"This is perfect, and that glaze is beautiful." He used his fork to scoop a bite of the flakey fish. "Damn, that's good."

"I have a dozen more if you want me to wrap them in foil for you to take home."

"I can't guarantee all of them will make it, but those are tasty."

We fell silent while we ate.

"When will you be home for a visit?"

"We have a week-long Fall Break the last week of September and then two weeks for Thanksgiving."

"I will try to schedule a trip to town to visit if that's okay."

"That's more than okay with me. I'll let Mom know you will join us, but that's not usually a busy time."

"Perfect," I said. "Did you get enough to eat?"

Troy smiled. "I'm stuffed, but it was delicious."

I carried the pan inside and picked up a small box and a roll of aluminum foil. "I'll wrap these smoked fish if you want to load the cooler with filets and berries."

We stored his goods on the boat, and I hugged Troy. "Good luck with school. Study hard, but don't forget to have some fun."

Troy nodded. "I will." He hugged me again, and I could see tears in his eyes. "Keep listening to messages on Saturday nights."

"I will. Be safe going home, and tell your mom and Erica I'll see them soon."

Troy started the motor, and I dropped the line inside the boat. He waved as he put the boat in gear and drove away.

I watched him disappear and walked back toward the cabin. I unfastened one of the crates with bags of fish and berries and carried them inside. I planned to try the vacuum sealer and get them in the freezer. I left a bag of filets in the sink for dinner and froze the rest. The sealer was miraculous and allowed me to stack bag after bag flat in the freezer. I rinsed out the Ziplocs and left them out to dry.

My eyes came to rest on the pancake batter in the fridge. "I think I'll go pick more berries." I slipped the shoulder harness across my body, picked up the shotgun, and grabbed several buckets on my way to the ATV. If I were lucky, I might bring in another grouse or two.

†

Several hours later, I had three buckets full of berries. I was tempted to drive farther into the grove to seek grouse, but Poe's cry alerted me to danger. A small black bear was on the far side of the blueberry patch a hundred yards away. I decided that was my clue to head home. The spruce would wait for another day.

"Thanks, Poe," I called out and drove quickly home.

After filling several small containers of berries to place in the refrigerator, I bagged the rest for the freezer. I picked up the fly rod and plucked a cold beer from the river as I sat on the dock casting for fish. It didn't take long to fill two buckets with fish which I prepped for the smoker. Now that I had refrigeration, I could store smoked fish in other ways beyond canning. I placed several carcasses on the smokehouse and dumped the rest downstream before deciding on a bath. It was still early, but the last two days had been busy, and I would relax for the remainder of the day. I lit the fire to heat the water and cut a dozen more sections of wood to add to my carving menagerie. I set them on the steps and went inside to make a coffee.

When I returned to the steps, Poe sat on one of the chairs at the firepit.

"Thanks for saving my bacon today. I had no idea he was so close. I reckon Troy is correct, and you're my guardian angel."

I sipped on coffee and whittled the piece of wood. I laughed when I saw a bear appear in my hands. "That's fitting, I guess." Returning inside, I retrieved clean clothes and walked to the bathhouse. The basket of dirty clothing was growing, and I needed to set up the washpot to take care of them soon. *Tomorrow while I harvest fish,* I promised myself. Then if the day was pleasant, I would travel to the first lake I found to look for grouse or other small animals. I planned to give the berry patch a wide birth for a few days while the bear ate his fill of the sweet berries. I relaxed in the tepid water and listened to the chorus outside while I reviewed the progress of the last two days.

July 12th – Day ten

It was great seeing Troy, and we got much work done. I now have the means of freezing and storing a variety of foods. I met my first bear today by accident. It could have been much worse if Poe wasn't watching over me and alerted me to his presence. I shouldn't be surprised that my carving tonight was a bear. My subconscious must draw on the animals I've seen to create the figures. I hope there won't be many more bears that make it onto my windowsill. Goodnight, Poe, and thanks again for being my protector.

CHAPTER EIGHT

After scrambling eggs and sausage for breakfast, I pulled on a light jacket and walked to the boat. I hauled in another dozen fish and decided to smoke a batch. Once the fire started in the smokehouse, I decided to ride to the lake. I strapped on the pistol and grabbed my shotgun before remembering I was supposed to do laundry. *I'll do it when I get back.* I smiled and climbed on the ATV. I lucked up and managed to shoot two grouse, and cleaned and stored them in the bucket before I reached the lake. I was driving slowly, looking for other game animals, when I heard a loud bang. The sound of a rifle. I slammed on my brakes and froze. The sound was close. Very close.

Do I continue forward to investigate, or do I return home? My curiosity got the best of me, so throwing caution to the wind, I crept forward until I reached the lake. Ahead I could see a figure bent over a large animal. A moose, I presumed. As I drove closer, I discovered the hunter was a woman in her mid to late thirties. I was more comfortable that the visitor was a woman, but if she could drop a massive moose, I wouldn't be a challenge for her. She turned when she heard the sound of my motor and reached for her gun. I slowed and raised a hand in a wave.

I stopped twenty yards away. "I heard a shot and thought I would investigate."

The woman frowned. "That could have been dangerous if I had been a poacher."

"I suppose. I didn't think of that. You aren't a poacher, are you?" I asked with a smile.

My smile appeared to disarm her slightly. "No, not even close. I am River Foster. I am a designated subsistence hunter for my Athabascan tribe."

"Pardon my ignorance, but designated hunter?" I asked.

"We are a small village. Most adult men work on fishing boats or away from home for months and cannot provide fresh meat for their families or the village elders. I have been elected as a designated hunter for years. The elders and women of the village harvest fish and small game, but the responsibility for red meat is mine."

"I didn't think it was the right season for hunting moose yet?"

River smiled. "I'm not a poacher. As a designated hunter, I am allowed to hunt outside the season designated for sport and other Alaskan hunters who subsistence hunt for only their families."

"That's interesting." I noticed she kept working on skinning the moose as she talked, looking up only briefly to see if I was still there. "My name is Tatum Chastain."

"Charles Chastain's daughter?"

"I laughed. Is there anyone in Alaska that doesn't know my father?"

"Probably not," River answered. "He's been a considerable benefactor in this area for years."

Then I realized there was more to my dad than I ever suspected.

"So, what are you doing out here?"

"Father has presented my brother and me with a test of resilience and creativity. He plans to retire next year and is having difficulty choosing his successor. We must survive in the wilderness using our skills and creative thinking for six months."

"That's an exciting concept. How long have you been here?"

"Just a few weeks. I have to remain until the new year."

"Well, since you're here, you might as well help. Grab the small tarp off my ATV trailer and bring it to me, please." She pointed me toward the vehicle I had passed without detecting.

When I returned, she pointed along the length of the moose. "Stretch it out as close to the moose as you can. I need to get these guts out before the bacteria starts to spread. "Hold the back legs in the air for me, please."

I blanched and felt my knees weaken when she plunged a large knife into the animal's sternum and carefully opened the abdomen. I held back the bile and saw the laughter in her eyes when she looked at me.

"Is this the first time you've witnessed this process?"

I nodded, afraid to speak for several seconds. When I was sure I wouldn't vomit, I spoke. "Yes, it is. I have hunted grouse and harvested fish, but neither has the odor billowing out in a steamy cloud from this beast."

River chuckled. "That's almost a poetic description. I can't afford to waste an ounce of this meat to laziness. Harvesting the meat and hide will take several hours, so I must work quickly once I drop an animal."

Forcing the bile back into my stomach, I asked. "What can I do to help?"

River made several more precision cuts. "Help me roll him onto his side."

I followed her lead and pushed the back legs toward the ground. The stomach sack rolled onto the tarp with an audible wet sound, and I had to look away as River severed the final connection to the animal.

She looked up at me and smiled. "Can you drag the tarp a hundred yards away from us so the scavengers will feast on those and leave us be?"

I nodded, grabbed the tarp's edges, and pulled as mightily as possible. Thankfully the ground was level, and the tarp slid across the grass. I dragged it as far as possible before dumping the smelly entrails off the tarp and walking back to River.

She looked up when I returned. "Relax, that is the worst part."

"What's next?"

She had severed the head while I was gone and was working quickly to remove the hide from the animal. "This part requires a practiced hand. You can help by watching my back and ensuring no predator sneaks up on me."

I looked into a large spruce tree and found Poe watching. "That's not a problem. My protector is with us. He alerted me to a bear in the berry patch yesterday."

"What?" she asked.

I pointed to the tree where Poe sat. "That's Poe. He has been with me almost from the beginning."

River smiled. "That is good medicine to be blessed with a raven." She continued to skin the animal, and when she looked up, she asked, "Will you bring me the bundle of drawstring sacks and the saw from my trailer."

I walked over for the supplies she had requested. "Do you process the meat as well?"

River shook her head. "I hunt and prep the meat, but the village women do the processing while I return to the hunt." She pointed to a bag. "Will you hold one of those open for me?"

I opened a bag as she placed the organ meat and backstrap into the sack.

"Would you mind helping me turn the moose? It will make the skinning go faster."

"Sure," I grabbed the rear legs and lifted them to help River access the hide.

"Thanks. I need a break."

I looked at River, who had blood dripping down from her elbows. She walked to the lake and rinsed her arms and the skinning knife. When she returned, she looked at me. "Do you have something to drink?"

I couldn't help but stare at the tall woman as she stood before me. Since I arrived, she had been bent down over the animal, and when she stood and stretched, I was surprised that she was nearly six feet tall. "Uh, yes, I have water. Do you need some?" I stammered.

"Thanks, but I've got my own."

I walked to the ATV, sat, picked up my water bottle, and took a long drink.

"Are you staying at your father's cabin? I thought I smelled smoke earlier."

"Yes, it's such a great spot. I've got a batch of salmon in the smoker."

"It is a beautiful location. I visited with Charles years ago."

"Where is home for you?" I asked.

"A two-hour ride north of here. I hunt, deliver the game, and then return to the woods to camp during my time in the area. I usually spend a few weeks here to thin out the moose, deer, and elk populations. Once the caribou begin migrating, I will move north or east to harvest as many tags as we have been allotted for the year."

"So you'll be in this area for a while?"

"Yes, as soon as I finish here, I'll deliver the meat, travel back to pitch my camp, and prepare for tomorrow's hunt."

"Would you join me for dinner later tonight, then? I have a small cot in the bathhouse that you could spread your sleeping bag across to have a roof over your head."

"Having a roof is not necessary to me. I prefer to gaze up at the stars as I fall asleep, but I'd like to join you for dinner. If I don't get back to work, it will be midnight before I return."

"Just tell me what I can do to help."

"Be ready to hold one of the more giant bags open. I'm almost done removing the hide. We'll bag it, and then I will cut the rib sections and the quarters with the bone saw. Once we get that meat bagged and loaded, it's a matter of cleanup, and I move on. Your help has saved me at least an hour, if not more."

"Thanks for allowing me to help. It's been very educational."

River smiled. "When was the last time you had red meat?"

"Not since I left Glennallen. I've focused on fish and fowl."

River cut a small roast section from the meat. "You can cut several steaks from that and have a few to store."

"Thank you," I replied, placing the roast into a bucket.

When all the meat was loaded onto the trailer, River turned to me. "All I need to do now is clean up, and then I'll be on my way. Delivery and round trip will be close to five hours. Is that too late?"

I looked at my watch. "That will be perfect. Thanks for the steaks. I'll see you around seven." I walked to the ATV and drove home.

†

That was an exciting morning. I placed the roast and grouse in the sink to brine while I filled the washpot with water and dropped my dirty clothes inside.

What to serve for dinner? I decided to prepare a combination of moose steaks, grouse, and fish on the Blackstone, accompanied by a rice medley and some frybread. I grabbed a handful of berries for a snack and made a compote of the crushed berries to use with the salmon. I would stick to the honey and garlic for the grouse. I'd never cooked moose, so I'd have to make a plan for that.

†

After adding some detergent flakes, I used a weathered boat oar to stir the clothes. I removed each piece and draped them across a chair or porch railing to dry. The sun was bright, so I had no doubt they would be dry in hours. I removed the grouse, placed them in a bag to chill, sliced several steaks from the roast, coated them with a dry rub, and added them to the refrigerator.

Time seemed to be creeping. I lit the fire for the bathhouse and drove to my fish line. I harvested ten more fish from the net before returning home. I rinsed the filets I would use for dinner and placed the remainder in the smokehouse. Time for a soak.

The water in the washpot was still hot, so I stripped out of my work clothes and dropped them inside. I had no worries about being seen walking naked to the bathhouse by anyone other than Poe. I would have a nice bath, eat a light lunch, and relax until it was time to cook.

I sank to my chin in the warm water and closed my eyes. What an exciting day this was turning into. River danced before my eyes as I relaxed. She was ruggedly handsome. She could never be mistaken for a beauty contestant, but the aura around her was intriguing. She reeked of power from her long legs to the ripple of muscles in her arms as she processed the moose. Her position was an honor to serve her people, and she welcomed the responsibility. I remembered how her dark eyes appeared to be laughing when I nearly lost my breakfast. The smell of the hot intestines filled my nose, and I quickly moved on from that memory. Watching her dissect the large animal was comparable to watching a skilled surgeon as she sectioned the meat into useable portions. Nothing went to waste.

Her face held lines of wrinkles around her eyes and mouth. Some could probably be from laughing, but I bet most were gained from worrying about feeding her people. It was a huge responsibility, and their survival depended on her skill. An underlying current of joy had become visible briefly as a smile washed across her face. It was a pleasant experience to witness, bringing a softness to her otherwise hardened exterior. I had dated many women, but the allure River projected spun my head, leaving me feeling dazed and confused.

After bathing, I began to drain the tub and sat on the edge to shave my legs. It was my first shave in the bush, but it felt good to be silky smooth again. As my hands moved down my body, I realized how much my physique had changed. My legs were taut from hours of being on my feet, and my arms were firmer than before. I thought it was amazing what hard work creates as I dressed in fresh clothes. No time in the gym could generate this feeling of well-being. I opened the cot in case River changed her mind and returned to the cabin.

My clothes dried well in the soft breeze, and I experimented with a moose steak for lunch. The rub was flavorful, but something was missing. I examined my pantry to find a bottle of apple juice that had not been opened, and I poured a small glass, storing the remainder in the fridge. I used Dad's small injector in the kitchen to infuse the meat with the sweet juice. I placed the steak in the fridge to rest while I collected my clothing. I didn't want to be caught with laundry strewn about the place by my first new visitor.

Poe flew onto the woodpile, and I returned inside for leftover fry bread to feed him.

"What did you think about the woman we met today?" Poe cocked his head at me and then began pecking at the offering. "Obviously, not as impressed as I was."

Returning inside, I placed a pot on the stove to boil rice and mixed the batter for the fry bread. River's arrival was still hours away, but I tried to keep my mind occupied. I removed the injected steak and cooked it slowly on the grill. The juice softened the texture and added great flavor to the meat. This would be the combination I would use tonight. I returned inside after my meal to inject the remaining steaks.

†

I fished the knife from my pocket and sat on the steps sipping coffee as I focused on what animal to carve. I wasn't sure I was ready for the shape of a moose, so a rabbit quickly formed in the wood.

When the time came nearer for River's arrival, I prepared the rice medley, left it warming on the stove, and set the table for two. The meat was in a pan, ready to go on the grill, and my excitement grew. I was surprised at how eager I was to share an evening with this woman.

My heart raced when I heard the sound of a motor approach, and River pulled to a stop.

"You made good time," I said as she stepped from the vehicle.

River's smile filled her face. "I could deliver while my mother was out fishing, which helped speed up my return. If she had been near, she would have insisted I share a meal with her, and I would have spent half the night talking with her."

"It sounds like you are close with your mother."

"It's been only the two of us for most of my life. My father died young working on a fishing boat."

I cocked my head. "That seems to be very common here. My young friend, Troy, his father also died on a fishing boat."

River nodded. "The oceans can be treacherous during crab and fish season. Several lives are lost each year, as a rule. If you're referring to Troy from Glennallen, he's a fine young man."

"He is and will be traveling to Anchorage soon to study at the university. He was out earlier this week to make a delivery and help me set up a few new systems."

River glanced around the yard. "You certainly look like you've been busy."

"I haven't had a dull moment for sure." I smiled. "Are you hungry, or do you want to relax? I have a cold beer I can offer."

"That sounds great. My body is still vibrating from the trail."

"Have a seat at the firepit, and I'll be right back." I walked to the dock and pulled a milk crate from the water to pluck two cold beers from inside. Offering one to River, I took a seat beside her.

"That was a smart idea for a beer cooler."

"Dad has only used this place for short-term trips, so I decided on some upgrades to survive into the winter. Troy brought out the water tank, and we installed a bush refrigeration system in the ground next to the cabin. I can use my small freezer to freeze items and then use the ground to keep them chilled. At least that's the theory," I stated.

"It will serve you well if set up correctly."

"It seems to do well so far." I smiled. "How long have you been a designated hunter?"

"Forever, it seems." River chuckled. "I started in high school to get classroom credits for maintaining our cultural existence, and I found I was good at it."

"Are you the only hunter?"

"No, there is one more. A young woman who is starting out. She is up north keeping an eye open for the caribou and hunting goats."

"How long do you hunt?"

"It varies from year to year, but I stay out as long as the weather permits. Rarely into January, but usually well into late December. Then I take time off to recharge, run my trap lines, and start over in the spring."

"That sounds like a nomadic way of life."

"It is, but I enjoy it. What about you? What do you do at your family business?"

"I'm the COO and handle most significant real estate transactions."

"That sounds exciting."

"It was initially, but I've become disenchanted with the corporate rat race. Coming here was not only a test for my father but an opportunity to do some self-discovery for me."

"Are you any closer to finding your future?"

"Not really, but I'm going to start dinner right now. You must be hungry after such a long day."

"I had some jerky along the way, but I could eat."

"Grab another beer and relax while I cook."

"Is there anything I can help with?"

"You can bring me another beer." I grinned. I started the Blackstone and returned inside for the pan of meats and fry bread mix. "I hope you're a carnivore. I haven't experimented much with the wild vegetables except lettuce and mushrooms yet."

"I thrive on protein," River replied. She handed me a beer and sat on the steps to watch me cook. "That's a nice setup."

"Thanks. I didn't think I would survive cooking on two burners. I've enjoyed using the grill and experimenting."

River nodded and took a long drink. Her eyes followed me as I placed the meat on the grill and returned inside to rinse the pan and get a plate for the frybread.

"That smells great," River stated when I raised the lid and poured the frybread batter on the grill.

"I couldn't decide which meat to serve, so you're getting grouse, salmon, and my first-ever moose."

River's eyes landed on the small container of wood sections, and she picked one up. "Have you started carving?"

I nodded. "I needed a hobby at night after I finished my chores. I've got a windowsill full of my menagerie."

"My mother does carvings she sells to help make our supply purchases. I'm sure she would share some ideas with you should you come for a visit."

"I'd like that. I never know what I am creating until it forms in the wood," I explained.

"That's exactly what she says." River smiled.

I could feel the pride and love she held for her mother in her words. I carefully turned the meats and added more of the seasonings to each. "Can you sell the hides and antlers from your harvested animals?"

"The villagers have first rights to any hides if they need them for clothing or other items. The antlers sell well in Anchorage and Fairbanks. I usually have Erica deliver a large load to each buyer at the end of the season."

I placed a cooling piece of frybread on the woodpile for Poe. He had sat atop the smokehouse preening for the last hour.

"Dinner is served," I called to him. "Ours too," I said as I carefully removed the meats from the grill and handled a platter of fry bread for River to carry. I placed the meat pan on the table and put the rice in a bowl. I reached into the refrigerator for the compote. "I have water or coffee."

"Water is fine for now," River said. "This looks incredible."

I served a portion of each meat and added the compote to the salmon. I handed River the rice bowl and placed several pieces of fry bread on my plate before passing. "Enjoy," I said as I scooped rice onto my plate. I took a bite of the moose and looked at River. She was chewing a taste of the salmon.

"The blueberries are a nice touch." She smiled and cut into the moose steak. "Wow, this cuts well. It has a tendency to be chewy." River took a bite and moaned her appreciation.

The sound sent a pulse through my body, and I felt my face flush with embarrassment.

River swallowed and took a bite of the grouse. "I can't honestly choose a favorite. They are all fantastic."

I released a soft sigh of relief. I didn't understand why I felt it essential to gain River's approval, but my heart swelled with pride.

"I do need to share your secret on the moose with Mom. Sometimes her steaks threaten to loosen a tooth."

I couldn't help but break into laughter. "I bet you eat every bite, though."

River nodded. "Don't you know it, but this is tender and tasty."

"Apple juice," I replied. "I injected some apple juice into the meat to let it break down some of the tissue. I tried a section at lunch, and it was chewy, so I returned to my magic pantry and found some juice. It worked out well."

"I'll agree with that. That's the best moose I've had in a while."

"Thank you."

"Thanks for preparing a wonderful meal. That really hit the spot. My diet in the bush is mostly game roasted over an open fire, so this was a delicacy for me."

I continued eating while reveling in her praise. After we finished eating, I cleared the dishes. "Coffee?"

"The perfect end to a great meal." She nodded.

We sat together sipping coffee, and her eyes drifted to the windowsill.

"The raven is stunning. Poe, I presume?"

"He was such a great model," I joked.

"You are quite talented. I hope you will continue to experiment with your cooking and knife."

"I know there will be long nights ahead that will be too bitter to venture outside for long, so carving should help pass the time."

"The time of long sleep, when the sun disappears to recharge. It will feel overwhelming at first, but your body will adjust."

"Just like the long days of daylight. I found myself waking at an ungodly hour until my body adjusted. It allowed me to jump on my chores, but I was sure ready for bed after dinner."

"You have canned well, and your fish cooler is well stocked. I'd recommend continuing to harvest and cut firewood as long as possible. Better to have too much than not enough."

"I'm estimating a few more weeks for the fish before the runs end, and then I'll concentrate on waterfowl and grouse."

"That's a good plan. I will be in the area for a few weeks yet and will supplement your red meat stores in exchange for a hot meal now and then."

My eyes flew open. "You do have a deal. Could I spend a day or two hunting with you to pick up some techniques and help?"

"I'd love the company," River answered. "The help is nice too."

"Excellent. One other question. Will you take my bags of roe to your village? I haven't acquired a taste for it, and it will be weeks before I go to Glennallen to resupply."

"Salmon roe is like gold. I'm sorry you don't care for the taste, but I will gladly accept any offer. The rich protein source is very welcome in my village."

"What time will you start out in the morning?"

"I will leave here around eight if that's not too early." River smiled.

"I'll be up, have run my net, and cooked breakfast by then."

"That works for me. I'll help you run your line and process the fish while you cook something for breakfast."

"Ham steaks and blueberry pancakes sound good?"

River's stomach growled at the mention of breakfast. "I think my stomach approves of the suggestion. Can I help you clean up?"

"I've got this. It won't take me long at all. I placed the cot in the bathhouse if you change your mind about being inside. Just let me empty my bladder; the place is yours." I left the cabin, and when I returned, River had washed the dishes.

"I'll see you in the morning," she said. "Thanks again for a great meal."

"My pleasure. I hope you rest well."

"Now that my belly is full, I will sleep like a rock."

"Goodnight then," I said and walked her to the door.

July 13ᵗʰ - Day eleven

Where to start? Today I met the most amazing woman by pure accident, which turned into a great arrangement. River will teach me to hunt the bigger game and process the meat in exchange for a hot meal and shelter. I feel like I'm ahead of schedule on my chores, so I'll tag along for as long as she allows. River will only be in the area a few weeks before she rotates to a different hunting location, so I will glean all the information I can from her. Surprisingly, Poe seems to like her, too. He didn't go into hiding like he did with Troy. Maybe he can sense something special in her as well. Time for bed. It has been a long but productive day.

CHAPTER NINE

River was awake and packing her trailer when I walked outside to use the bathroom. "Good morning. Did you sleep well?"

"Very much so. I decided to take your offer of the bathhouse. That cot is much more comfortable than the ground."

"I'll be ready to check the lines in just a few minutes." I pulled on a light jacket and walked into the bathhouse.

River was waiting on the dock when I emerged. "Good morning, Poe," I said as I walked by the smokehouse. "Breakfast will be served soon."

I climbed into the boat, followed by River, who secured the mooring line. "It looks like we will have a fine day for hunting." She smiled as she sat.

I spread out three buckets for the fish when we approached the line.

"That will hold a lot of fish," she replied.

I shrugged. "This has been a great line, so don't jinx me," I teased.

"Sorry," River said and bent over to grab the first float as I idled down the line. When we reached the end, two and a half buckets were filled. "I shouldn't have doubted. That was a good haul."

"Pretty typical each day so far, so I'll fish until there's an end to the run. I sometimes sit on the dock and flyfish, just for the thrill of the fight. It's great to land one of these massive fish. I can see why Dad became addicted."

"Do you think he'll spend more time here once he retires?" River asked.

"I think he plans to. Not full-time, but longer than a week or two at a time."

When we reached the dock, I handed the buckets to River after she secured the boat. "I'll bring a filet knife and some bags for the roe and start on breakfast. Hungry?"

"Starved," River replied.

"Okay, I'm on it. Please leave a bit of flesh on a carcass for Poe's breakfast. I usually put one on top of the smokehouse for him."

River nodded. "Will do. The rest in the smoker?"

"Yes, I'll add some wood before we leave."

†

Coffee was the first item on my agenda. I mixed pancake batter and whipped six eggs, then split a few sausages to warm on the grill. When I carried the food outside to start cooking, River was busily processing the fish. She looked up and smiled when she heard me begin cooking. We finished around the same time, and after hanging the fish, she carried two bags of roe.

"Where do you want these?"

"You can place them in the refrigerator for now to cool. If we add water to your cooler, will they be safe until you can deliver them tonight?"

"I'll add some salt, and they should be fine," River replied.

"There are two other bags in the milk crates you can take also. That should help hold the temperature down."

"Do you have a rifle?" River asked.

"Yes. One I haven't shot yet."

"Bring it today in case we find a group of animals."

I nodded, unsure if I could pull the trigger on such a beautiful animal. I packed my daypack and met River at the ATV. She looked at the rifle slung over my shoulder.

"Nice," she replied. "Ready?"

I nodded. "Where to?"

"Back to the lake we met at yesterday. It has plenty of animals coming to drink. Maybe we will be lucky enough for another moose."

†

We parked the ATVs under a large tree and stalked quietly toward the lake. Ducks and geese floated noisily on the lake, but no sign of game existed.

"Now what?"

118

"We wait," River answered and pointed to a fallen tree that concealed them from view but allowed us to scan the lakeshore.

My head jerked up when I heard something massive moving through the brush. I gasped softly when a huge moose bull stepped to the water's edge and sniffed the air before leaning down to drink.

"He's a beauty," River said. "Do you want to try a shot?"

My heart lodged in my throat. I didn't want to disappoint River. An animal that size would provide over a thousand pounds of meat.

"I don't know what to do," I whispered with a quiver of excitement and trepidation.

"I will help you," River answered as she moved behind me. "Lift the rifle to your shoulder."

Her warm breath on my neck made it impossible for me to breathe.

River felt me tense and used her hands to steady my aim. "You want to hit him just behind his front leg. Understand?"

I nodded, unable to speak.

"Relax and breathe. Then slowly pull the trigger."

I was almost sure I closed my eyes when I pulled the trigger, and the gun butt slammed into my shoulder. When I opened my eyes, I saw the animal stumble and fall to the ground.

"Great shot," River said.

I nodded, but I could feel the tears welling in my eyes.

River cocked her head at me. "You just fed several families for weeks. Be proud of that and appreciate the animal's sacrifice so we can survive."

I wiped a tear back and followed River to the ATVs.

"Let's get busy." She smiled as she climbed onto her vehicle.

When we arrived at the moose, I was surprised he was larger than the one River had harvested yesterday. She loaded me up with tarps, bags, and the saw. "Same as yesterday. I'll turn his body until you can place the tarp beneath him."

I was more prepared for the disemboweling, but that didn't keep me from grimacing and holding my breath when the entrails dropped onto the tarp. I quickly carried them away and rushed back to River. She had removed the head and looked up at me. "Come closer, please."

I watched as she dipped a fingertip into the blood and drew a line down my forehead. "You must celebrate the animal sacrifice for your first kill." She smiled at me. "You did well. I should have told you to pull the rifle tighter."

"Yeah, I'm going to have a heck of a bruise."

"Another memory," River said.

"Painful one, too," I joked.

After storing the organ meats in a bag, River looked at me. "Are you ready to learn how to skin? Because of their thick hides, a moose is great for teaching."

"I'll give it a try," I answered.

"Let me see your knife," River asked, reaching toward me. She checked the sharpness of the edge and used a sharpening rod to add a new edge, then repeated the same for her knife. River was patient as we worked shoulder-to-shoulder to remove the heavy hide. I didn't take long under her instruction to learn to separate the coat from the carcass. Working together, the skin and meat were harvested in record time.

"You are a good student," River said. "A great hunting partner, too. Thanks for your help."

I smiled, proud of my accomplishment and hearing her praise for a job well done. "Do you have time to return to the cabin for the roe and some smoked fish for your journey?"

"That can be arranged," River said, placing the saw back in the trailer. "Let's wash up, and we can head back."

I hadn't realized how bloody I had become until I placed my arms under the water, which was tinted red. I dried my hands on my pants, and after taking a drink, we drove home.

†

I walked inside for a box and foil while River gathered the roe. I opened the smokehouse and lined the box with aluminum foil. "Will you take these to your mother? Eat some along your ride home, too?"

"That's not a problem. Mom will be pleased to not have to cook tonight," River replied. She placed a filet across her handlebars and picked off a chunk. "Damn, that's great. Especially for a *Cheechako*," she teased.

I smiled back at her. "How long before I'm not a newcomer?"

"Years, but you've certainly made a good start. I need one other thing."

"What?"

"Hand me your rifle," she requested and ejected the shell that had been used on the moose. She slipped it into her pocket and looked at her watch. "A little earlier tonight if I can escape Mom."

121

"I'll be here," I replied. "Any special requests for dinner?"

"Anything you want to cook. See ya."

I watched as River drove away and went to the bathhouse. I looked at my image in the mirror and smiled. The blood stained my skin, and I wiped it off. "I'm definitely not the same woman I was in Chicago."

†

I opened the refrigerator and pulled out the remainder of the moose roast. I placed it in a pot to boil and drank a cup of coffee while starting a supply list. The iPad was resting on the counter, and I spotted a small book beside it and picked it up before returning to the table. The Blackstone came with a small recipe book I had forgotten about. I opened the book and flipped through the pages. "Here we go," I spoke aloud when a biscuit recipe jumped out. I scanned the list of ingredients and was overjoyed that I had everything I needed. They would be a pleasant meal addition and work well with the camp stew I planned for dinner. Butter would be possible now that I had refrigeration, so I added several new items to supplement my essential supplies.

I stretched and walked outside after chopping onions, carrots, and potatoes. My eyes scanned the property. The firewood was in good shape, but I could use more alder for the smokehouse. The meat would take at least another hour to stew, so I grabbed the chainsaw and a rope length to drag several alders back to the cabin. I could section and split them while the stew continued to cook.

Thirty minutes later, I pulled into the yard with three large alders. I removed the brushy limbs, tossed them into the firepit, and walked inside to check the meat. It was simmering, and a nice broth was forming. I removed the roast, cubed the meat, and browned it in a frying pan before adding it back to the broth with some oil and flour to begin making the gravy.

After splitting the rounds into sections for the smokehouse, I went inside for a drink and began making biscuits. I had never made biscuits that didn't come from a can, but it wasn't as difficult as I feared. I lit the Blackstone, and when it reached the desired temperature, I placed the pan of biscuits inside and closed the lid.

While the food cooked, I decided to enter my journal early.

July 14th – Day twelve.

Another milestone today. I became a big game hunter. I killed and helped process my first moose today. The guilt was tough to swallow until River pointed out he would feed several families for weeks, and the herd would grow stronger by culling him. It was still challenging to pull the trigger for the first time. And painful. It was an experience I will carry with me for days until the bruise fades. I'm trying my hand at my first stew and batch of biscuits. The forgotten recipe book that came with the Blackstone has several dishes I would like to try to create. I made a large pan of biscuits to have leftovers tomorrow. I plan to spice up some of the sauce to make a gravy to smother the biscuits. Just thinking about it has my mouth watering. The geese honking drew me from my chair, and I watched several birds land in the river. I need to ask River about the best time to harvest them before they fly south to winter. River. I am amazed at how often she fills my thoughts. She is truly a remarkable woman.

My heart raced when I heard the sound of her return.

†

"You have a new fan," River replied. "Mom nearly passed out when I opened the cooler to show her the roe and the box of smoked fish. She insists I bring you home tomorrow for dinner after we make a delivery."

"Confident we will make a kill."

"I never come home empty-handed. It may be birds, but I always have something."

"That reminds me. When should I harvest some geese and ducks before they leave the area?"

"Yesterday," River answered and laughed at the shocked look on my face. "Soon," she replied. "This time of year, filling your bush cooler with geese and ducks won't take long. We can start early in the morning and see what birds and game we can harvest. I'll clean whatever birds we get while you run your fish line."

"Can we take a bird and some berries to your mom?"

"Nope," River answered with a straight face. "She might not allow you to leave," she said, smiling. "Be prepared to bring some fresh vegetables home. She won't accept another gift without a barter. Her garden has been plentiful."

"I'd like that. I miss fresh vegetables."

"Prepare to have corn, cabbage, squash, onions, and potatoes. I'm not sure how her tomatoes fared this year."

"Sounds perfect. I eat all of those. Can your mom afford to give them to me? Will it cut you short this winter?"

"Mom would be hurt if you didn't accept her barter. Besides, we have enough canned vegetables to last several winters."

"Is there anything I have that she would enjoy?"

"She ate the heck out of your smoked salmon. Maybe more of those since you have found your honey hole."

I smiled. "That's not a problem. The smoker is full again."

"You can smoke moose or venison for longer storage, too," River said. "You need to take some as we harvest."

"I don't want to jeopardize the village food source."

"They won't miss a few roasts. Besides, with your help, I can process the meat more quickly, allowing me to hunt more often."

†

After sharing a beer, River looked at me. "Are you ready to share what you are cooking? The smell is driving me crazy."

"Let's go," I replied and walked onto the porch. I lifted the lid, pulled out the biscuit pan, and turned off the gas.

"Wow, those are beautiful," River said.

"Place them on the table and bring the plates to the stove, please," I said as I handed her the plate and walked to stir the stew.

"I hope I'm not drooling," River said as she held the plates for me to fill.

"No pressure there. I hope it meets your expectations."

"I have no doubt it will."

I brought a jar of honey to the table, but the rich gravy made it unnecessary. I smiled as I watched River sop every drop of gravy from her plate. "Seconds?"

"Maybe just a bit more." She grinned.

"Take all you want. I'll jar up the rest for another meal. I've got biscuits and sausage gravy planned for breakfast."

"That will start us off right in the morning. Did you have a cast net by chance?" River asked.

"Yes, it's in the shed. I've never used it. Why?"

"It may come in handy at the lake tomorrow to bring birds close enough to shore. I'm not excited about going in after them." River grinned.

"Mind a suggestion?" I asked.

"Not at all."

"The smaller lake by the woodlot is shallower, and I've seen plenty of birds there. If nothing else, it may be easier to retrieve them. If they aren't present, we can try the other lake."

"That's a good plan. I'd also recommend you take your shotgun when you check your line. Geese, in particular, enjoy floating down the river."

"I've noticed that these last few days."

"I can even lug a canoe down here if we need it," River offered. "Let's see how tomorrow goes."

†

"Do you need to use the restroom? I'll turn in early for a fresh start in the morning."

"Sounds good," I said and left the cabin. I was disappointed River wanted to retire so soon, but I imagined she was tired from all the exertion.

I was surprised when she met me outside of the bathhouse. "There's one more thing," she said. She reached beneath her shirt and removed a length of rawhide. River had drilled a hole in the cartridge of my first kill and made it into a necklace. "You can wear this to honor the moose you harvested for my people, or hang it inside the cabin for good luck and a memory of today."

I slipped the rawhide over my head, and the cartridge, still warm from River's body, rested between my breasts. "Thank you," I said and felt tears glistening in my eyes.

"You are to be thanked for feeding my people and giving honor to the animal."

I nodded and walked into the cabin before my tears could fall.

After parting for the night, I placed the leftovers in a jar and climbed into bed.

†

I warmed the biscuits on the stovetop while I made the gravy. I glanced out the window to find River processing the morning's catch. She must have gotten up early, too. I turned the gravy on low and poured coffee to walk out and greet her. "You must have gotten up exceptionally early," I said, offering her a cup of coffee.

"I did. I couldn't get back to sleep, so I decided to get to work. One last fish and you will be set today. Yesterday's fish look great."

"Breakfast is ready whenever you are." I sipped my coffee. "Does it feel colder to you today?"

"Yes, it was brisk on the boat ride. We need to bundle up when we head to the village. It might be late when we get back. Do you mind riding with me? I don't see a need to take both ATVs."

"I don't have a problem with that. Should we drop some of your gear before we go to lighten the load?"

"Yeah, that's a good idea. Let me get these fish in the smoker, and I'll wash up for breakfast."

"More coffee?" I asked, picking up the empty cup.

"Yes, that hit the spot."

†

After making coffee, I split open biscuits onto two plates and covered them with gravy. River arrived just as I placed them on the table.

"That was good timing," she stated. "Looks delicious."

"I hope it tastes as good as it looks. There is plenty, so eat your fill."

After eating, I cleaned the kitchen while River loaded the cast net onto the trailer. She slipped a camo hoodie over her work shirt and waited for me. I grabbed my shotgun and ammo belt and climbed in behind her.

"Ready?"

"Yes, ma'am." I placed my hands on River's hips to steady myself as we started down the trail.

She stopped the ATV yards from the lake as we surveyed the surface. A large gathering of geese floated calmly across the water. "Are you loaded?"

I nodded. "All set."

"Let's stalk as close to the lake as we can. Take your safety off, and start blasting away when I tell you to go. If we are lucky, we can bag a few before the birds take flight. Keep shooting until you are empty."

"Got it," I whispered as we crept toward the shoreline.

"I will shoot to the left, and you can cover the right. If birds get up, we can bring them down before they escape." River paused. "Ready on three. Remember to tuck the gun into your shoulder." She winked. "One, two, three."

The air rang with gun blasts, and the smell of spent gunpowder filled my nostrils. I looked across the water. Eight birds floated in the water.

"Good shooting," River said. "Reload in case the others decide to return."

I stuffed the spent shells in my pocket and reloaded, placing the gun on safety.

"It looks like the birds are floating to the opposite shore. Let's ride around and see if we can reach them with the net."

Twenty minutes later, we had retrieved all eight birds. River taught me how to remove the feathers until we heard an odd noise in the distance.

I looked at her. "What's that?"

"An elk, bugling," she answered. "Not far away either. Let's be still and see if it will approach the lake." River exchanged her shotgun for a rifle, and we knelt in the tall grass surrounding the lake.

Several minutes passed before River tapped my arm and pointed across the south end of the lake. "That's a nice male," she whispered.

I watched as she calmly lifted the rifle to her shoulder and took aim. I could see the pulse throbbing in her neck as she leveled the gun and fired.

"Got him," she said.

I could see the sparkle in her eyes as she discharged the cartridge and slipped another into the chamber.

"Let's load these birds and process the elk. We can finish them later and put them in your smokehouse or fridge."

"I want to take half to your mom."

River smiled. "She is going to so love meeting you. Let's get busy."

†

The elk wasn't as large as the moose; working together, we processed it quickly. I needed less instruction from River, and she appeared to appreciate my willingness to help. When he was loaded, her eyes continued to sparkle with excitement.

"Let's go back to the cabin. I'll finish cleaning the birds while you unload the hunting supplies we won't need until tomorrow, and prepare the goodies you want to take to Mom. It won't take me long. Do you want all four in the smoker? There will be room once you remove some of the smoked fish."

"No, let's put one in the fridge for now. We can figure out how to cook it later this week."

We went into action as quickly as we arrived. I stored the hunting supplies in the shed and placed my shotgun inside. River had a cooler on her trailer that I filled with salmon filets, berries, and four geese. I filled a foil-lined box with smoked salmon and loaded it on the trailer while River hung the birds in the smoker. After filling our water bottles, I took them to the smokehouse, where River had finished hanging the birds.

"Go wash up, and let's have a salmon snack before we hit the trail."

"That's a good idea. Be right back."

"Do you have a medium-weight jacket?" River asked.

"I do. I'll go get it," I replied. "Do you need anything?"

"No, I'm good. Thanks."

I slipped into the jacket and climbed on behind River. "You might want to hold on tighter in some areas. The trail gets rough in sections, and we'll cross two creeks along the way. I'll try not to get you muddy, but no guarantees."

I wrapped my arms around her waist and enjoyed her warmth as I tucked in close. The position brought my face close to her head, and I could smell the clean scent of the shampoo she used.

"Wait," I said. "I need to leave food out for Poe."

River nodded toward the smokehouse. "He'll be busy with those for hours."

"Thank you."

"No problem. Ready?"

"Yes, I am."

†

River pulled out of the yard and drove the trail next to the river. I leaned into her when we reached a point farther than I had ventured.

"I've never been this far north."

"It's a beautiful ride. Let me know to slow down if you see something you'd like to look at."

"I will." I found myself resting my chin on her shoulder as we rode. I enjoyed wrapping my arms around her body, and the feel of her so close was marvelous. I could feel her muscles contract as she steered the vehicle through rough patches, and I knew she gathered strength from these daily workouts. River was such an enigma. She was handsome but never mentioned anything about her personal life or partner. She talked warmly of her mom but no one else. There were moments when I caught her watching me, but she would turn away when she realized I had noticed. Working closely together, our hands and bodies frequently came into contact, but she neither shied away nor leaned into the touch. It frustrated me that I could not read her. She appeared aloof, but I could sense a fiery passion inside of her. River loved her life and her home. That was apparent, but everything else seemed a mystery to me. Maybe meeting her mother would help answer some of the questions that burned through me.

I was lost in the feel of our bodies pressed together and hadn't realized River had slowed to a stop. She pointed down the creek we were sitting in.

"Our great waterfall," she teased.

"It's not mighty, but it is beautiful," I said.

"Wolf Creek. The spring flow is much greater with the melting snow, but the levels are down."

River continued driving, and when she crested a hill, I saw smoke rising in the air, and then a small village came into view. She slowed to a stop. "The town of Wolf Creek and my home."

"Busy place." I saw people toiling in gardens and filling smokehouses, doing laundry, and small children chasing each other in the streets.

River crept into town and stopped in front of a small lodge. "I need to drop this elk with the elders for disbursing," she told me. The children crowded around the ATV, and several pairs of curious dark eyes smiled at me. "Don't be rude. Introduce yourselves to my friend Tatum," River told them as she climbed off the ATV.

"I'm Reba," a beautiful little girl said. "I'm Kevin," her play partner announced. "Are you a hunter, too?"

"She's the great white hunter," River announced. "She killed that big bull moose I brought in yesterday."

"He must have been a monster," Kevin said. "River could barely lift the quarters."

"Don't tell stories on me now, Kev," River teased.

"Well, you did grunt loudly." He laughed.

"You need to grow strong quick so you can help me," River said. "Can you handle a bag?"

"I can," he answered and carried the organ meat bag inside.

"And you, little missy, can you help me with these ribs?"

"Yes, River."

River handed Reba a corner of a bag, but she handled most of the weight. "Should I grab a quarter?"

"Front will be lighter," River said.

"I picked up a bag with a front quarter and followed her inside."

"Greetings and welcome home, River," an elderly woman spoke. She looked at me with curiosity. "Tatum, daughter of Charles Chastain, we welcome you."

"Thank you," I replied and took the wrinkled hand she offered,

"I am Nanesha, an elder of the Wolf Creek people. River tells me you bring her great luck."

"I'm not sure about that, but she's taught me a great deal about hunting," I replied.

"Your mother is still raving about the smoked salmon you brought home and the richness of the roe."

"Good. We brought more today," River said. "I'm sure Mother will share if you'd care to stop by for a visit."

"I might see you later today after I assign this latest meat you have harvested."

"Any word on the caribou yet?" River asked.

Nanesha shook her head. "Not yet. I fear the herd has migrated farther north this year."

"I hope not," River said. "I will hunt harder to bring in as much red meat as possible. The game seems to be plentiful this fall."

"Thank you. It was nice to meet you, Tatum. Please visit as often as you can."

"I will," I replied, returning to the trailer to help carry the remaining bags.

†

"Are you ready to meet my mom?" River asked.

I nodded. "I'm looking forward to it."

"Climb on," River instructed. The small girl looked up at her. "Come see me in a little bit. I have something for you."

Reba's face beamed. "I will, River."

River put the ATV in gear and drove slowly through town, greeting the people sitting on porches or working in garden plots. There were about two dozen homes clustered together. River stopped in front of one and turned to me. "Here we are."

The door flew open, and a portly woman rushed out. "Here you are. I was beginning to worry."

"It's only two, Mom. We made good time and brought an elk in to share."

The woman's face beamed with pride. "You do well."

River bowed her head in respect. "Thank you, Mom."

I felt the woman's eyes shift to me. "You must be Tatum. You look so much like Charles." She smiled. "I am Nikita. Welcome to our home."

"Thank you. It's a pleasure to meet you."

Nikita's eyes landed on the trailer. "Do you need help unloading?"

River smiled. "We've got this, but you can hold the door for us." River picked up the heavier cooler. "Will you bring the box?"

"Sure will," I replied.

I picked up the box and followed River inside a small but comfortable home. She placed the cooler on the kitchen floor. "You can put that on the counter," she told me.

"Oh, that smells delicious. More of your smoked fish?"

"Yes. River said you enjoyed them, and I had extras to share."

"They are delicious," Nikita said. "Thank you."

"That's not all," River said, opening the cooler lid.

Nikita's eyes widened when she saw the four geese, fish filets, and blueberry bags. "I promised Reba a special treat, so I want to send some blueberries home with her."

"Send a bag home with her. She and her family will enjoy the tasty treat," Nikita stated.

"I can send more," I offered. "If brother bear has left me some."

"Be careful," Nikita warned. "They will eat everything they can get their paws on right now."

"I've only seen one so far, but I'm certain there are more."

"I hope you're hungry," she told River. "I've been cooking all morning. I've got baskets of vegetables to send back with you, Tatum."

"I'm looking forward to that."

River lifted a lid on a frying pan. "Where did you get these?"

"I've been saving those pork chops for a special event."

I felt honored. I knew pork wasn't easy to come by in the area.

"Pour some drinks, and we can eat," Nikita said as she placed bowls of steaming food on the table.

"This is incredible," I replied as my eyes surveyed the table. Rice, gravy, cornbread, and various vegetables filled every available inch of the surface. "Where do we start?"

"I don't know about you, but a pork chop is calling my name." River placed a chop on her plate and passed it to me.

When there was no room left on my plate, I began eating, and it was difficult to choose a favorite. "It's so great to have fresh vegetables. I didn't arrive on time or have the necessary garden equipment."

"The gardens here have produced well this year. I've canned more this year than ever before," Nikita replied.

A soft knock sounded on the door, and Nikita said, "Come in."

Reba moved through the door and walked over to River. "You said to come to see you."

"I did," River said. "Excuse us for a few minutes."

Reba followed River into the kitchen and waited patiently as she wrapped six smoked fish in foil and placed a bag of berries in the bottom of a plastic grocery sack before placing the fish on top. "Take those home to your mama for me, please."

Reba tugged at River's shirt sleeve until she leaned down. Reba kissed her cheek and whispered a bit louder than she realized. "She's pretty."

River chuckled. "Yes, she is," she whispered. She handed the child the bag. "Go before I take those berries back."

"Thanks, River," Reba said. She giggled as she raced toward the door.

River returned to the table to finish her meal.

†

"I'm going to explode if I don't stop," I said as I smiled at Nikita. "That meal was absolute heaven. Thank you."

"It's the least I could do to thank you for all the goodness you're sending us. After this meal settles, we can get you loaded for a return trip. I know River is anxious to get back before it turns colder."

"I'll be traveling to Glennallen next week. Is there anything you need from there that I can pick up for you?"

"Let me think about it, and I'll send a list and money with River in a day or two."

We chatted for several minutes until River began to fidget.

"Before you go, please tell me your secret for the moose steak you fed River. She raved about it for an hour. Mine has a tendency to be tough, but she eats it anyway."

"Apple juice. I injected the meat with some juice and let it sit in the refrigerator a few hours before cooking." I smiled at her. "She enjoyed the blueberry compote on the salmon too. It gives it a whole other taste."

"I will definitely add apple juice to my list."

"Do you have an injector?"

"Yes, I'll need to locate it." Nikita grinned.

"Do you need to relieve your bladder before we go?" River asked.

"That's probably not a bad idea."

"Second door on the right. I'll load the trailer, and we can be off after I go."

†

When I walked out to the ATV, River returned inside. "Oh my gosh, are those Brussels sprouts?"

"Yes, I have more than I can use. A few stalks of broccoli too. More potatoes and cabbage will grow before the end of the season. I will save some for you."

I smiled. "I've found a real honey hole for salmon, and I have enough for the winter. Do you prefer filets or smoked fish?"

"I'll take any you care to send."

"Berries too?"

"Oh, for sure. I can come down and help pick if there are many left. Just let River know. I haven't been out of the village for a while."

"Are there any other berries I should look for? I've found several patches of morel mushrooms too."

"You may have cranberries and cloudberries near you. River will be able to identify them for you."

"I'll scout then and ask River to bring you down to harvest for a day or two."

Nikita smiled. "Would it be okay to bring Reba? She worships River if you couldn't tell."

"That would be great," I replied.

River returned and hugged her mom. "I'll see you tomorrow."

I hugged Nikita and thanked her for the fantastic meal.

"Thanks for all the goodies. I'll see you soon."

"Your mom and Reba will come down to help me harvest berries if I can find a few more varieties," I explained. "Mushrooms, too."

River's face lit with a smile. "That sounds good."

†

The daylight was growing shorter, and the temperature dropped quickly. I regretted not bringing a pair of gloves with me. River must have read my mind. She took my hands and placed them in the pocket of her hoodie, and within minutes, they were toasty warm again.

We unloaded the vegetables and carried them into the kitchen when we returned to the cabin. It was still relatively early, and neither of us was ready to retire. "I think I'll get a start on these vegetables," I told River.

"Do you want some help?"

"I'll never turn down your skills with a knife," I teased.

"I'll add some wood to the smoker and grab a couple of beers if that's okay."

"Perfect," I said. "I'll set up the vacuum sealer while you're gone and get some water boiling."

†

We sliced and packaged vegetables for hours, discussing River's life growing up in Alaska. She had led a hard life, but the village highly respected her. I could easily pick up on that after today's visit. Reba's adoration of River was cute, too.

After sealing a final bag of sliced carrots, I stretched and turned to River.

"That's a fantastic piece of equipment. That might make a good Christmas present for Mom."

"It makes storage easier, and you can boil items in the bag." I smiled. "I use it to store leftovers that can quickly turn into hot meals. The flat bags store easier and save room."

"Can I get one in Glennallen?" River asked.

"Yes, that's where mine came from."

River grinned. "I will look into that."

"What's the plan for tomorrow?" I asked.

"I need to look for another moose or elk," River replied.

"I've got enough geese. Do you want me to try for more while you hunt the bigger animals?"

"That would be great. You can scout for berries if you don't find any birds."

"I'll listen for a shot and find you to help harvest the meat."

"Thanks. That does speed up the work."

"No problem. I'll run the fish line while you make a delivery and prepare a hearty meal for your return."

River smiled. "That sounds good." She stood. "I'll see you in the morning. Rest well."

"You too."

I wiped down the counter and table and opened the iPad.

July 15th – Day thirteen.

These have been two of the most exciting weeks of my life. I find life at the cabin more pleasurable with every new adventure. Today we traveled to River's village, and I met her mom. She was a lovely lady who cooked the best meal I've had in a long time. Sent a trailer full of vegetables home with me too.

I paused my typing and felt a smile grow on my face.

River thinks I'm pretty. It took the innocence of a child to learn that revelation, but it made my heart race. I find myself falling deeper for River every day. I would generally be terrified to be attracted to someone so quickly, but there is something different with River. I can only hope that she feels the same. I understand she shelters her emotions, so I may need to push the envelope and be the aggressor if we want to have a relationship.

She may not want to pursue something physical with someone who may be gone in a few short months, and I couldn't blame her for that. Damn, how I want that woman. What to do?

I chuckled and ended my entry. "Time will tell," I said and closed the iPad.

CHAPTER TEN

A fine rain was falling the following day when I woke. I removed a slice of fry bread and placed it on the porch for Poe, but he was nowhere in sight. Neither was River. Maybe she wasn't up yet. I returned inside to start on breakfast. I chopped onions, mushrooms, ham, and sausage to add to whipped eggs for omelets. There were six remaining biscuits that I split and placed on the stove to heat. I poured another cup of coffee and walked to the door.

My heart swelled when I saw River processing fish and talking with Poe, who was curiously close to her. I brewed another cup of coffee, pulled on my slicker, and joined them. "Good morning, Poe."

River looked up at the sound of my voice and smiled. "Hey," she said.

"You got an early start."

143

"The rain woke me, and I couldn't fall back to sleep."

I noticed her breath turn into puffs of vapor as she talked. It was cooler this morning, and the dampness added to the chill.

"It's a bit brisk this morning," I said as I handed her the coffee.

"Yes, it is, but I don't think it's permanent. I wouldn't be surprised if the sun came out before afternoon, and we'll sweat. It's that time of year."

"I've got breakfast ready to cook when you're done."

"I won't be long. Add another layer of clothes so you don't get chilled this morning," River suggested.

"I will." I returned inside, added a thermal shirt under my work shirt, and refilled my ammo belt while waiting for River.

When I heard her boots on the porch, I walked to the stove to start the omelet.

"That smells good. Good lord, I hope we're sharing that," she joked.

"Yes, that's the plan. Do you want some honey or syrup for your biscuits?"

"Honey will give us more energy," River said as she retrieved a jar from the pantry.

"Are you warm enough sleeping in the bathhouse?"

"It's not bad at all right now."

"When I start heating the house at night, I hope you bring the cot and join me where it's warmer."

"I will if I'm still in the area."

I turned away from her to hide the pained look on my face. I hadn't given thought to River changing hunting areas soon. I reckon it was inevitable to prevent the depletion of animals in the area.

We ate breakfast in silence. I wasn't sure I was prepared to discuss River not being here or being able to control the emotional distress I felt. I knew I had grown strong enough and planned well for winter, but I was becoming accustomed to her presence.

We parted ways on the trail, and I drove to the lake to look for geese. The flock had doubled overnight, and I took aim and unloaded my shotgun. I used the net to retrieve four birds and processed them quickly after reloading my gun. After placing the geese in buckets, I climbed onto the ATV and drove past the lake to scout for berries. There was still a good supply of blueberries. I picked a handful for a snack. Still sweet and juicy. The chill wind made my eyes water as I scanned for evidence of more berries. A sea of red was ahead, and I pulled into an area where the ground was covered with round red berries. I picked several handfuls and placed them in a basket. I wouldn't waste time picking them if they were not the edible cranberries Nikita described. I sat on the ATV, enjoying the view of the mountains. It had been quiet for hours until the air exploded with a gunshot. The cool air carried the sound from miles away. I knew River was hunting at the larger lake, so I headed in that direction.

I was surprised when I neared the small lake to find the geese had returned. I quickly took four more and tossed them into a bucket. I would clean them once I saw what River had shot.

When I located her, she was bent over skinning a bull moose. She had already removed the entrails and moved them from the kill site. At least I missed that part. She looked up and smiled when she heard my approach.

"I shot four more geese on my way. As soon as I clean them, I will help you."

"Thanks. Good job with the geese. I've seen several groups flying south today, so they probably won't be around much longer."

"I found some berries that I think are cranberries. I brought some to show you. Plenty of blueberries are left, too."

"I've seen prints that suggest brother bear is visiting the gut piles, so he's probably gorging on those for now."

"He's still a few months from entering a den, right?"

River nodded. "The first snowfall will be a cue for him."

†

"What are your plans for the rest of the day?" River asked as she loaded the last bag and placed the geese in her trailer.

"I think I'll work on dropping more trees. I'm doing well for food stores. Maybe I can shoot a grouse or two for more soup now that I have vegetables."

"That's a good plan."

"Now that you've confirmed the cranberries, invite your mom and Reba down, and we can pick while you hunt."

"I will," River said. "I'll be back as quick as I can."

"Be safe," I said, watching her pull away before turning toward the cabin.

†

At home, I ate a smoked fish, serviced the chainsaw, loaded the shotgun, and made my way to the woodlot. I had downed three dozen trees before realizing how many I had and stopped for a break. The work was getting less taxing, that was certain. My arms no longer ached from the constant vibration of the saw. I took a break for a long drink of water and spotted a grouse not far ahead. One shot, and he would soon land in my soup pot. I grinned. I cleaned him and trimmed limbs from the trees until I saw another grouse. Two in the bucket would be great, so I called it a day after cleaning him. I would work on cutting rounds once the fishing ended.

After cutting the breasts into cubes, I added diced vegetables and seasoning to the pot. I also boiled some rice. The biscuits had turned out well on the Blackstone, so I made another large pan to cook. Once the rice finished, I used the burner to cook some dried beans. I would vacuum-seal them and have them for other hot meals. I laughed at myself, thinking I was becoming a squirrel hoarding food for the wintertime.

I walked to the dock and plucked a beer bottle from the crate. The first sip had ice crystals in it from the cold water. Damn, that tasted good. I sat on the steps sipping the beer and considering the emotional onslaught I had gone through earlier in the day. I couldn't blame River for protecting herself from hurt if I chose to leave at the end of the year. I sensed self-protection was a big issue for her. The thought of what-ifs began to creep in on me. *What if I didn't return to Chicago? Would my father be disappointed if I didn't return? Can I make it long-term in Alaska?* Too many questions with no hint of answers filled my brain.

I stirred the soup and beans before returning to the porch to check the biscuits. They looked good, so I picked up a piece of wood and pulled out my knife. Poe landed on the railing closer to me than ever before.

"Hello, my friend. Are you beginning to trust me, or are you reminding me dinner time is close?"

He stared back at me with bright yellow eyes and remained silent. A goose developed in my hand, and I brushed away the shavings and walked inside to make a coffee after placing him on the windowsill.

†

An hour later, I heard the sound of a motor and walked out to watch River and Nikita pull into the yard and park by the bathhouse. Reba clung to River, and when the ATV stopped, she jumped off and ran over to me.

"We're having a campout," she squealed with excitement.

"I know," I replied, and opened my arms for a hug. "I'm glad you're here."

"Me too, Tatum," Reba answered.

River smiled at me. "I see you have stolen the heart of my godchild." She grinned. "We couldn't get here fast enough."

"Godchild?"

"Reba is my best friend's daughter," River explained.

"That's interesting. Welcome, Nikita."

"Thank you, Tatum. It's good to be here where the air is fresh and clean."

"I'm going to get us set up in the bathhouse. Mom will take the cot, and Reba will sack out with me. You better not kick, though," she teased Reba. "Come, you can help me unload."

"Come inside," I told Nikita. "Are you all hungry?"

"We could eat. I love how you have this place set up. Different from your father's trips."

"He only stayed for short trips, and the cabin wasn't prepared for winter accommodation." I lifted the lid. "I have soup, beans if you want some, biscuits on the grill, and we can add some smoked fish, too."

"I do love your fish."

I handed Nikita a pan. "Will you bring us some from the back of the smokehouse?"

Nikita nodded and exited the cabin.

River and Reba entered as I poured the soup into a large bowl. I placed a ladle in the bowl.

"Here, let me get that," River said. She took the bowl from my hands, and our eyes and hands met briefly.

"Thanks," I replied, turning away before my blush rose. "I cooked a pot of beans to freeze if you want some, and rice for the beans or soup. Your mom is bringing in some fish, too."

"The soup with some rice and fish should be plenty. Keep your beans to freeze."

"That works for me. I had time and a free burner, so I thought I would cook some. Oh, there are biscuits warming on the grill, too. I'll be right back. You can pour some water, please."

I passed Nikita coming through the door. "I forgot the biscuits. Be right back." I left a fresh biscuit out for Poe and returned inside.

†

Reba filled her belly with soup and honey-filled biscuits. Soon after, she was asleep in River's arms.

"I think I'll take her out and put her to bed," River said.

I nodded. "Would you two like to share a beer with me?"

"I'm not far behind Reba, but maybe tomorrow night if we haven't worn out our welcome?"

"Stay as long as you can. I have found enough berries to keep us busy for a while."

River smiled. "Do you need to use the bathroom before I put her down?"

"Yes, I think I'd better. You can grab the beer when you finish, and I'll pick up the kitchen. I think the beans are cool enough to bag."

Nikita grinned. "I'll wash the dishes if you want to tend to the beans. I'd like to see how that gadget works."

"Don't worry about the dishes. I can do them later."

"Nonsense, you prepared a great meal."

†

Nikita began washing dishes and noticed the carvings on the windowsill. "Are these your handiwork?" she asked, pointing to the figures.

150

"Yes, I figured I needed a hobby to relax with occasionally."

"That raven is exceptional," she praised.

"That's Poe. You will probably meet him tomorrow. He's quite the character."

"A good luck omen for you, too," Nikita said.

"You know, I hadn't thought of that. But, my harvests have been plentiful since Poe arrived." I showed Nikita how to seal a bag of cooked beans. "You want to try?"

"Sure." She smiled. "That is easy, and they stack much better this way."

"You are more than welcome to borrow mine anytime you wish," I told her. "Did you bring a shopping list?"

"I did, but I may still add an item or two before we leave."

River brought in two beers and sat at the table to watch Nikita and me finish packaging the beans.

"That is a nifty machine," Nikita said.

"Thanks for helping me," I replied.

"My pleasure. I think it's time for me to put these old bones to bed."

River kissed her mother's cheek. "I won't be long."

"Goodnight," I told her. "I'll see you for breakfast in the morning."

†

After her mother left, River looked at me. "Thank you."

"For what?"

"Allowing her to help and showing her to use that nifty machine, as she called it."

151

I chuckled. "I enjoy having your mom and Reba here."

"Tired of me already?" River looked at me with a glint of humor in her eyes.

"Not yet, but Reba is a charmer," I teased. "How will she do picking berries tomorrow?"

"She'll probably eat more than she puts in the bucket, but she'll have a helluva time doing it."

"With two and a half of us picking, we should be able to harvest quite a few to take to the village. Do I need to help you process a kill tomorrow?"

"No, keep picking the berries while you can. They will fade quickly with the weather."

I nodded. "Blueberry pancakes and ham steaks okay in the morning? I figure we can pack some ham biscuits for snacks."

"Wonderful plan. I'm getting hooked on your cooking," River said.

I yawned. "Sorry, I kind of overdid things this afternoon. I cut down three dozen trees in no time, and I'm starting to feel it."

"Get some rest, and I'll see you at breakfast. I may take Reba along to check your nets if that's okay. You and Mom can share some coffee and prepare breakfast."

"Goodnight, then," I said, walking River to the door.

July 16th – Day fourteen

I am as confused as ever regarding my growing feelings for River. My heart pounds when she looks at me with her dark eyes and smiles. Is love growing, or do I admire her for her strength and skills? Definitely an enigma to me. Nikita and Reba returned with River today. We will harvest berries and other goodies to return to the village. Reba is adorable, and she dotes on every word coming from River. I don't know why I was surprised River was her godmother. It's apparent the love between them is mutual, and Reba brings out a new layer of tenderness and caring in River's personality. Why am I so confused? It's been a long day, and tomorrow will be fun, so I'll end this here for tonight.

†

I decided on a large batch of blueberry pancakes for breakfast. I also heated ham slices to add to the leftover biscuits for snacks. My mouth watered as I cooked, and I added cheese, pasta, and other items to my shopping list. I found experimentation fun for someone who had never been interested in creating in the kitchen. I looked up from the grill when I heard the boat motor approaching, and it was difficult to tell which of them was smiling the brightest.

Reba climbed onto the dock and rushed over to me. "Tatum, we caught twelve fish. They are big, too."

"How big?"

Reba spread her arms as wide as she could.

"Monster fish." I chuckled. "Are you hungry?"

Reba nodded. "Are those pancakes?"

"Blueberry pancakes, just for you. Do you want to help?"

Reba nodded.

"Let's go wash your hands at the sink then," I said, holding a hand out for her.

When we returned, Nikita and River were processing the fish for the smokehouse, and the two were nearly finished. I called across the yard to them. "Chef Reba and I are almost done preparing breakfast, so come wash up to eat while it's hot."

"Go ahead, Mom. I'll be right there," River said.

Reba enjoyed learning how to flip the pancakes and add the finished products to the growing plate of food. "There's one more we need to make," I told her and poured a smaller pancake onto the grill.

"What's that for?" she asked.

"Breakfast for my friend, Poe. He loves pancakes, too."

Poe sat perched atop the smokehouse preening as he watched the flurry of activity.

"He likes them, too?" Reba asked.

"Loves them. Poe will tap on my window if he thinks I have forgotten him." I waited until she pulled the pancake from the grill and let it cool for a second. "Do you want to feed him?"

"Yes," she answered excitedly.

I handed her the cooling treat and lifted her to the top of the woodpile. "Place it on top for Poe, please."

Reba placed the food on the woodpile, and I returned her to her feet, and I handed her a smaller plate of ham pieces. "Can you carry that for me? We can stuff some biscuits with the ham for a morning snack."

"Yes, I can," Reba said and proudly carried the plate inside.

"I placed the platter of pancakes on the table and set the ham on the counter before lifting Reba. "Will you help me make coffee?"

"Yes," she answered with glee.

154

I showed her which buttons to push, and we had three cups made when Nikita arrived. "Do you want some juice?"

"Please," Reba answered. "We don't get juice often in the village."

I poured a small glass and placed it before her. "Syrup or honey?"

"Syrup." She grinned.

"Do you need help cutting the pancakes?"

"I've got this." Reba picked up her fork and used it and her fingers to cut a bite of pancakes.

River walked inside as Reba took a bite. "Whoa, save some for me," she teased Reba.

"There is a big stack, River. We won't run out."

"Did I really see you cooking pancakes?"

"Yes, you did. I even made one for Poe."

"He's already enjoying his, too," River said, pointing out the window.

Reba giggled. "That's funny."

†

"Are you ready to go berry picking?" River asked Reba as she prepared her equipment to hunt.

"I'm happy about it," Reba answered.

"Pick more than you eat. You and Tatum used a bunch on breakfast this morning."

"I will," Reba said.

"No worries. We will come home with buckets filled with berries," I told Reba.

"Mom has her twenty-two in case you scare up any rabbits for a stew pot," River told me. "They should be plentiful in the berry patches."

I nodded. "Good luck this morning. We'll see you later today." I handed River a bundle of ham biscuits. "Don't forget to snack to keep your energy up."

"Thanks," River replied and stored the biscuits.

†

Nikita and I placed buckets in her sled. I found a smaller bucket for Reba to use. "That should work. Are we ready to go get some berries?"

"Yes," Nikita nodded. "Let's start with cranberries since you already have blueberries. "They will be easier for Reba to pick, too."

"Just follow me, then." I climbed onto my ATV and drove beyond the woodlot to the cranberry field.

When a sea of red berries came into view, Nikita sighed. "We won't have trouble filling these buckets." She grinned.

"No, not at all," I agreed.

†

After picking berries for hours, Reba grew sleepy and napped inside the sled. "No worries. She'll be recharged in less than an hour."

We filled five large buckets and placed them by the ATVs. Nikita pointed out a large rabbit feeding on the berries. "One for the pot?"

"Sure," I answered. "I'll keep picking if you prepare the rabbit for eating."

Nikita aimed her rifle and downed the rabbit with one shot. I worried the noise would wake and startle Reba, but she slept through the sound of the smaller caliber rifle. Nikita retrieved the animal and gutted him.

"I will skin him later. Maybe we will get a few more to make warm gloves for the winter."

"I bet those would be nice. The fur is so soft," I remarked.

After filling the remaining buckets, we returned to the cabin. "Tomorrow, we can work on more blueberries."

Reba rubbed her sleepy eyes and looked at the two rabbits Nikita had harvested. "Those will make a good stew."

"We will send them to your mother," Nikita said. "She can make a nice stew when you return from your camping trip."

I took out one bucket of berries when we returned, intending to send the rest to the village. Nikita frowned. "Just one for you?"

"One will be plenty. It will give me several large bags. I prefer the sweeter blueberries," I said with a wink to Reba, and then I carried the bucket inside to rinse the berries. "Reba and I can store my berries if you want to check on River. I'm surprised we haven't heard a shot yet."

"Me too," Nikita said. "I will go check. Do you need anything first?"

"I have my assistant, so I should be good."

"Do you mind if I use your ATV? I don't want to lose any berries."

"That's fine."

†

Reba and I chatted while I rinsed the berries, and then she scooped them into Ziploc bags for me. "Thank you for all your great help. Are you having fun?"

"I am." She grinned.

"When River returns, I will ask her if we can use any leftover meat bags to transport the berries. That way, I can pick more and not worry about them arriving safely in the village."

"Mommy has a stack of cloth bags she uses when we carry things back to the village. Maybe we could borrow some of them."

"That's smart. I'll ask River to check for us. Great idea."

Reba swelled with pride.

"Do you go to school yet?"

"This year, I can start," Reba said. "I'm so excited to learn my letters and numbers."

"I'm sure you will make a good student."

"If not, Mommy says she'll tan my hide. She's one of the teachers at our school."

I chuckled. "Uh oh, Mom will hear everything you do in school."

"Yeah," Reba answered.

After adding the berries to the bush cooler, I looked at Reba. "What should we do now?"

"I don't know. Can we check for more fish?"

"We can, but I must make some room in the smokehouse first." We walked to the smokehouse, and I removed two of the geese. "While these cool, will you help me wrap up more smoked fish? I don't know about you, but I'm getting slightly nibbly."

"My stomach has been growling," Reba said.

"We can definitely fix that. Let's go get some fish."

We filled a large pan with fish and ate a section each while waiting for the geese to cool for deboning. I would keep the breasts and send the drumsticks and wings to the village for seasoning soup. I sealed the meat I would keep and packaged the rest in a Ziploc. After dropping the packages into the cooler, I turned to Reba. "Let's go check for fish."

"All right," she cried out and rushed ahead of me to the boat.

"Wait for me," I said and hurried inside to get my shotgun. We could look for geese or ducks on the river if we didn't have many fish.

I climbed into the boat, stored the gun, and reached for Reba. "All set?"

She smiled at me and nodded.

Before we reached the net, I spotted several geese and shot two before they took flight. I maneuvered the boat close. "Can you be careful and pick up the bird?" I held my breath as Reba leaned over and plucked the bird from the water. "Great job! Ready for another?"

"Yes," Reba replied, wiping the cold water from her hands. "This is fun."

Four fish were in the net, so we continued upriver to search for more birds. Finding none close, we returned to the cabin. River and Nikita were arriving as we docked the boat. "Welcome back," I called to them. "How did you do?"

"She got another nice moose," Nikita answered. "Did you get more geese?"

"Two and four more fish," Reba said proudly.

"Good job." River smiled at her excitement. "Let's get them cleaned and ready to go. Do you want to ride home with me?"

"Will I get to come back?" Reba asked, concerned.

"Of course. You are a part of this hunting party," River told her.

"Do you have any meat bags you aren't using?" I asked.

"I think there are three. Why?"

"Nikita and I can transfer the cranberries into them for transport, and if she's up for it, we can pick blueberries while you're gone."

"Great idea. Mom, will you grab some of the bags?"

"Absolutely. Let's get these bags filled," Nikita said to me.

I propped my shotgun against the ATV.

†

It took all three bags to hold the berries we loaded onto River's sled. "Reba said her mom has some bags we could use," I told River as she placed the geese and rabbit in her sled. "We also have a large bag of wings and drumsticks to send, too. Reba, will you get those?"

Reba flew around the side of the cabin and returned with the large bag.

I looked at Nikita. "Would you possibly have some shredded cheese and sour cream?"

"I do. River, will you bring it back with you?"

160

"That sounds interesting," River said.

"My creative juices are flowing again," I replied.

"Anything else?"

"Some lettuce if you can find some."

"Pick a couple of heads from the garden," Nikita told River.

"We'd better get moving then," River said, reaching for Reba, who tucked in front of River.

"Be careful, and we'll see you soon."

†

We watched them pull away, and then Nikita turned to me. "More berries?"

"Right behind you." I slung the shotgun over my shoulder and climbed onto the ATV.

Picking the blueberries off the bushes was easier instead of the ground, and we worked quickly to fill the buckets. I shot three grouse, and after field-dressing them, we returned home.

"I think it's time to have a beer and relax for a little while," I replied, placing the birds in the sink to soak.

"I won't argue, but I prefer a coffee. It's been a long but productive day."

"Yes, it has. We accomplished a lot today," I answered. "Coffee does sound good."

†

As the day faded, I thought it was time to prepare dinner. I expected River and Reba to return within the hour.

"What can I do to help?" Nikita asked.

"Will you cut the grouse breasts into small strips?"

"That's easy enough," Nikita said.

I walked to the pantry and removed a variety of seasonings to mix in a bowl.

"What are you planning tonight?"

"I thought we would have some soft grouse tacos for something different," I answered.

"That sounds interesting."

"I'll grill the meat and then make some flour tortillas. We can dice up the lettuce and dress them with cheese and sour cream," I said as I sliced an onion into thin strips. I added the meat and onion to the box and covered them with spices. "Will you make us another coffee and join me on the porch while the meat cooks?"

"I'll be right there," Nikita said.

I grabbed the oil bottle and the meat bowl before walking to the grill to start heating.

Nikita handed me a coffee, and we sat on the steps while the grill heated.

"Has River always been a designated hunter?"

Nikita chuckled. "Ever since she was a small child, I found it impossible to keep her out of the forest. River loved everything outdoors, and keeping her in school as she grew older was difficult. Her soul longed for the hunt," she told me. "Finally, an elder who had been a designated hunter for years took her under his wing and taught her everything he could about hunting and tracking animals. I would go days sometimes without seeing her. Especially after Becca."

I must have had a confused look on my face. "It doesn't surprise me River hasn't talked to you about Becca. She was her first love, and when Becca went to college and never returned to River as promised, it destroyed her. She would disappear for months and return looking haggard and nearly starved to death. For a while, I wasn't sure River would survive the hurt, but as the seasons changed and spring arrived, she decided to begin life anew." Nikita sipped her coffee. "That's when she became a full-time designated hunter."

"She's an amazing person," I said softly.

"River thinks the same of you, but she's terrified of growing close to you. I feel she fears she couldn't survive another great heartbreak."

I stood, added more oil to the griddle, spread the meat to cook, and then returned to sit beside Nikita. "I won't deny I have feelings for her, but until I decide my future, I will not compromise her heart. I'd rather we remain friends than make her suffer."

"I am deeply grateful for that. River is all I have left, and I don't want to lose her."

"I have so much soul-searching to do yet. I love it here and feel confident I have learned enough to survive a permanent move. However, I don't want to disappoint my father by not returning to the business."

Nikita smiled. "I don't know him well, but any parent would want their children to follow their dreams. He may be more jealous than disappointed. Not unlike you, Charles is in his element here."

I stood and walked to the grill to stir the meat and allow Nikita's words to sink in. When I returned, I said, "I am terribly conflicted about what to do. I'm probably still in a honeymoon phase, but I've never felt so free and vibrant. The air is filled with beautiful scents and sounds instead of polluted with the noise and congestion of the city. I'm not sure I can go back to who I was. I like this version of me much better."

"I may be biased, but you are the most impressive *Cheechako* I have ever met." She grinned. "I believe you will survive and thrive here if you choose."

"Thank you for your vote of confidence. It means a great deal coming from you." I walked inside, rinsed the bowl to place the cooked meat, and covered it with foil. "Do you think they will return soon?"

"Very soon," Nikita said, pointing at the headlight coming down the riverside trail.

"Damn, I'd better get busy."

"What can I do to help?" Nikita asked.

"Dice the lettuce for the tacos and set the table while I cook the tortillas." I lowered the heat on the grill and mixed the batter.

"Here we go," I whispered as I poured the first batter onto the griddle. "My first attempt at tortillas." I lowered the lid as River and Reba stopped in the yard. "Welcome back."

"I don't know what you've been cooking, but the air is filled with spices," River said.

"Nikita and I have been busy. We're making soft grouse tacos."

"That sounds delicious."

"Don't jinx me." I handed Reba my coffee cup. "May I get a refill and a plate for the tortillas?"

"Be right back," Reba said.

"Good trip?"

"The elders insist I kidnap you. Our meat lockers haven't been this full in years." She smiled.

"You've done all the hard work," I insisted.

"I got word the caribou are finally beginning to sprinkle in. After tomorrow's hunt, I will move north until we fill our permits, but I will be back."

"I plan to travel to Glennallen next week, so I may stay an extra day or two."

Reba rushed out with a plate, and Nikita carried the hot coffee. I looked at Reba. "Shall we check this test run?"

"Yes," she said, nodding her head vigorously.

I lifted the lid and breathed a sigh of relief when I was welcomed by the sight of four beautiful tortillas. "Wow, I couldn't have asked for better."

"They look fantastic," Nikita said. "I'm almost done with the lettuce. Will you help me put the cheese and sour cream on the table?" she asked Reba.

River held the plate as I removed the tortillas and added more batter. "Starving?"

"Hungry, yes," she answered.

"There will be plenty," I promised.

After cooking sixteen, I asked River to carry them inside while I cooked one more for Poe. He hopped onto the woodpile and pecked at the offering.

"Let it cool some first," I warned.

July 17th - Day fifteen

The soft tacos were a huge success; after everyone ate their fill, we decided to retire early. Everyone had started their day early, and we had accomplished much working together. At the end of the hunt tomorrow, River will be gone for a week or longer as she hunts the caribou that have begun to migrate several days north of the village. I will be sad to see them leave, but I will prepare for a trip to Glennallen to occupy my thoughts. The conversation with Nikita gave me a greater awareness of who River has become, and I appreciated her insight. Reba has been a pleasure getting to know, and I will miss her excited laughter around the cabin. Hopefully, she and Nikita will return with River soon.

†

I kept a bucket of blueberries and sent the rest to the village. Nikita, Reba, and I also processed bags of chaga and all the mushrooms we could find. River finished the trip with an elk, and after we loaded down the two sleds with meat, fish, and berries, they returned to the village. Nikita had left a small list of supplies and some cash to purchase the goods. The change would make it into one of her canning jars when they were delivered. I made a cup of coffee and reviewed my list of items. I would load two empty propane tanks and top off the boat and ATV to fill three more gas cans with some remaining for the trip. I didn't cherish running out and paddling my way into Glennallen.

I harvested the net and began to see production slowing down. I would place the five fish in the smoker, and if not successful before leaving in the morning, I would pull out some frozen filets for Elizabeth and Erica. I would also take bags of berries, mushrooms, and chaga to them.

Deciding to cut some rounds, I serviced the chainsaw and made a note to add bar and chain oil and gas mix to my list for my trip to town.

I cut rounds for hours until the daylight faded and returned home to light the bathhouse fire for a nice bath. After days of manual labor, I was beginning to offend myself. Biscuits were left over from breakfast, so I heated those and drank a cup of coffee while waiting for my water to heat. The silence in the cabin reminded me how much I missed River, Nikita, and Reba. Poe brought me back from my thoughts when he tapped on the window for dinner. I laughed and split a biscuit to place on the woodpile for him. "You must return to being a bird for a few days while I'm gone. There will be fish carcasses and some biscuits, but if you devour those, you are on your own, buddy."

I carried clean clothes to the bathhouse and removed my soiled clothing. I pulled the necklace off and hung it by the sink. I had become accustomed to wearing it and enjoyed the pleasant reminders of that day. Sliding into the warm water, I relaxed and had nearly fallen asleep when a clap of thunder boomed outside. Night had fallen and brought a thunderstorm with it. I dressed quickly and made a dash for the cabin. Poe had grown accustomed to nesting in a small wicker basket under the Blackstone. I looked in on him and entered the cabin. It had grown cold with the approaching rain, so I started a fire in the stove. I left the stove door open until I was sure the wood had caught fire, and I became mesmerized by the dancing flames. Until another clap of thunder rattled the windows.

I made a cup of coffee and flipped open the iPad.

July18th – Day sixteen

River, Reba, and Nikita returned home today. River will travel north to hunt the caribou migration, so she may not return for a while. It was eerily quiet until a rainstorm moved into the area tonight, bringing colder temperatures. Lit the fire in the stove for the first time tonight. I have everything ready for loading in the morning for the trip to Glennallen. I will run my fish line and then drive south.

I'm looking forward to my first solo adventure. I tried the radio tonight, but the static was too powerful to hear the music. Poe is nested in a basket under the Blackstone. I'll hunt a few rabbits to add the pelts to keep him warm. What did he do before I arrived?

After packing a small travel bag, I climbed inside my sleeping bag versus sleeping on top of it for weeks. I felt like I had slipped into a warm cocoon as I snuggled in and fell fast asleep.

CHAPTER ELEVEN

The rain had moved through during the night, leaving everything fresh and glistening with raindrops. The cooler temperatures had remained, and I put a heavier coat on over my favorite hoodie. I knew it would be colder on the water.

After running my line, I packaged some fresh filets and loaded the gas tanks to refill in town. The berries and other supplies were added, and I was on my way after leaving biscuits out for Poe. "I'll see you soon," I said, pulling away from the dock. I feared he would follow me like he did to the woodlot and hunting trips, but I think he realized I was going to town. He sat on the smokehouse and watched me disappear.

The water was higher from the rain, and the current was swift. I had to stay on my toes to watch for stumps, rocks, or downed trees. The last thing I wanted was to go for an unexpected swim.

I had only been gone for three hours when I began to see signs of the small town just north of Glennallen. "Damn, I must be cruising." I chuckled when I turned a bend twenty minutes later, and the Trading Depot dock came into view. Erica saw my approach and walked out to greet me.

"Welcome back," she said.

"Thanks, it's good to see you."

"How are things going for you?"

"Almost too good to be true," I replied. "I keep waiting for a disaster."

"Don't go talking anything up," she warned. "Troy said you had made tremendous progress."

"I feel like I've got a good supply of fish and game, and I work on firewood regularly. I may run out of the yard to store everything I've cut."

"You'll be surprised how quickly it can vanish, so keep a good supply. Do you have a list for me?"

"I do," I handed the list to Erica. "I need propane and gas, too," I replied.

"Will you be here a day or two?"

"Yes, at least two."

"I'll get Buck to inspect the boat, replace the plugs, and check the lines if that's okay."

"Sounds perfect." I reached down for a box of supplies. "I brought something for you and Elizabeth," I said, handing her a box of fish, berries, mushrooms, and chaga.

Erica grinned. "What do you think of chaga?"

"My first experience was wow, so I've diluted it a bit since."

"It can be overpowering if you've never experienced it before. I've got to run an errand. Would you like a ride to the bed and breakfast?"

"That would be great." I handed her the box of goods for Elizabeth and tossed my bag onto the dock before climbing out of the boat.

"It looks like bush life suits you." She smiled.

"It's a lot of hard work, but I enjoy the adventure."

"Drop in tomorrow so we can catch up on everything you've been doing."

"I will," I promised and slipped out of the truck when we arrived at the B&B.

†

"Dang, you look good," Elizabeth said when I walked in. "You seem happier."

"I am," I answered, placed the bag on the floor, and handed Elizabeth the box. "I brought you some goodies."

"Oh, yummy. Those smoked fish smell delicious. Are you up for some coffee?"

"Sounds great."

"Let me get a key for your room, and I'll brew a pot. Same room, okay?"

"Perfect," I answered. I walked down the hall and dropped the bag onto the bed before emptying my bladder. I caught my reflection in the mirror as I washed my hands. "I don't look like the same person, and I damned sure don't feel the same."

I joined Elizabeth in the kitchen, and she tempted me with a slice of pie. "How have you been, and how is Troy doing in Anchorage?"

"It's difficult determining who has the worst withdrawal symptoms. Troy really dislikes the hustle and bustle of the city. He has been visiting some family while there. Hopefully, when the orientation period is over, he will enjoy things more once fall classes begin. It's way too quiet around here for me with him gone." Elizabeth sighed. "I told him he could return until classes start, but he insisted it was way too expensive. It was unfortunate that was the only orientation period left."

"I have always been a proponent for education, but coming here has taught me so much more than any university ever could. Is it essential for him to attend? You could teach him the business here, and he could get on with the Park Service."

Elizabeth smiled. "I truly expect him to make the same suggestion after staying for a semester. I don't like him being unhappy. I wanted him to experience it for himself so he wouldn't regret not trying."

"That's a wise decision. Troy seemed excited to attend but won't benefit from staying if he's unhappy."

"That's very true. So tell me about you. How are you faring?"

"Better than I ever dreamed possible. I've got food stored to the gills, and I think I've harvested half of the dead-standing trees in Alaska."

Elizabeth's warm laughter filled the room. "How long will you be able to stay?"

"I was thinking two or three days. I left a supply list with Erica, and I'd like to hit the grocery store while I'm here."

"I will be going tomorrow, so you can ride with me or take the truck if you prefer," she offered.

"Going with you will be great. I've become creative in cooking meals and want to add a few more items to my pantry."

"You are having fun, aren't you?" She grinned.

"I've never been so happy."

†

We talked for several hours before my stomach started growling.

"What can I make you to eat?"

"Would you join me at the diner? I've been thinking about a bison bacon burger all morning."

"Oh, that does sound good. Pork chops or fried chicken for dinner?"

"Either would be great."

"Or we can have steak if you want red meat."

"Chicken or chops are fine."

"Well, let's go get that burger for you."

†

When we returned from the diner, Elizabeth looked at me. "I'm sure you left early to make such good time. Do you want to relax and maybe watch some television?"

"If I'm honest, I couldn't care less about what's on television anymore. I hope that doesn't sound horrible. I've got Poe, some friends from an Athabascan village, and my Glennallen friends. I don't need to watch all the depressing news."

"Who is Poe?" Elizabeth asked.

"He's a beautiful raven who arrived a few days after I settled in. He's quite the character and a good protector. He alerts me if there are bears or other predators around."

"That's interesting."

"Ever since he arrived in my life, it's been filled with a bounty of fish and game. I found one honey hole for salmon and never had to move my nets. I've hunted geese, grouse, and rabbits. I even shot my first moose under River's guidance."

"River Foster?"

"Yes, do you know her?"

"We've never met, but she's a legendary hunter known as the Alaskan Amazon due to her height. Unusually tall for an Athabascan woman."

"That's River. I met her when I was grouse hunting, and she has taught me a lot about how to process and store meat." I smiled. "I managed to stockpile plenty of food for the winter, so I've been assisting her with hunting and foraging for her village in exchange for my education. I've got my bush coolers, refrigerator/freezer, and pantry stuffed with fish and fowl that I have processed and canned. I've bartered some of my fish and other goods for fresh garden vegetables, so it's been a win-win situation."

"Listen to you," Elizabeth teased. "I'm proud of you, and I'm sure Charles would be, too."

174

"I think he would be. I know I'm proud of myself. I had serious doubts, but this is where I'm meant to be."

"Long-term?"

"Possibly, if I can last through the winter," I admitted as much to myself as Elizabeth.

"I've got a bit of work I need to get done. I'll start cooking around six if that's good."

"I may stretch out and take a nap," I said.

†

I surprised myself by falling asleep and was glad I had set the alarm. I rinsed my face before going in search of Elizabeth. I sat in the kitchen while she cooked.

"When will Troy be home?"

"The Fall Break is still a long way off. It might end up being torture for him." She chuckled. "Will you plan to come to town for a visit?"

"I'd like to. I might need more supplies by then, and I would love to see Troy."

"He called when he arrived in Anchorage and asked about you. He wanted to know if I've seen or heard from you. If you don't come for a visit, I'm sure he'll come to find you."

"Let him know I'll be here."

†

"Do you want to shop early in the morning?" Elizabeth asked.

"If you don't mind. I told Erica I would drop by tomorrow."

"That's fine. We can shop, then you can drop me off and go to the Depot."

"Thank you, and thanks for a great meal."

"My pleasure. Having company at the dinner table for a change was nice." She stood. "See you at seven for some breakfast?"

I nodded. "Nothing heavy, though."

"Are you kidding me? If you grocery shop hungry, you'll sink your boat."

"Good point." I grinned. "Breakfast it is, then."

†

The hot shower felt fantastic, and I took advantage of the opportunity to shave. I had to change blades, but I finally had my legs silky smooth again. I brushed my hair, surprised at how quickly it had grown past my shoulders. *Should I get a haircut while in town or just let it grow and tie it back?* I decided to let it grow. I would pick up some hair ties at the store tomorrow.

I didn't bring my iPad, so I would add some longer entries when I returned home. The soft bed was comfortable, but I missed the sounds of home.

†

"Fried or scrambled eggs?" Elizabeth asked when I entered the kitchen.

"Fried, please."

"Grab some coffee, and I'll have breakfast right out. Elizabeth cracked three eggs and then carried toast and a platter of bacon to the table."

"Oh, how I've missed bacon," I groaned as I took a bite. "I think I'll buy some now that I have the means to store it."

"This will probably be the last opportunity for fruit that doesn't cost an arm or a leg, so grab what you can," Elizabeth warned.

"Will do." I broke the yolk with the toast and sopped it up with the bread. "I may have to try my hand at baking some bread. My biscuits and fry bread are good, but there's nothing like toast with fried eggs."

"I understand that. Troy loves his dippers, as he calls them."

"Let me brush my teeth, grab my list, and I'll be ready," I said, placing my dishes on the counter.

"I'll meet you at the truck," Elizabeth said, placing the dishes in the machine.

†

We both grabbed carts as we entered the store. I loaded my cart with the more oversized items on the bottom, placing three cases of beer and a bulk pack of toilet paper. The larger bulk items, flour, spices, etc., were cheaper through the Trading Post, so I focused on smaller items at the grocery store. Twelve boxes of angel hair pasta, elbow macaroni, spaghetti, and Alfredo sauces came next. A large container of powdered Parmesan cheese, several pounds of butter, and a block of Gouda cheese were added. Powdered ranch dressing also made it to my cart. I added a few products from the hygiene aisle, including hair ties and scented candles. I thought my vegetable collection was sufficient, so I moved to the fruit section and picked out several bundles of green bananas, a flat of strawberries, and a bag of yellow apples. Several family-sized jars of peanut butter were added. My sweet-tooth cravings added a dozen boxes of instant pudding and big bags of chocolate chips. Cookies were easy to make from scratch. I couldn't resist the fudge brownie mix staring at me, so four boxes were added. The grocer added meats to the counter, so I picked out a dozen packages of thick sliced bacon.

"Someone is bacon hungry," he teased with a wink.

They were pricey, but I picked up more sausage links and another small ham. When Elizabeth found me in the freezer section, she smiled at the items in my cart.

"One more selection," I said, picking out a few pints of ice cream. "For tonight." I scanned my list. "Nuts."

"What did you forget?"

"Nuts," I repeated.

"Two aisles down." Elizabeth laughed.

After making a few nut selections, I looked at her. "We better leave before I do sink my boat."

"We can store your cold items, and you can take the rest to the Depot. I wouldn't advise taking the beer. It might be too tempting for teenagers.

"I'll just leave it in the truck if that's okay?"

"Fine as wine."

I separated my cold items when we returned to the B&B and took the rest to the Depot.

†

Erica helped me carry in the boxes of groceries to place with my other supplies. "This isn't too bad." She smiled.

"I have some cold items at the B&B and some beer I'll bring when I leave."

"That's a smart move. So, things are going well?"

"I can't complain. I work hard, eat good, and have had some opportunities to explore." I told her about meeting and befriending Poe, River, Nikita, and Reba.

"It sounds like you are blending in well to bush life."

"I think so, and I'm enjoying the solitude and peacefulness."

"Buck has the boat serviced and ready to go when you are. Do you plan to leave tomorrow or stay another day?"

"Originally, I planned for another day, but I promised Elizabeth I'd come back to visit with Troy while he's home from school. Although I'm sure I'll be back before Troy returns for a visit."

"Troy will love that. He really admires you."

"He seems to be a great young man. I'm sad he is not enjoying his time in Anchorage, but I understand why he misses it here. I was excited to visit town but I'm eager to return home."

Erica broke into a smile. "This place has got into your blood, hasn't it?"

I nodded. "Two months ago, I wouldn't have thought it possible, but yes, it has."

Erica handed me a receipt. "Come whenever you're ready in the morning, and we'll get you loaded and on your way. Thanks for the smoked fish, by the way. I had some for dinner last night, and they were fantastic."

"Thanks, Erica."

"Hey, I noticed you had another vacuum sealer on your order. Did you wear that one out already?"

I chuckled. "No, it's been perfect. This one is for Nikita and the village to use."

Erica smiled. "Good deal."

†

I stepped out of the truck at the B&B and felt a chill in the air. The sun was shining, but there was an iciness to the breeze. I found Elizabeth at the table sipping coffee and watching the weather report.

"Is there a weather front moving in?"

"It's not showing anything, but I can feel something in the air."

I poured a cup of coffee and joined her. "Is there a normal pattern for when the snow flies here?"

"It can start in June and snow through May, so no. Nothing consistent. Some years are lighter than others, and sometimes the river doesn't freeze solid."

"If it doesn't freeze, is there someplace else for a bush plane to land to bring supplies?"

"Some things can be air-dropped into an open field. Erica has a boat with an ice-breaking wedge on the front. She can usually make it upriver, but travel takes twice as long."

"So, I need to inventory my supplies closely for a resupply trip or two before the ice begins?"

"Exactly, especially your fuel and gasoline. It wouldn't be safe to drop those." Elizabeth grinned. "How are your batteries on the solar panels holding up? You might want to consider buying more to add more storage capability."

"Erica can order those for me, right?"

"If she doesn't already have them in stock." Elizabeth smiled and handed me a cordless phone. "Speed dial number one."

†

Erica ordered twelve storage banks for me, and she suggested Troy bring them out while he was home. "They will be too heavy for your small boat," she explained. "You can top off all your fuels and maybe add an extra bottle or two for emergencies."

"That sounds great. I'll see you in the morning."

"Would you loan me Troy for a day or two while he's home? I will need extra hands to install those battery banks."

"He will jump all over that and would be disappointed if I say no," Elizabeth teased. "You can ask him yourself when he calls tonight."

"I'd like that."

"So, you're heading back tomorrow?"

I chuckled. "I'm starting to feel antsy. I'm usually working all day long. I want to bring in as much firewood as possible before the snow flies on the regular."

Elizabeth smiled. "I understand."

"I'm sure I'll be back at least one more time before Troy comes for a visit. Is there any fish or fowl I can bring you? I've got all the geese I need and can smoke more fish."

"I'll take anything you care to bring," Elizabeth replied.

"Deal. Is there any help you need around here?"

"You can't sit still, can you?"

I shrugged. "No, ma'am."

"Come on then. I need to go to the wood lot for some wood for the fireplace. The men will load, but you can help unload and stack when we return. I've got gloves and a wheelbarrow."

"Sounds good." I rinsed our coffee cups and pulled on my jacket.

†

I showered the following day and loaded my bag and cold groceries in the truck. Elizabeth insisted on feeding me breakfast before driving me to the Depot. We quickly loaded my goods while Erica's crew added the rest.

"I'll see you in two weeks."

"Yes, you will," I promised and hugged her.

†

The skies were overcast with a threat of rain, but my heart felt lighter as I drove north on the river. I kept my slicker close in case I needed to put it on quickly and secured a tarp over my load of supplies. I felt the shoulder rig pressed tight to my chest, and with each bend in the river, I began to feel like myself again.

I floated into geese on the river and shot three. I would take as many as possible to Elizabeth as she was entering the

182

season when fresh meat would become expensive, so any supplement I could provide would help. I'd process them and add them to the smoker when I got home.

I watched several eagles flying up the river and diving into the water to take flight with a salmon in their talons. A mother bear with two cubs was fishing in the shallows. We locked eyes as the boat floated past. "Easy, Mama, I'm just going home." She watched me warily until she was sure I wasn't a danger and then resumed feasting on the salmon floating in the shallow water.

My heart raced when I saw the downed tree on the riverbank within a quarter mile of home. I pulled up to the dock and tied off before unloading the geese and the numerous boxes I would carry into the cabin. I added a case of beer to the crates and brought the cold foods to store in the refrigerator. The rest could wait until the geese were in the smoker.

Poe called to me from the smokehouse, either welcoming me home or fussing at me for leaving. Which, I wasn't sure, but he enjoyed the buttered biscuit I fed him. I missed Troy's dolly, and carrying my supplies to the porch for unloading took many trips. I looked at the boxes and decided it was time for a break before I began storing the goods. I made a cup of coffee and looked at the boxes, deciding where the contents would end up.

I had barely finished storing the gas and fuel tanks when the rain began to fall. "I guess I work inside for a while," I told Poe, who sat on the railing to watch me. The dry goods were added to the pantry, and I smiled when I opened the box with the sealing machine. There were many more than the dozen boxes of bags that I ordered. I took out the four boxes I needed and resealed the box.

I dug around the kitchen until I found a hammer and a few nails. I had bought a gun rack to store the guns off the floor, and I hung it on the wall next to my calendar and placed the two rifles and my shotgun on the rests. "Perfect." I would hang my shoulder harness and ammo belt on the bottom level. There was also a small drawer to hold some of my ammunition. I was beginning to feel like a hunter.

When the last box was emptied, I decided I had done enough for the day, and some food and beer were in order. It was still misting, so I took a small pan to the smokehouse for several pieces of fish and plucked two beers from the crate. I broke off some fish for Poe and returned inside. After devouring the fish, I opened the iPad to add an entry for missed days and then call it a night.

July 21st - Day nineteen

I've spent the last few days in town resupplying and visiting friends. Troy will be home for Fall Break in late September, and I will return for a visit. Then he will bring a heavy fuel and battery bank delivery to help me prepare for winter. Poe seemed glad to see me return. All the supplies were stored, and I had a great meal. It's good to be home. I could feel the tension of the small town draining from me as I rode home. Many times today, I wondered where River was and whether her hunting trip was going well. If I'm honest, missing her added to my anxiety, and I can hardly wait to see her again. I will catch up on chores tomorrow and stay busy until she returns.

I removed my shoulder rig and placed it on the gun rack, and when I pulled off my work shirt, I removed the necklace to hang it with my pistol.

CHAPTER TWELVE

I packed an apple and some jerky in my daypack after breakfast. After checking the fish line, I would attach the sled to begin hauling rounds back to the cabin. I didn't plan to split them, but they would be accessible in an emergency. The fish line was starting to provide less, but four fish were present that went into the smokehouse. I would pull the line in two weeks or whenever it stopped producing, whichever came first.

I pulled on the shoulder rig and a sweatshirt before selecting the twenty-two along with an extra clip of bullets. I could bring a rabbit or fresh grouse home for dinner if lucky. As it ended up, I managed both. I cleaned them on a trip back to the yard with a load of rounds and put them in the sink to soak. I hauled three more loads and was taking a break when I sensed movement across the woodlot, and Poe called out. A substantially sized bear stood on his hind legs, looking at me from the blueberry patch. He seemed curious about what I was doing but made no move to approach. I watched him for several long minutes as he swayed back and forth.

"The berries are all yours today, brother bear," I shouted at him. When he dropped to the ground, I figured I had hauled enough wood for the day and would allow him to forage in peace.

I had collected several long thin limbs and decided to slice them into sections small enough to carve when I returned home. It had been days since I had whittled anything, and brother bear inspired me. I sliced a bucketful of pieces and carried them to the porch after storing the equipment for the night. I spread the rabbit pelt across the railing to dry and placed the carcass in a pot to boil for a stew. I would grill the grouse, and coat part tonight in the powdered ranch dressing and the other half in Parmesan cheese.

I lit the grill and walked to the dock for a beer. While dinner was cooking, I carved a piece of wood. Brother Bear stared back at me, standing on his hind legs, just as he had earlier in the day. I smiled at the carving. Tomorrow I would scorch and stain him black to add to my collection. The flavor of the grouse breasts was impressive, and I vowed to hunt more grouse in the days to come.

†

After lighting the stove for the evening, I booted up the iPad and began my entry.

July 22nd – Day twenty

It seems longer than three weeks since I arrived in the bush, but my life here is settling well. After long workdays, I can relax, knowing I'm as prepared for winter as possible. I plan to continue to hunt to improve my skills and to supplement my diet with fresh meat when possible, but I am comfortable that I have plenty to survive. I hope my confidence is warranted and that I'm not underestimating my food stores. I miss River. It's been less than a week, but I have grown accustomed to her presence in camp. If the weather remains pleasant, I will travel to the village to deliver Nikita's supplies and surprise her with the food sealer. That might also be an excellent reason to try baking cookies from scratch. I bet Reba would love some chocolate chip cookies. Who am I kidding? I would love some, too. Maybe I could get a hint of when River might return from her northern hunting trip. This could be an excellent time to travel south since I haven't explored that area yet. So, that is the plan. I will hunt early for another flock of geese to take to Nikita and experiment with my baking skills.

†

The trip to the lake produced five more geese, and I picked up several more grouse for my cooler. My first batch of cookies was a bit crunchy on the scorched bottoms but still edible. I would eat those and cook more for Reba. When the second batch of cookies was cooling, I mounted my ATV for a drive south. Less than a mile from the cabin, I spotted a large nest atop a tree and found an eagle perching. I sat and watched for several minutes, but there was no sight of a mate or young bird in the nest. The bird was majestic, and I knew it would form a carving soon. Hopefully, the mate was out hunting and had not fallen into peril. Driving farther, I came to a small pond, and I could see a beaver den. Several animals were swimming along the border, adding small limbs to secure the foundation. I had no clue if they were edible, but I made a note to tell River about them.

When the wind picked up and the air began to cool drastically, I returned home. The low-hanging clouds were full of moisture, and as I sat carving, snowflakes began to fall and then turned into sleet. My life in Chicago was filled with snowy and icy winters but filthy from human traffic and pollution. I bet the snow blanket would be pristine, almost blinding white, when it arrived. Elizabeth told me the snowfall was unpredictable, and I turned believer thirty minutes later when it disappeared altogether. I would have to wait another day for that first blanket of snow.

July 23rd – Day 21

A few snow flurries today that turned into sleet and were gone. Added some geese for Nikita. Will load up supplies and pay her a visit in the morning. Saw eagles and beavers on a short drive south. The second batch of cookies turned out well. First, not so much. More practice is needed.

†

I ate some brown sugar oatmeal for breakfast before loading up the sled and heading north. I got an early start, so

I felt confident I could get there and back at a reasonable time. After stuffing a few more "crunchy" cookies in my pocket, I grabbed my rifle and left camp.

The waterfall at Wolf Creek had grown with the recent precipitation and was even more beautiful as I passed. I could see leaves in the forest changing colors as vibrant reds and yellows dotted the tree line. I knew I was getting close to the village when I smelled smoke, and my heart pounded excitedly. Maybe River would be home.

I pulled into the yard and found Nikita snapping beans on the porch.

"Well, this is a pleasant surprise," she said as she placed the bowl aside. "I wasn't expecting you, or I would have a nice meal prepared."

"No worries. I thought this would be a good day for a ride, and I wanted to bring your supplies from town."

"Great, did you have enough money?" she asked.

"You nailed it," I answered. Nikita would hopefully find her cash when she opened her canning jars later. "I've got a few geese if you want them, too."

"Goodness, yes," she answered. Nikita walked out to the sled. "A few? That's more than a few."

"If you can't use them all, you can share."

"I won't have any problem finding homes for those. They are some nice birds."

"Tatum."

I heard my name called and saw Reba running toward me.

"There's my assistant. Can you help me carry supplies inside? I brought something for you, too, but you must promise to share."

"Okay," she said.

I handed Nikita boxes of canning jars and gave Reba a smaller package to carry. I carried the geese into the house, then returned for the sealer machine and storage bags. I handed a smaller bag to Reba. "Wait until you get inside."

"Smells good whatever it is." She smiled. "Thanks, Tatum."

"Don't thank me yet."

I lifted the box when I saw a curious look on Nikita's face. "This is for you."

"A vacuum sealer? Are you kidding me?" Nikita called out.

"Nope, and boxes of bags to use with it. It will save you some storage space."

Nikita hugged my neck. "Thank you so much. I loved using yours."

"Same model, so you can get right to work."

"Can I open my present now?" Reba asked patiently.

"Not a present, but yes, you may."

"Chocolate chip cookies. My favorite. Thank you, Tatum."

"I've been teaching myself how to bake from scratch. Round one of the cookies got a bit scorched, but these turned out well."

"Do you want one?" she offered to Nikita.

"Maybe just one," Nikita said and fished out a cookie.

"Yummy," Reba said and pulled my arm so I would bend down for a kiss.

"I'm glad you like them," I said.

"Very much. When can we have another campout?"

"Whenever you're ready," I answered. "Not many fish getting caught these days, but I think I've found some cloudberries."

"Those make excellent pie fillings," Nikita said. "Not the sweetest berry, but with some sugar added, they make delicious pies. I haven't seen any close for a while."

"I rode south yesterday and found a nice patch. Along with some eagles and a beaver lodge."

"I'm glad you're doing some exploring," Nikita said.

I shrugged. "I've got plenty of food stores for winter and cut down half the forest in firewood." I nodded to the box of geese. "The geese still seem plentiful, so I will hunt those when possible."

"Your gifts are very much appreciated by the village. If that's okay, I'll freeze some of these birds and share the rest with the elders."

"I know they won't go to waste."

"Is there anything you need?" Nikita asked.

"No, I am in good shape. I'll probably make at least one trip before Troy returns from college. Plus, I intend to make a trip to visit Troy when he's home from college, then he will deliver some bigger battery banks and my last round of fuel before winter."

"I hope you know you are welcome here anytime," Nikita said. "We don't have luxuries, but anything we have, we are willing to share."

"That means a great deal to me. Unless a tree lands on the cabin or god forbid it catches on fire, I should be good."

Nikita nodded. "The trail should remain clear for months yet."

I couldn't resist asking. "What have you heard from River?"

"Her hunting partner brought in their first four caribou yesterday. I hope they will collect the last of the permitted animals soon."

"How many do they have left?"

"The village is only allocated nine this year. That's why it's so essential River hunts all she can."

"I've seen plenty of evidence the moose and elk are still near. I've watched River and helped her several times. I will see if I can bring in some meat."

"If you can wait one more day, I will come to help if River has not returned."

"I can wait. I'll do more scouting. Can you get meat bags and a bone saw to use?"

"I know I can," Nikita said. "I just need to finish harvesting some vegetables. Can Reba come, too?"

"We can have a campout." I shot Reba a grin.

"Yes," Reba said and pumped her fist.

"We have to ask your mom first," Nikita said.

"Ask me what?"

I turned to the door to see a beautiful woman, who apparently was Reba's mom.

"If I can go on another campout with Nikita and Tatum," Reba pleaded.

The woman turned her warm brown eyes on me. "So, you're the woman Reba raves about? I'm Sonya."

"Nice to meet you." I offered my hand to her.

Sonya shook it with a smile. "Everyone is right. You do look like Charles."

I broke out laughing. "I never knew I was related to such a famous person."

"Look, Mommy, Tatum made cookies. Do you want one?"

Sonya could see the smear of chocolate chips on her daughter's cheek. "Are they good?"

"Yummy," Reba said and handed her a cookie.

Sonya bit into the cookie. "This is good."

"So, can I go with Nikita tomorrow for a campout?"

"How can I say no, when you bribe me with cookies. Don't eat too many, or you will spoil your supper."

Reba nodded.

"I'm going to hit the trail. So, see you the day after tomorrow?"

"We'll be there," Nikita said.

"It was nice to meet you." I told Sonya.

"I'll see you soon," I said and hugged Reba.

"Be safe and stay warm."

†

The ride home seemed faster than usual. Maybe it was because I was excited about a visit from Nikita and Reba or the idea I had to make some jelly. I had buckets in the sled and daylight left, so I drove straight to the berry patch and filled two buckets of blueberries and more cranberries. I could use the pulp to make preserves or in pancake batter and compote. I bet Reba would enjoy making some jelly. I had cases of jars left, plenty of sugar, and paraffin. Jelly it is.

I rinsed the berries and put them in the refrigerator to chill. My stomach reminded me I was hungry, so I ate some cookies and then checked the line for fish. There were six nice fish on the line. I added four to the smokehouse and placed two in the sink to brine for the grill. My eyes landed on the rabbit pelt on the railing. It was slowly drying, so I coated the underside with salt and hung it in the smokehouse to speed up the process.

Sitting on the steps sipping a beer and watching Poe dance across the yard, I felt a smile grow. Never in a hundred years would I have imagined living and thriving in the Alaskan bush. But there I was.

I sprinkled the filets with brown sugar and drizzled maple syrup to give them a nice glaze. Two ears of corn were grilling nicely, and when they were done, I buttered them and sprinkled some dry ranch dressing on them. I served the meal and placed small portions on the woodpile for Poe. The fresh corn was delicious, and I ate dinner on the porch steps.

July 24th – Day twenty-two.

The visit to the village went well, and I have made plans with Nikita and Reba for a visit. I grilled the first of the fresh corn, and it turned out wonderfully. I will plan some excellent meals for Reba and Nikita using some of my new supplies. Some fun activities, too, when we finish picking berries, and if we successfully bring in meat, we will send some back to the village. Hopefully, River will return soon.

After adding the journal entry, I climbed into bed.

†

The day dawned brisk and beautiful. After eating a banana with a bowl of oatmeal, I geared up and started out for the day. I would hunt for more grouse and geese while scouting for signs of moose, deer, or elk for a hunt. By midmorning, six geese and five grouse were added to my sled. I saw signs of a moose near the lake and sat briefly to see if he would arrive to drink, but I feared the sound of my gunshots had warned him off.

I was pleasantly surprised when I returned to find Nikita sitting on my steps and Reba playing in the yard. Nikita looked at me and shrugged.

"I hope it was okay to come early. Reba was wearing Sonya and me out with her excitement. Sonya promised to harvest the remaining vegetables I was working on if I'd bring Reba early." Nikita chuckled. "She's a bit excited."

"I have some birds to process, and then we can hunt berries. Maybe that will help Reba wind down some. I want to try my hand at jelly if you think she would like that."

"Probably so, and I know I would," Nikita answered.

Reba ran over and hugged me. "I missed you," she said as she kissed my cheek.

"I missed you, too, and I have all kinds of things planned for us."

"Things I can help with?"

"Well, you are my number one assistant," I teased, and her face beamed. "First, though, I need to care for these birds. Can you get more buckets from the shed and load them in the sled for me?"

Reba nodded and rushed across the yard as we watched her. "Oh, to have that much energy," Nikita said. "Let's tend to those birds."

†

When the birds were dressed and cooling, I looked at Reba. "Are you hungry?"

"A little," she answered.

"Can we have a snack of smoked fish for now? I will cook a big meal tonight."

Reba nodded.

"That sounds perfect. I'll grab a pan and some fish," Nikita said.

†

"Are you ready to pick some berries?" I asked Reba.

"Blueberries?"

"Not at first. I found a patch of cloudberries I want us to harvest first. Then more blueberries," I replied. "There's something else I want to show you, too."

"What?" Reba asked.

"It's a surprise. Ready?"

Reba nodded and climbed behind Nikita.

We drove south, and I turned off my ATV when the eagle's nest appeared. I pointed to the large nest at the top of the tree. "Let's watch and see if anyone is home."

Fortunately, moments later, the male eagle arrived at the nest carrying a large salmon. "I guess it's lunchtime for them, too," I whispered.

"Look," Reba squealed when an eaglet appeared in the nest, eagerly pecking at the fish.

Nikita looked at Reba. "The baby is too young to tear and eat fish. One parent will chew on strips to make them soft enough for the baby to eat while the other continues hunting."

"Wow," Reba said as the female took flight, spreading her powerful wings to continue the hunt.

†

We picked cloudberries until we had three buckets filled.

"Enough?" I asked Nikita.

"I think so. Let's check the blueberries."

We returned home with two more buckets of blueberries. The bushes were beginning to look bare, but I was pleased with our managed harvests. "I think we've cleaned out the patch's blueberries, unless they bloom again. We should have plenty, though, for the winter."

We poured the berries into the sink to rinse, and I grabbed a few bananas for a snack. I looked at Reba. "I will need your help. Do you need a nap before we get started?"

"No, Tatum," she answered.

"Do you like peanut butter?"

"I love peanut butter," Reba said.

"We will make some no-bake peanut butter bars while our berries cook. They need a lot of stirring. Can you handle that?"

"What can I help with?" Nikita asked.

"Will you slice some Brussels sprouts in half? Then, chop some onion and cut a few potatoes into thin slices. That would be a big help for dinner."

"Easy peasy," Nikita said.

198

I placed peanut butter, honey, and powdered sugar in a bowl before Reba. "Will you stir this while I check our berries and prepare a dish for us to use?"

I watched closely from the stove as Reba stirred the mixture. She struggled at first with the thickness of the peanut butter, but as the honey and powdered sugar began to blend, it was easier to stir. Nikita saw me watching and smiled. Reba was having a blast.

While we worked, I sliced several apples into wedges and cut slices from the Gouda cheese block for a snack. Nikita remarked on the sweetness of the apples. "These would make an excellent pie if you have plenty."

I pointed to the pantry. Two twenty-pound bags hadn't been opened. "I think we can make a pie or two."

†

When the mixture was complete, I dropped the contents of the bowl into a dish and handed Reba a spoon. "Spread this out in the pan as evenly as possible while I juice the berries." I removed a potato masher from the drawer and used it to crush the softened berries to extract as much juice as possible, then poured the contents through a strainer to remove the pulp. I placed the liquid back into the pot, added sugar, and lowered the heat to simmer the mixture.

Nikita had finished chopping and removed a case of jars from the pantry. She looked at me and smiled. "I saw what you did with the money. Thanks."

"No problem at all." I smiled.

Nikita rinsed several jars and placed them on the counter to dry. "Do you have a small pot to melt the paraffin?"

199

"I do," I said and pointed to a cabinet before checking on Reba. "Wow, that looks great. Let's add one more thing." I sprinkled a light coating of powdered sugar across the top.

"Now what?" Reba asked.

"Now they chill in the refrigerator for a few hours. We will have some for dessert tonight." I opened the door, and Reba placed the dish on a shelf. "I do believe those are going to be tasty."

"I'll keep stirring if you take a break for a few minutes," Nikita said.

"I'll sit at the table, but I can prepare the Brussels sprouts and vegetables for cooking. How's your stirring arm?"

"It's good," Reba answered and sat next to me.

"I added olive oil and brown sugar to the sprouts. Will you mix those for me?"

Next, I added the oil to the potatoes and sprinkled on some of the ranch powder.

"That looks interesting," Nikita said from her position at the stove.

When she finished mixing, I asked Reba to chill our veggies in the fridge.

"I think this batch is ready," Nikita said. "Do you have oven mitts and a funnel?"

"Mitts, yes. I don't have a funnel, though," I answered as I removed the thick mitts.

"Free pouring it is, then. Will you place four jars in the sink, and I will fill them?"

I spaced the jars in the sink and watched Nikita pour the thickened juice into the jars, leaving space at the top for wax. Then she carefully placed them on the cutting board to cool.

"Reba and I can continue making jelly to free you up to cook dinner," Nikita said.

"Is that a hint you're getting hungry?"

"I think we can get another pot on to cook and take a coffee break before you start cooking."

"What can I help with?" Reba asked.

"You can play gopher," I teased.

"Gopher?" Reba asked, confused.

"Yep. We'll ask you to go for this and go for that." I smiled.

"Got it." Reba laughed.

I made coffee while Nikita placed more berries on the stove. I looked at the jelly. "That will go well with some biscuits." I bagged up the pulp and put it in the fridge. My eyes landed on the strawberries, and a breakfast idea began to form.

†

When we finished eating, Nikita and I stored the leftovers and sipped a coffee while dinner settled. I saw that Reba's eyes were growing heavy. "Will you help me bring your bags and the cot here?"

"We aren't sleeping in the bathhouse?" Reba asked.

"I shook my head. It's getting too cold at night. Nikita can sleep on the cot, and you can bunk with me. I will push you out of the bed if you start kicking." I grinned.

"I'm so tired. I don't think you have to worry about that tonight," Reba said.

"Let's go then, and we can have some dessert and hit the sack."

"We'll get the bags if you bring the cot," Nikita offered.

After taking the cot inside, I told them. "I'll be right back." I walked to the smokehouse and removed the rabbit pelt. It was still warm as I tucked it inside Poe's basket. "There you are, my friend," I said and returned inside. "Who's ready for dessert?"

"I am," Reba replied.

"I made more coffee," Nikita said.

I removed the dish from the fridge, cut large squares of the peanut butter treat, and placed them on small plates. I watched Reba's eyes widen with delight as she took the first bite.

"These are good." She smiled.

"Easy to make, too," I said. "Maybe you can make some for your mom."

"She would love these. Daddy, too, when he comes home."

I looked at Nikita. "He'll be home for Thanksgiving. He's offshore now."

"Ah, I see."

†

"Change into your sleep clothes and climb into bed," Nikita told Reba, whose head had started to bob.

She climbed from her chair and hugged us before changing clothes and crawling into my bed. I lit the fire in the stove to keep the edge off and changed clothes. I hung my shoulder rigging and necklace on the gun rack. Nikita returned from the bathhouse and bolted the door behind her. I scooted Reba over in the bed and turned off the light. "Good night," I said and climbed onto the bed. Reba was warm and snuggled closer when she felt me enter the bed. *So precious*, I thought as I closed my eyes.

CHAPTER THIRTEEN

Neither Nikita nor Reba had ever had crepes for breakfast, so it was a new experience. Nikita sliced strawberries and bananas while Reba watched me make the sweet pastry. "Now what?" Reba asked after I had cooked two dozen of the thin treats.

"Now, we get to fill them and eat them," I told her as we carried the plate to the table and walked to the pantry for more ingredients. "Can I make my favorite for you?"

Reba nodded and watched me closely as I placed a crepe on a plate, added slices of strawberries and bananas, drizzled chocolate syrup over the concoction, folded the edges together, and handed her a fork.

"Voila," I said, "*bon appetit.*"

I began making one for myself. "All we're missing is some whipping cream, but I don't have the right ingredients."

Nikita followed our example and made her first crepe.

"You can stuff them with fruit, berries, meat, or other yummies. Some people only eat them with maple syrup, but I like adding stuff to mine."

"These are delicious," Nikita said.

"Fun to make, and except for the fruits, are not expensive. We could have used some of the berries, but I wanted something special for our first bush crepes."

"Great decision," Nikita said, wiping chocolate syrup from her lips.

†

Nikita and Reba cleaned the kitchen while I loaded the sleds for a hunting trip. I emptied my bladder and rushed inside.

"Bundle up," I said. "It's cold this morning." I put on a thermal shirt under my work shirt and pulled on my necklace and shoulder rig. I removed the rifle from the case and made sure it was loaded.

"Ready?" I asked as I pulled on my hat.

Nikita nodded. "I made a thermos of coffee. I have a feeling we will need it this morning."

After driving to the big lake, we parked in the shelter of the trees. Nikita poured me a cup of coffee, and I walked to the shooting stand River had shown me and waited. Minutes turned into hours without a sign of game. I was sure Reba was probably cold and I was ready to return to the ATV to send them home when I heard movement. I held my breath as a bull moose approached the lake. I pressed the safety off and located him in my scope. Just a few more steps, and I would take a shot. "Boom" filled the air as the moose dropped to the ground. I returned to the ATV to find Reba asleep in Nikita's arms.

"Got him," I whispered. "Do you need to take her back home?"

"No," Nikita answered. "I'll place her in the sled and cover her with a blanket. The sun is coming out, which will help warm the air."

We drove to the moose, and I pulled my heavy coat off and draped it over Reba. I would be warming up quickly as we began to harvest the moose. I relied on my experience with River to guide me through gutting the animal and removing the head. While I began skinning, Nikita disposed of the entrails and then returned to help. Once the hide was released, we rinsed our hands and took a coffee break.

"He will provide a lot of meat," Nikita said.

"How are those massive ribs cooked?" I asked.

"They are cut into more manageable sections and slow-cooked for hours on a grill before adding the sauce."

Sawing the carcass into quarters was more exhausting than I realized, making me appreciate River's strength even more. Once the meat was bagged and loaded onto Nikita's sled, I picked up a large roast to place in a bucket.

"Dinner tonight," I said.

Reba climbed behind Nikita, and we drove to camp.

"Why don't we share a meal before you and Reba take the meat to the village? We made good time, and you will make the round trip in time to be back for dinner."

"That is a good plan. Maybe some smoked fish?"

"That is fast and easy," I agreed.

†

Nikita was loaded with moose and geese, and they were preparing to leave when we heard the sound of a motor. I was relieved to see River's ATV coming down the trail, but seeing her when she arrived made my heart ache. She looked exhausted.

"What's this?" she asked, pulling next to Nikita.

"We got a moose this morning, and Tatum has been hunting geese. Reba and I will make a delivery and return for dinner. You missed a great breakfast," Nikita teased.

"Tatum made crepes," Reba said. "They were so good, too."

River forced a weary smile. "Do you want me to make a delivery? I asked Sonya where you were, and she said you two had decided on a campout."

"We've got this. You look horrible and exhausted."

"Thanks, Mom." River frowned.

"Meaning you're tired and hungry. You haven't stopped for weeks."

"I thought we would chase those damn caribou to the Arctic, but we finally caught up to them. I'm glad that's done for a year."

"Get something to eat and rest. Maybe Tatum will let you use her bath. Some hot water may revitalize you."

"Absolutely. I'll start the fire and get the water going." I walked to the bathhouse.

"I can't believe you all got a moose," River told Nikita.

"Not you all. Tatum shot him and did most of the hard work. You've taught her well. Now get some rest, and we'll see you later." Nikita waved to me as she pulled away.

"Be safe," I called out. I looked at River. "Go wash up, and I'll get some food into you while the water heats for your bath. Will a beer, some fish, and leftover veggies hold you until dinner?"

"That sounds great," River said. "Thank you."

I turned on the grill to heat the leftover veggies from dinner and then carried several fish and a cold beer to the cabin. "You can start on the fish, and I'll have veggies warm in a few minutes."

"Thanks, Tatum."

When I had carried the plate of veggies to the table, I made a cup of coffee. "How have you been?" I asked when I sat across from her.

"That hunt was challenging this year. We had to go farther and longer than ever to fill our permits. I missed your cooking and having a roof over my head." She smiled. "My campfire cooking is nothing compared to this. How have you been?"

"I've been good. I had a great visit with Elizabeth and Erica and picked up supplies. It was good to come home. I took Nikita's stores and some geese I had harvested to town, and we agreed they would come out to pick berries and hunt if we can."

"That was an impressive antler rack and stack of meat."

"What can I say? I have a great teacher." I smiled.

"This is the best meal I've had in days. Thank you."

"Leftovers and smoked fish were easy. You will have a hearty meal tonight. Would you mind if I make a suggestion?"

"Not at all," River answered.

"Take a nice soaking bath, then stretch out on my bed for rest."

"I'd rather help you with dinner and chores," River replied.

"The chores are done for the day, and you know how I am about too many cooks in the kitchen."

"Do I look that rough?"

"You look exhausted," I replied. "I've got one more thing I want you to try, and I'll go check your water to see if it's ready."

I pulled out the dish of peanut butter bars and placed a large piece on her plate. "Reba and I made these yesterday."

"Damn, you and Reba made these? This is delicious."

"I added the ingredients, but Reba did all the labor. She did very well."

"She's a great kid." River smiled.

"Yes, she is. Can you eat more fish?"

"No, I'm saving room for dinner." River smiled, and there was a return of a sparkle in her tired eyes.

"I'll be right back then."

†

When River left to bathe, I took the roast out and sliced it into steaks, injecting them with the apple juice and covering them with seasonings to chill in the fridge. I put eight ears of corn on the stove to precook before placing it on the grill and began chopping vegetables.

I drank coffee as I prepped for dinner, and my kidneys cried out for relief. I hated to disturb River, but it was too cold to drop my pants outside. I walked to the bathhouse and tapped on the door.

"Come in," River called out.

"I'm sorry to interrupt your relaxation, but my kidneys are screaming at me," I said as I entered.

"No problem," River said. "I'm beginning to feel human again, but would you mind scrubbing my back. I've reached everything I can."

"Sure. Give me a minute." *Breathe*, I reminded myself as I walked to the toilet. My body was on high alert that a naked woman was in a bathtub just feet from me. I refused to gawk as I passed by.

After washing my hands, I took a deep breath and turned to the tub. River had soaped a washcloth and offered it to me as she leaned forward. I was shocked by the large bruise on her back as I gently began caressing her skin. "What happened to get this bruise?"

"A lapse in caution. We were racing after the herd, and I hit a rock, and it flipped me off the ATV. My landing could not be confused for gracefulness."

"Does it hurt bad?"

"No, it's just a fading ugly color, so don't hesitate to give me a good scrub. It feels good."

I bathed from the base of her neck down her back to the water's edge. "There, all bright and shiny again," I said, returning the cloth to her.

River dropped the cloth in the water and took my hands in hers. She placed a gentle kiss on each palm. "Thank you. That did feel great."

I was surprised by her gesture and felt a blush rising. "You're welcome. You have about ten minutes left of warm water, so I'll leave you to finish bathing. Do you need anything?"

"I'm good. Thanks. This was exactly what I needed."

"Hopefully, it will help you sleep."

"I have no doubt it will."

†

I waited until River was settled on the bed to mix batter for brownies and prep a biscuit pan. I placed them on the grill to cook, picked up a chunk of wood, and began whittling. Brother Bear appeared this time with all four feet on the ground. I checked the grill, and the brownies and biscuits were cooking well. There was only a handful of veggie scraps, but I carried them to the smokehouse for Poe. "I'll add to this later," I promised.

I added a salmon and a rabbit to the collection. The brownies looked done, so I carried them inside and placed them on the counter to cool. River was curled on her side, and I could hear her soft snoring. I crept around the kitchen as quietly as possible, gathering the food and supplies to cook supper. I covered the grill with oil and added the steaks and chopped veggies. I would put the corn on last as it was partially cooked in advance. A stick of butter in a container would melt slowly as the food cooked. I planned to brush some on the corn and sprinkle powdered Parmesan cheese to flavor it once it was grilled.

I was sipping on a beer waiting for the food to finish, when I heard the door open slowly. River slipped through the door. "You've got something smelling good."

"It should be ready soon. I would think Nikita and Reba will be back soon."

River looked at her watch. "I agree."

"Would you like a beer?"

"I'm good," River said, sitting next to me.

"How much more meat will you look to harvest?" I asked.

"I think another moose or two or a couple of elk will finish the season's red meat. I'd like to process a quarter for you to have some red meat in your cooler."

"I don't need a quarter, but I'd take a few roasts to cut for steaks. I don't eat as much red meat."

"I'll make sure you have what you need for steaks."

"What's next for you once the hunting is done?"

River smiled. "A couple weeks of rest, and then I start on winter projects."

"Like what?"

"I'll work on cleaning up antlers and take them to Glennallen for shipping to a buyer in Anchorage."

"I had already decided to go to Glennallen at least one more time before my visit when Troy's home from school. He will deliver a big fuel load and a dozen more battery banks. They are too heavy for my boat to handle. He will help me install them, too, so I can store more power in case the solar doesn't charge as often as they do now."

"That's a bright idea."

I walked to the grill to turn the food. "Could I take a load since my boat will be relatively empty? Then Troy could also take a load when he returns."

"That's not a bad idea. I'm unsure how many I will have ready to go for the first trip."

"Is that something I can help with? I learn pretty quickly, and I'm in good shape here."

"It would be fewer distractions if I worked here. Are you sure you wouldn't mind?"

I shook my head. "Not at all."

"All right. I'll start bringing loads here when I return from town."

"Nikita and I can haul some, too," I offered.

River nodded. "Speak of the devil."

"We can make a plan after dinner. That's a lot of your annual income, isn't it?"

"Those and any furs I can trap. That pays for our fuel and any supplies we can't get from the land."

"Welcome back," I said as Reba rushed over to us. "Are you hungry?"

"Yes, I am," she said.

"Will you help Nikita set the table and pour some drinks? River can help me bring the food in."

Nikita walked up carrying two boxes of jars.

"Let me get those, Mom." River took the boxes.

"Donations from the elder council in exchange for some jelly if you make more."

"We've got many berries left, so I like that plan."

"Reba and I will help. I brought a bag of sugar to use, as well. Carry those, and I'll grab the sugar and get the table set."

Nikita waited for River to disappear inside. "She looks better."

"She ate a big lunch, had a soaking bath, and just woke from a nap a few minutes ago."

"Good job," Nikita said. "Thank you. She looked exhausted."

"I think she still is, so maybe we can convince her to take a day off tomorrow."

"Yeah, good luck with that," Nikita said and winked at me.

River returned. "Reba is eyeing that pan of brownies."

"I guess we'd better eat so she can have one." I began removing the steaks and placing them in the pan River was holding. "Will you bring three bowls out?"

†

"That was a delicious meal," Nikita told me.

"I'm glad you enjoyed it. River and I talked before you returned and we want to know what you think of an idea." I told her the plan was to prep the antlers for transport from here.

"That does make good sense." She smiled at me. "Why don't you two go to the village and start hauling the racks here? Reba and I can work on some jelly while you're gone."

It wasn't exactly a day off, but it wouldn't be as physical as hunting. "I like that idea."

"Me, too," River agreed.

"Will you help me with jelly?" Nikita asked Reba.

"Yes, I will. Could we have crepes again for breakfast?" Reba asked me.

"That could be arranged," I answered. "I lit the fire for the evening. Are we ready to call it a night?"

CHAPTER FOURTEEN

Nikita sliced berries and bananas while River and Reba emptied out the sleds. I cooked the crepes and enjoyed watching Reba educate River on how to fill her pastry. The trip to the village was fast since we weren't carrying a load, and several women, including Sonya, helped to pack the sleds for transport.

"Is Reba being good?" Sonya asked me.

"She's excellent. A hard worker. She's helping Nikita with jelly today."

"Thank you for teaching her some kitchen skills. She was so excited about the peanut butter bars you two made."

"Reba did a good job and is excited to make some for you and her dad."

"Would you mind if I send a case of jars and a bag of sugar if you have berries to spare?"

"That would be perfect."

"I'll be right back then," Sonya stated.

"You okay with that?"

"Absolutely," I answered.

River tied down the sleds.

"One more load after these?" I asked.

"I think so. I'll hunt tomorrow and pick up the rest when I deliver."

Sonya returned with the jars and a bag of sugar. "Are you sure you don't mind?"

"Not at all. Any preference for flavors?" I asked.

"I heard you've found cloudberries." Sonya smiled. "Blueberry if you have berries to spare."

"I don't see a problem with that at all," I told her.

"You've brought so much to the village. Is there anything you need?" Sonya asked.

"I've been tearing up the fresh corn Nikita gave me. I'll take some if you have extras, but not if it cuts your family short."

"Corn grows like crazy here, so sending some won't be an issue. I'll get some together for your next trip to town."

"Thank you."

"Are you in any rush to have Reba back?" River asked. "She's having a blast."

Sonya chuckled. "That doesn't surprise me. I'll send some clean clothes for her. Will you be back tomorrow?" Sonya asked.

"Yes, I hope to bring in more meat and pick up the rest of the antlers," River said. "The meat locker is almost full. Anything special you'd like?"

"A few more geese for holidays," Sonya said.

"That's no problem. I'm getting good at hunting geese," I answered.

"We are so happy you are." Sonya smiled.

"We'll see you tomorrow," River said. "Ready?" she asked.

"Right behind you."

†

"I want to go check for geese," I said after we unloaded the sleds.

"Want some company?" River asked.

"Always," I answered.

"I'll grab my shotgun and tell Nikita we'll be back."

"We can take my ATV. No need to take both," River said.

I nodded and picked up our water bottles.

†

"River and I are going to check for geese. Are you two okay?"

"We are jellying up a storm," Nikita answered. "We'll keep going until you get back."

"How are the berries holding out?"

"We could use more cloudberries and cranberries but have at least two more buckets of blueberries."

"Do we need to pick more?" I asked.

"Reba and I will do that tomorrow while you deliver to the village."

"Sounds like a plan. I'll start some dinner when we get back. Did you eat some lunch?"

"We did and enjoyed the rest of the peanut butter bars," Nikita answered.

"I guess we better make more, then." I smiled at Reba. "Maybe some cookies, too."

†

With both of us shooting, we returned with a dozen geese.

"This should take care of Sonya and a few others." I grinned as we processed the birds.

"Yes, it should. I hope I can get an elk in the morning," River said.

"Are beavers edible?" I asked.

"It's an acquired taste, but popular meat with some elders. Have you seen some?"

I nodded. "I found a sizeable beaver colony in a pond a few miles south."

"I'll load a few traps when we get to the village tomorrow. The pelts and tails are prized for clothing items."

"Good to know. Are you getting hungry?"

"I could eat," River answered.

"If you can finish here, I'll get started on some dinner."

†

"May I borrow the sink for a few minutes?" I asked, returning inside.

219

"Sure. I think it's time for a coffee break. Reba, will you ask River if she wants to join us?"

I removed a large pack of grouse breasts from the cooler and rinsed them in the sink before putting them in a bowl. I looked at the stack of jar cases on the counter. "Empty or full?"

"Those are all full," Nikita grinned. "We are getting jelly down to a science."

Reba rushed inside. "River will be here in a few minutes," she told us.

"I'll start some coffee then," Nikita said.

"How's that mixing arm of yours?" I asked Reba. "Ready to make more peanut butter bars?"

"Yes, I am." She climbed into a chair at the table.

"Let me season this meat, and we'll get you set up."

"Cool." Reba smiled.

I poured a mixture of seasonings on top of the meat and mixed them, coating the meat, then set them in the fridge. I placed a large mixing bowl on the table and added ingredients for the peanut bars. "Have at it," I told Reba and handed her a spoon.

I sat and sipped coffee, watching her work. River entered and sat with us.

"That tastes good. You two have been busy," she remarked.

"Reba and I will pick more berries tomorrow while you hunt."

"Your mom is sending clean clothes for you tomorrow," River told Reba.

"Does that mean I can stay longer?" she asked excitedly.

"As long as Tatum says you can," River answered.

Reba looked at me.

"As long as you want."

"At least a few more days," Nikita said. "We'll finish the jelly, but you will start school soon."

"I know. I'm excited to tell my friends everything I've learned here." Reba smiled. She looked at me with a serious face. "Can we have more corn tonight? That was so good."

"I believe that can be arranged," I answered, removing a package of corn and placing it on the stove to boil.

"What can I do to help?" Nikita asked.

"Put two boxes of the angel hair pasta on the stove with a little oil and salt, and make sure it doesn't clump together, please."

"I can handle that." She looked at Reba. "We can pick up the kitchen and set the table, too."

After finishing my coffee, I picked up the bowl of meat and walked to the porch. I flipped a bucket over to sit next to the grill.

"What can I do?" River asked.

"Just keep me company right now. You can bring the corn in in a few minutes."

"Beer?" she asked.

"Why not." I grinned back at her.

†

I diced the breasts while the corn was grilled and added meat to the pasta with Alfredo sauce. I had to admit it looked and smelled delicious.

Nikita and Reba had the table ready to go when I placed the pasta in the center and returned for the corn.

"I hope you don't mind, but we used one of your instant puddings and added some bananas," Nikita said.

"That sounds delicious," I said. "You can use anything you find in the pantry. You don't need to ask. You're family," I told her.

"Thank you," Nikita answered.

"Parmesan or ranch on your corn tonight?" I asked Reba.

"Ranch?" she asked and cocked her head.

"Yes. I'll coat one and let you taste it. If you don't like it, I'll put Parmesan on one for you."

I covered an ear with a light coating of ranch and handed it to her. I watched her eyes grow wide when she took a bite.

"That's good."

"So, it's a keeper for you?" I asked.

"Yes, it is." She smiled with buttery cheeks.

I sprinkled an ear on my plate. "You two are on your own," I said, passing the corn.

†

"I can't eat another bite," River groaned.

"I saved room for some pudding," I teased.

"I can make an exception for pudding." River laughed.

"Uh, huh. I thought you might."

†

River carried a stack of wood for the stove and lit the fire. "Has everyone been staying warm enough?" I asked. "I've got extra blankets if needed."

222

"Toasty warm," Nikita said.

"Me, too," Reba said.

"You are a little heater," River teased her. "I don't even need a blanket when you bunk with me."

"Okay, so we're berry picking and hunting tomorrow, but what's for breakfast?" I asked.

"Blueberry pancakes?" Reba asked.

"That's easy," I said. "Goodnight, everyone."

"Goodnight, Tatum," Reba said and kissed my cheek.

I was going to miss that when she returned home. I was becoming spoiled by her attention and appreciation of life.

†

I placed a package of bacon on one side of the grill and started pouring batter. By the time the bacon was done, I had cooked a huge stack of pancakes.

River and Reba had loaded Nikita's ATV with buckets and baskets for berry picking. When we were ready to leave for the morning, I handed a cloth bag to Nikita.

"Will you harvest some chaga for me? I promised Erica I would bring some next week."

"That's easy," Nikita said.

"Can you two eat the leftovers for lunch if you get hungry?" I asked.

"We can, but don't worry, after that breakfast, we may not be hungry for a while."

"Take some apples and bananas for a snack. I've already packed a bag for us."

†

"Hunt first and then come back for the geese?" I asked.

"That's the plan. Grab your rifle, and let's go," River said. "I have a good feeling about this morning."

"Let's roll then," I said, climbing behind her.

After driving to the big lake, we parked the ATV under the trees and walked to the shooting stand.

River's intuition was spot on when a small herd of elk came to drink and graze around the pond's edge.

"There are several nice-looking bucks," she whispered. "Do you think you can take down the one on the right?"

"I think so."

"I'll shoot to the left. Don't forget to tuck the butt tight to your shoulder." River grinned. "Ready?"

I nodded and lifted my rifle.

"On three. One, two, and three."

Our shots echoed in the cool morning air. "Nice shot," River said. "I'll get the ATV."

I watched the rest of the herd scatter into the trees.

"These two should finish out the season," River said when we pulled up next to the bucks. "We need to remember to cut you a few roasts."

The meat and supplies filled River's sled, and we returned to the cabin. We loaded the geese and cases of jelly in my sled and rode to the village.

†

We dropped the two elk, four geese, and three jelly cases at the elders' lodge. The meat storage locker was packed with meat quarters and appeared full.

"We can't hold anymore for now, so enjoy a nice rest, and thank you for all your hard work. The people will eat well this winter."

I followed River to Sonya's, where we delivered more jelly and eight geese. "It feels like Christmas," Sonya said when we carried the goods inside.

"Nikita and Reba have been making jelly like crazy, and they are picking berries today for more."

"That sounds great. I've got buckets of corn ready for you," Sonya told me.

I chuckled. "Don't be surprised if Reba asks you to sprinkle some dry ranch powder on her corn. She has grown fond of that."

"That sounds interesting," Sonya admitted. "Let's get you loaded and back on the trail. Thank you both for everything. You've saved me a lot of money on groceries."

"Trading for vegetables is a great bargain," I said.

"Let me grab Reba's clothes, and you'll be set."

"I have a partial load of antlers left and want to throw some traps in. Tatum has spotted a beaver colony. I'd like to trap for a few. It's still early to begin trapping, but maybe I'll catch some. Is there anything else you need?"

"Yes, there is. Will you, Tatum, and Nikita join us for Thanksgiving? Thanks to you, we have much to be thankful for."

River looked at me. "I'd love that."

"Thank you." Sonya handed River a bag of clothes for Reba. "Send her home soon so she can get ready for school."

"I will," River said. "We'll see you soon."

"Thanks again for the goodies," Sonya said.

"Thanks for the corn. It's some of the sweetest I've ever eaten."

†

I was sad to see them go, but two days later, Nikita and Reba returned to the village with a sled full of jelly and, hopefully, some beautiful memories. They had only been gone an hour when I realized how quiet the camp was without Reba's laughter. I had never considered becoming a mother, but having her present the last week had me questioning my decision.

River was sitting at the fire pit, working on a set of antlers, when I decided to go pull the fish net for the season. It had stopped producing, and we decided to travel to Glennallen in two days to visit and drop off a load of antlers.

"I'm going to pull the net," I announced after finishing my coffee.

"Do you want my help?"

"Thanks, but you keep going. I've got this, and after I have the net stored, I will come to help."

River nodded. "Be careful."

CHAPTER FIFTEEN

I started the boat motor, and while it was warming, I prepared the storage box for the net. I was amazed at the enormous number of fish I had harvested from a single net, and thinking of all the people who had enjoyed the fish or would soon, made me smile. After untying the bowline, I climbed aboard and started upriver. The cold wind chilled my cheeks as the mist rose above the water.

When I reached the line, I pulled up the first anchor and placed the net in storage as the boat idled. I only had a final section of the net to retrieve when I lost my balance. Time slowed as my body approached the freezing water, and my mind whirled with thoughts of self-preservation. *Get out fast*, my thoughts screamed at me as I broke the surface, and my body was shocked by the intensely frigid water. My attempt to remain calm failed miserably, and I found my arms and legs flailing as I reached for the boat, and my foot got caught in the net. The ten-pound anchor felt like a hundred pounds as I pulled on the net to free my foot. I felt the intense cold draining my energy, and I knew if I didn't get out of the water soon, I wouldn't make it. I grabbed the side of the boat, pulled with everything I had left, pulled my trunk into the boat, and finally, my feet. My teeth chattered as I reached for the throttle and raced toward camp. I was out of the water, but grave danger persisted. I could hear Poe's voice screaming as he led me back to camp. As my vision faded, I saw him diving at River to get her attention. I gunned the motor to beach the boat and stumbled out of the boat, desperate to make it to River. My world went black when I felt my body lifted in her arms.

†

When enough strength returned to open my eyes, I saw River in the kitchen, her upper body devoid of clothing except for a sports bra. She was stirring a pot on the stove, and I could faintly hear the sputtering of the coffee maker. My body shivered violently despite the pile of blankets I was covered by. I felt panic wash over me when I realized I couldn't feel my hands or feet. I opened my mouth to call to River, but only a weak croak escaped my throat.

When she turned toward me, I could see the look of concern on her face, and something I never thought I'd see in River's eyes. Fear. She saw my eyes were open, picked up the coffee, turned off the stove, and pulled a chair beside the bed. "Welcome back."

"What?"

"Relax and let your body repair itself. If I prop you up, can you sip some coffee?"

Still unable to speak, I nodded.

I watched River place the coffee on the chair and climb onto the bed behind me to take me in her arms. Her body warmth was heavenly as she wrapped her arms around my waist. I rested there while she reached for the cup and brought the steaming liquid to my lips.

"Slow, small sips," she warned.

The coffee felt like fire going down my throat, and I winced.

"Okay, too soon for that," River said, pulling the blankets tightly around our bodies.

My head rested on her chest, and I could feel her heart pounding. I tried to keep my eyes open, but the blackness swallowed me again.

†

In the darkness, I dreamed of River. The beauty of her smile as she watched Reba or we worked together on a project. I could fight it all I wanted, but I was deeply in love with her. Time away from her was punishment, and I prayed for my sentence to end so I could be back in her presence. I lived for the moments we touched, even if it was a brief brush of hands as we worked together, or had my body wrapped around hers as we traveled. I wondered if she felt the same. She sheltered her heart and emotions so well it was challenging, but I glimpsed a flicker now and then. I felt the shivering subside and learned I could wiggle my toes. River was still wrapped around me like a human blanket, her face

229

buried in my neck as she dozed. Her warm breath on my neck sent a surge of much-needed warmth rushing through me. River must have felt my movement. I felt her startle and lift her head.

I managed a weak smile as I turned to look at her. "What happened?"

"You decided to go for a swim, and it almost didn't end well."

I could see the tears in her eyes, but she didn't loosen her hold on me.

"I was concentrating on work when Poe started dive-bombing to get my attention. I've never heard a bird so distraught, but his efforts paid off. I saw you beach the boat and stumble toward me." She brushed the hair from my face. "Do you remember anything?"

I looked at her and felt confusion. "Intense cold and pain, but no detail."

"It was miraculous you found the strength to climb back into the boat. Cold water drains strength from muscles quickly," River explained.

"Is that why I feel like I weigh a ton right now?"

"Probably. Are you ready to try some coffee or soup? I'll make a fresh cup."

I nodded. "Just run the coffee back through the maker."

I was disappointed when she removed her body from around mine, but coffee might help me bounce back faster. Soup too, but I wasn't sure about that. I watched River carry the cup back to the kitchen and looked around the room. My clothes and several layers of River's clothes were strewn across the floor. A shiver raced through me, but not from cold. I imagined the touch of River's hands on my body as she undressed me, which had a pleasant warming effect. Shit. River undressed me, and I wasn't present for the moment. I had to hold back a chuckle at the silly thought.

"Do you feel like you can sit up?"

I wrapped the blankets around me and pulled myself to a sitting position.

"Can you feel your hands yet? I will hold the cup if you need me to."

"I can do it." I reached for the steaming cup of liquid.

I was sipping on the heavenly brew when I heard tapping. I looked up to see Poe tapping on the window glass.

"Thank you, Poe. Thank you, too, for saving me," I told River.

"Just let me know when you need a swim, and we'll go to the warm springs."

I could see the sparkle of laughter in her eyes. That was much more pleasant than the fear I saw in them earlier.

I looked back at Poe. "Will you give him the leftover pancakes?'

"I will." River stood and carried the food outside. "Thank you, Poe." I heard her tell him.

River returned and started the soup warming again. "I don't have your biscuit making skills, but I could handle making some fry bread," she offered.

"The soup will be plenty. I'm not sure I'm ready for that, but I'll try." I turned to lean my back against the wall to watch River as she began picking up the scattered clothing.

"I didn't damage the boat, did I?"

River chuckled and shook her head. "The boat is fine. You even managed to pull the rest of the net home with you."

"Really?"

"It will take a few minutes to untangle it from the prop, but it's salvageable."

"I honestly don't know what happened. I was almost done hauling it in, and then I hit the water."

"I'm glad you made it back safely. You gave me a helluva scare."

"Can we keep this between us?"

River smiled. "Yeah. That's not a problem. That was a hard but valuable lesson to learn."

"If Dad got wind of it, he'd make me come home for sure."

"Do you not want to go?" River asked.

"No, I don't think I do." I surprised myself with the admission, but I had been thinking more about it lately. I was happy. Happier than I had been in a long time.

"That's encouraging to hear. I think you've done incredible things for a *Cheechako*." River smiled.

"Thanks for your vote of confidence."

"I'm serious. You have performed incredibly for someone from the city. That's highly commendable. I've known Native peoples who haven't been able to thrive like you have."

"They were probably just not as stubborn."

"There is that," River said and returned to the stove. "Do you think you're ready to try some soup?"

"I think so, but can I sit at the table?"

"Yeah, but you need to dress warmly. I'll grab a clean shirt from my pack and give you a few minutes," River replied.

I waited until she closed the door and then raced to get dressed. I didn't understand why I was suddenly shy. River had undressed me and seen me in all of my glory, even if it was an emergency situation. When River returned, I had dressed in several warm layers and pulled on dry boots.

"Feel better?"

"Much. Thank you."

"Let's get some soup into you." River served two bowls of soup and brought them to the table. "Go slow."

I took a tentative bite and reached for the salt and pepper. "Needs some spice."

"Easier to add than take away," River said, reaching for the salt. "Hit's the spot, though."

†

"I think you need to take things easy tonight," River said.

"I'm feeling much better since I ate."

"That may be true, but you've had a traumatic event, and the effects can be prolonged. I'd feel better if you slept longer and stayed warm."

"What are you going to do?"

"I'm going to work on more antlers, so we'll have a nice load to take to town."

"Out at the firepit?"

"Yeah."

"If I bundle up and we light a fire, may I sit with you and help?"

River looked at me. "You won't accept no, will you?"

I shrugged. "If you insist, however, I'm not much for lying on a bed."

"How about a compromise? Sit with me, but relax. You can keep us in coffee and supplies."

"I can do that," I answered, pulling a wool cap on my head and putting on my heavy coat.

River lit a fire while I made cups of fresh coffee and carried them outside.

"You've got a nice pile ready for town."

"I think I've got enough for a boatload, but although I know it is a long ways off, I want to work on as many as possible when Troy comes to deliver."

"I will help tomorrow. Do you have any idea what you want to eat for dinner?"

"Let's keep it simple with some pancakes."

"That works for me." I settled into a chair and watched River work until my eyes grew heavy.

When my head snapped up, I saw River looking at me.

"Now will you go stretch out for a bit?"

"Yes, but don't let me sleep long."

"I'll work a couple more hours, and then we can rustle up some dinner."

"Do you need more coffee?"

"I'm good. I need to go get rid of some."

"I'll warm the seat for you," I teased and walked to the bathhouse.

†

The rest and food emboldened my spirits. River began setting up her cot when we decided to retire for the evening. "Will you sleep with me tonight?"

She whipped her head around to look at me. "What?"

"Will you share a bed with me tonight? It was comforting to be held in your arms earlier today."

River smiled. "You didn't have to take a polar bear plunge for that. You could have just asked."

I smiled at her. "I'm asking now."

She nodded and lit the fire in the stove before removing her outer layers of clothes. I changed into my sleep clothes and climbed into the bed holding the covers open for her. River turned off the lamp and eased into the bed. I turned away but pulled her hand around my body, pulling her close.

"Is this comfortable for you?"

"Very," River answered, and tucked the covers behind her.

I was immediately enveloped by the warmth of River's body. "You are so toasty warm," I softly moaned. "That feels nice."

"For me, too," River whispered her warm breath inches from my ear.

"Goodnight, River."

"Goodnight. Wake me if you get cold or feel bad. You are not one hundred percent out of the woods yet."

"I will," I answered with a sleepy voice.

†

I woke to find the bed empty of River and turned to search for her. I could hear the coffee pot brewing, and River entered the cabin seconds later.

"I hope I didn't wake you," she said.

"No, not at all. My bladder says it's time to get up." I grinned.

"I know, I just relieved mine. I'll get the coffee ready while you're gone. Bundle up. It's cold." River added wood to the stove.

It must be cold if she was relighting the stove. I dressed and walked to the bathhouse. I couldn't believe how much the weather had changed overnight. I rushed back into the cabin and hovered around the stove for several minutes.

"You weren't kidding about it being cold."

"I bet it's probably twenty degrees cooler than yesterday."

I nodded and accepted the cup of coffee from her. "Are you planning to work on more racks today?"

River smiled. "I'll bundle up. They won't clean themselves. I prefer you stay inside again today, if you will. You don't need a chill. It will be cold on the river when we go to town tomorrow, but we can't change that."

"I'll do some baking today and make my list for groceries and other goods. Is there anything you need?"

"Remind me to pick up some new socks. Nikita says mine are no longer repairable."

"That's easy enough. What about ammunition? You must go through a lot in a season."

"The village elders provide that yearly as part of my agreement to be a designated hunter."

"That makes sense. Are you starving yet?"

"No, I can eat a banana, which will hold me for a while."

"I want to make a big pan of biscuits and some gravy this morning. The leftover biscuits can be filled with meat or jelly for tomorrow's trip."

"I'll clean my large thermos, and we can take some coffee with us," River suggested.

236

†

When the biscuits were ready to cook, I mixed a batch of brownies to bake before sitting down to make my list. I looked at my pantry, and it didn't appear I needed much in the way of basics. Sugar was probably my most depleted spice since we had made jelly, so I added it to my list with another few boxes of paraffin. The peanut butter bars were an easy-to-make protein snack, so I added a case of peanut butter to my list. More cookie-baking supplies, too. I added a muffin pan to my list, as I had yet to find one. The berry pulp would make delicious muffins, and I could also make cornbread muffins.

I made fresh coffee and carried a cup to River. "The biscuits are doing well. Are you warm enough?" I asked. My breath puffed out in vapor as I spoke.

"Yes, I'm good. Thanks." River took the hot coffee. "After breakfast, I will begin loading the racks onto the boat. I assume you want to get an early start tomorrow."

"I would like to, yes, so we can arrive, get our shopping completed, and visit with Erica and Elizabeth."

"Do they know I'm coming with you?"

"Yes. Both are excited to see you."

"I'm looking forward to it," River said. "It's been a while since I've been in town. I'd like to take a bath to look presentable."

"Start your fire before you come in for breakfast. It will take longer for the water to heat in this cold. I'll go start on some gravy."

The mention of a bath reminded me to add some hygiene supplies to my shopping list. Socks for River, too. As I crumbled the last link of sausage into the gravy, I wondered if I could replenish the sausage, bacon, and ham. I wouldn't starve without them, but it was nice to add variety to my diet. If I couldn't get them in town, I would see what I could have shipped and return for them later. That reminded me to ask River to use the bone saw to cut the large hambone into sections to season beans. Nothing would go to waste.

I called River when breakfast was ready.

†

"Before you put your bone saw up today will you cut the ham bone for me?" I asked.

"No problem. Once I finish loading, do you feel up to taking a ride with me? I'd like to see that beaver colony."

"Sure. It's not far from here," I answered. "Then you can bathe, and we will relax for the rest of today."

"That's the best plan I've heard all day," River replied.

I poured the leftover gravy into a jar and allowed it to cool while waiting for River. I laughed and added jars to my list. I had placed several jars of jelly into a crate for Erica and Elizabeth and would take the last fish from the smokehouse after sharing some with River for lunch.

River returned inside when she finished loading the boat. "I left room for our bags and a few boxes I know you want to take to town."

"That's perfect. Did you check the bathwater?"

"It's getting there slowly. I added more wood. I'll check again when we return."

†

I was disappointed not to see the eagles but pointed the nest out to River. The beaver lodge had grown huge when we reached the pond, and many animals were swimming around it.

"I can harvest several and not affect the population here," River said. "The area looks ripe for martin and other small fur-bearing animals. I will set a few beaver traps when we return from town and will set my other lines once the snow begins to fall."

A howl broke the air as we sat watching the beavers.

"Wolves," River said.

"I've heard them a few times but have never caught a glimpse of any," I replied.

"You rarely do," River said. "They typically hunt in the forest and shy away from human contact. They were hunted almost to extinction years ago, and the packs have just begun running strong again."

"I'm proud that you don't overhunt," I said.

"Never take more than you need and let your hunting areas repopulate. I try to change regions often for that reason. There is so much wilderness for hunting that never sees humans."

I shivered.

"Let's get you back inside and warm," River said, starting the ATV.

She pulled to the cabin to let me off and then stored the vehicle in the shed.

When River returned inside, I had stoked the fire. "Will my tolerance for cold return?"

"Eventually, but you must remember you took quite a shock to your system and will need some time. In the meantime, stay bundled whenever you venture outside."

"I will," I promised. "I thought we could eat some smoked fish for lunch after your bath, and I'll box up the rest for the ride to town."

"I've already added a large string of chaga for Erica." River smiled. "It wouldn't hurt to have a cup tonight to help bolster our immune systems."

"I've got some already ground." I handed River a pan. "Will you bring us fish on your way back?"

"I will." River selected clean clothes and walked to the bathhouse.

†

For the next seven weeks, River and I worked on continuing to forage, tanning some of the hides from her recent kills, and preparing the antlers for sale in Glennallen. River brought many of her traps to cure in my clothes washing pot and taught me what she would be doing in the upcoming trapping season. We made our planned trip to town to replenish supplies and visit briefly with Erica and Elizabeth. Never in my wildest dreams did I think I would find myself in domestic bliss, but working in partnership with River and sharing her company every day was exactly what my heart needed. We worked hard every day, and it was great comfort to fall asleep in her arms every night.

CHAPTER SIXTEEN

The iPad sitting on the counter caught my attention. I hadn't made an entry in weeks. Life had been hectic, but now it was time to make an entry.

I needed the calendar to determine what entry this would be.

September 21ˢᵗ – Day eighty-two.

Where did August go? I have failed miserably in posting in my journal, but so much has happened. I don't know where the time has gone. I don't remember it being that long since I made my last entry, but the calendar doesn't lie. So much has happened over the past three months. I have learned a great deal since stepping onto the land, and I don't feel like the same woman I was. I have become...different.

241

Stronger and more independent than ever, but in ways I didn't think were possible. I don't have to rely on a grocery store or takeout for delicious food. I hunt and gather my own. My body has changed too. I am leaner and feel the healthiest I've ever been.

Poe continues to bless me with his presence and was critical to my survival when I took an unexpected swim. Nikita, Reba, and I had a wonderful time making jelly, picking berries, and enjoying the beautiful late summer weather. I miss Reba's presence and laughter, but she had to prepare to start school. Then there is River. I feel my breath catch when she looks at me with passion in her eyes, and I can feel the growing connection between us. Our time apart when she hunted caribou was miserable for me, and I couldn't wait for her return. I finally admitted to myself and River that I didn't want to leave. I need to consider how I will bring up the topic with Dad. He is the last person on earth I want to disappoint. I'm ready, or at least hope I am for whatever winter brings. My food stocks are plentiful, and the cabin has become my fortress. With the addition of more power banks, I shouldn't need to worry about power during the dark days. The big question is, again, River. As the seasons change, will she choose to stay with me or continue her life and other projects? I fear that the time for a decision will come all too soon.

Will I be prepared for a future without her in it? So many questions, but no answers. It will be an exciting fall. I will do my best to not wait weeks to enter again, but for now, I will close.

I read the entry and stared back at the blinking cursor. What an adventure in self-discovery this had become.

†

I placed a biscuit on the woodpile for Poe and filled the rest with bacon and ham slices while waiting for River. The first of the hambones simmered in a pot of beans I would store in jars for this winter. I had rarely eaten beans since I had a plethora of fish, game, and fresh vegetables, but I was sure they would add much-needed protein during the cold winter days.

†

River carried in the fish for lunch. "Those beans smell good."

"I thought we might have some with some cornbread and onion slices for dinner."

"That sounds great to me. Are you planning to jar the rest?"

"I am as soon as they cool."

"I can help you with that," River offered.

I left some fish on the woodpile for Poe and returned inside. "I know he survived before I arrived, but I worry about Poe."

River chuckled. "You've made him a nice condo with that basket and rabbit pelt. He's probably never had a nest so lovely. Make some extra cornbread tonight that you can leave out for him. We will only be gone a few days."

"I know," I said and rinsed our dishes. "What are you planning to do this afternoon?"

"I thought I might grab a few chunks of wood, do some carving with you, and maybe nap later."

I reached over and placed my hand on her forehead. "Are you feeling well? You never willingly nap," I teased.

†

I carved a rabbit and looked over to find River intently working on a piece. "Are you ready for some coffee and a snack?"

"I thought I smelled brownies cooking earlier. Was I dreaming?"

"No, you weren't." I made coffee and cut two large portions.

River took a bite. "Moist and fudgy."

"I thought they might be a nice change. I'll wrap any we have leftover for the ride to town."

"Assuming there will be some. May I have another? Maybe not quite as big."

I brought River another brownie. "Are you good on coffee?"

"Yeah. Thank you. I hope you added more mixes to your list. These are a real treat."

"I did," I replied, brushing the bits of wood into my hand and placing them inside the wood stove. "What are you working on?"

"I hope it resembles a beaver when I finish," she answered.

I placed the finished rabbit on the windowsill and reviewed my list. "Is there anything, food or snacks, you'd like me to buy at the store?"

"Let me think," River replied.

I walked to the pantry and peered inside. "What's your favorite cake?"

"Yellow with milk chocolate icing."

I added those to my list. "Do you think we can get a few gallons of milk? I've got powdered, but I only use it for cooking."

"I don't see why not. You have room in your fridge and could freeze some in your bush cooler."

"I think I'll add a few more fish packages to take to town to free up some room."

"I don't think you lack food," River said. "We can always hunt small game if you run short in the winter."

I liked that River used the word "we" in her statement. That gave me hope that she had plans to stick around.

When River finished her beaver, she added it to the shelf.

†

The quick trip to town went well, and when we returned to the cabin, we began unloading the boat. "It feels so good to be back in the bush," Troy said.

"It's good to have you here, even for a short visit. Have you talked to your mom about school yet?" I asked.

"We've danced around the topic a few times," Troy replied. "I never dreamed I would be so unhappy in the city, but I feel trapped."

"Share that with your mom. She would never want you to be unhappy."

"I know. I just don't want to disappoint Mom."

"I understand, but have faith that she would be more disappointed if your heart isn't in college."

"Honestly, I'd use the money for a boat or property instead. Outside of town, but near enough, I can still help Mom. I can make deliveries for the Depot, hunt, and trap to supplement income."

"Would you consider working for the forestry service?"

"That's always a possibility, too. Or even a hunting and fishing guide. Mom gets a lot of interest for that from the bed and breakfast."

"See, you have many options," I said.

"He won't live to see them if he gets electrocuted hooking those power banks into your system," River teased.

"That's a good point. We will go store the supplies and start on some dinner. Any preferences?"

"I love your grilled salmon," Troy said.

"I think I have a few left on my stringer," I replied.

"Give me a holler if you need some muscle," River said, following me from the bathhouse while Troy added the new power banks.

We walked to my stringer and removed the four remaining fish. River took them and began processing them for dinner. She looked at me and smiled.

"You know, it probably wouldn't work well for salmon, but I bet we could make a fish pen to store some other fresh fish in the area. Whitefish, maybe trout."

"That sounds interesting. What would I need?"

"A few metal fence posts and some chicken wire. We can pick those up next spring." River smiled.

†

I boiled rice and mixed up a cake batter while River stored the groceries and fuel supplies. The filets were soaking in the sink while I diced some onion and mushroom for the rice. When I opened the fridge, I saw a container of blueberry pulp. I placed a portion in a smaller bowl and added a touch of sugar to make a compote I'd use on the fish. I set the bundt pan with my first cake mix in the wood stove oven and crossed my fingers.

River returned inside. "We had a few biscuits left that I gave to Poe for dinner."

"Thank you." I smiled. "Coffee?"

"Please," she said and rinsed her hands. "All the fuel is stored, and I think Troy is almost done."

"I hope he'll sleep in here with us. It's too cold on the boat or in the bathhouse," River said.

"I've already told him he's sleeping on the cot here," I said.

"Good. You know that now that you have a mini power plant, you could get a small ceramic heater for the bathhouse. It may make bathing more pleasant."

"What a great idea. I'll get Troy to ask Erica to order one, and we can pick it up when it arrives. I can't believe we didn't think of that sooner."

"Charles will laugh when he sees the resort you have made from his fishing cabin."

247

I frowned. "Just a few much-needed upgrades," I said in my defense.

River took me in her arms. "I meant that as a compliment, not a criticism. He will be impressed."

I relaxed, and she kissed my forehead. "What smells so good?"

"I'm making you a cake," I answered.

"Oh, hell yeah. I will stack more wood on the porch unless you need me for something."

"You just can't sit still, can you?"

"Nope, not when there's work to be done. I'm feeling snow in the air, and I want plenty of wood within easy reach."

†

"You should have enough power to run anything you want," Troy said when he entered the cabin. "The new banks are already charging well."

"If you grab some beers from the crate, I'll start the fish," I said, picking up the fish pan and cooking supplies to follow him outside. I looked at River. "Will you grab us some buckets for seats?"

"I'm already ahead of you." River smiled.

†

River's eyes lit up excitedly when I turned over the bundt pan, and the cake slid perfectly onto a plate. I drizzled the melted icing over the top of the cake and placed the rest on the table. "Who wants milk?"

"Oh, hell yeah," Troy said.

I poured glasses of milk and joined them at the table.

"I didn't think dinner could get any better, and then you serve this," Troy said, taking a large bite. "Oh, my gosh, this is almost sinful."

River nodded. "It is delicious. Thank you."

"Thanks for all your hard work today," I said.

"Keep this up, and I won't want to leave," Troy teased.

"Just wait until you have crepes for breakfast in the morning," I replied.

"I don't think I've ever had them," he said. "I love your cooking, so they will be fantastic."

After two slices of cake, Troy and River were finally satisfied.

"That milk was perfect with that cake," River said.

"I'm glad you both enjoyed it."

"Don't be surprised if you hear me in the kitchen in a few hours for more," Troy warned.

"I will send some back with you for the ride home," I promised. "I don't think you can eat it all before then."

"That almost sounds like a challenge," River teased. "We put a good dent in it tonight."

†

Troy fell quiet after breakfast, and I could tell he was stalling his return home. "How about we make a deal?" I asked.

"I'm listening," Troy said.

249

"I've already accepted an invitation to the village for Thanksgiving, but you'll be home for a few weeks, right?"

"Yeah, for two," he answered.

"If I can make it down the river, I will come for a visit and cook crepes and a cake for you."

Troy's eyes lit with excitement. "I'll buy whatever supplies you need if you do the cooking."

"Deal," I said and offered him my hand.

He took my hand and pulled me into a hug. "Thank you."

"I packed some cake and a few crepes for your trip." I handed him a small package. "Be safe and have that talk with your mom."

"I will," Troy said.

We walked him to the boat and watched him disappear downriver.

"Now what?" I asked River.

"I was thinking of splitting more wood this afternoon. Tomorrow, I'd like to take a short trip and wonder if you will accompany me?"

"Like you even have to ask," I teased.

"For this one, I do. We'll be gone for several days and sleep in a trapper cabin. Nothing even close to this place, but hopefully, it will still keep the cold out." She shuffled her feet. "I need to check my northern trap lines and do any maintenance before the season starts."

"Will we be able to cook?"

"I thought we could take some of your beans and soup to heat. There's a small wood stove, but nothing fancy."

"Bathroom?"

"A very primitive outhouse, but it has a door and roof. You won't roost there, or your butt will freeze."

"I think I can handle that. Let me grab a notepad, and I'll list the items we need to take. Your sled?"

"Yes, it's larger than yours." River smiled. "Thanks for agreeing to go. I hope you won't regret coming along. It will be cold."

"You wouldn't put me in a position that would place me in harm," I said.

"We live in Alaska. There's always a potential for harm," she reminded me.

I punched her shoulder. "You know what I mean."

"Like outrun you if we get chased by a bear?" She grinned.

"Or trip me," I joked back.

"There is a potential for seeing a bear or wolves where we are going, but I will keep us safe."

"That's all I could ask for. I'll be right back."

†

"If we don't stop soon, we will have to pull a second sled," River teased.

"I know," I replied, placing eggs in a pot to boil. "What time do you want to start out in the morning?"

"Early, so we can stop by to check on Mom. We can't stay long because it's quite a ride to the trapping cabin."

"One final pit stop," I teased. I placed a jar of soup, dumplings, and beans into a basket. "We have some cake left for tonight, but should I make some peanut butter bars? They should travel well."

"I'll never turn those down."

251

"I'll make fresh biscuits for biscuits and gravy in the morning and some meat biscuits, too," I said. "We can start out with something hot in our bellies."

"I'll load the sled while you fix breakfast," River said.

"What guns do I need to take?"

"I will have my rifle and shotgun. Bring your twenty-two in case we see rabbit or grouse. I can roast either of those on the campfire spit."

When River settled enough to eat, I made omelets. "I'm excited to go on a trip with you," I told her.

"I hope you rest well tonight. Tomorrow will be a long day."

†

We had become accustomed to sharing a bed, so I turned toward River when we turned in for the night. "Is there anything about this trip we haven't planned for?"

"Just one thing," River answered. "We need to add your fly rod to the sled. The camp sits on a beautiful lake, so there may be an opportunity to fish if it's not frozen over."

"Awesome," I replied and snuggled into River's warmth. The last thing I remember was feeling her arms wrap around me.

†

After eating, I jarred the gravy and placed it in the food basket. I broke open two biscuits for Poe. "We will be back soon," I told him as he cocked his head back and forth.

He had perched atop the smokehouse, watching River curiously as she packed the sled.

When we pulled off, he followed us briefly and then turned back. We made good time arriving at the village; and as expected, Nikita wanted to feed us.

"We can only stay a short time. We've still got many miles to go."

"I've got fresh bread and ripe tomatoes. Stay and at least have sandwiches with me," Nikita pleaded.

River looked at me.

"I love homegrown tomato sandwiches."

"Just the sandwiches. Maybe some chips, too," River amended her statement.

†

"Those sandwiches were terrific," I said, placing two more in the food pack.

"You'll stop on your way back for a proper meal, right?" she asked.

"In three days," River promised as she topped off the gas tank.

"I'll see you then," Nikita said, smiling as we rode away.

"That was painless," I said to River as we left the village.

"Yeah, and those were good sandwiches."

†

We rode for hours, and I began to notice changes in the landscape. The mountains loomed much more prominently, and we passed open tundra areas. River pointed out several animals along the route. So many eagles in the area surprised me, but they were beautiful to watch as they rode the thermals looking for a meal. River slowed when we approached a bend in the river, and saw a mother bear with a half-grown cub feasting on salmon on the opposite shore. She observed us until we passed and resumed eating. River pulled to a stop when something caught her attention.

"What is it?" I asked as she climbed off the ATV.

"You'll see in just a second."

Curious, I watched River enter the tree line and emerge carrying a large set of moose antlers.

"How did you see those?"

"I've found them here before. Moose typically shed in the same area every year," River explained. "There may be more, but we don't have time to hunt them today." River placed them close to the trail and approached the ATV. "We'll pick them up on the way home."

"No one else will get them?" I asked. Years of city life had taught me well that anything of value left unsecured would disappear in minutes if unattended.

"No one else will be here." River grinned. "Do you need a few minutes to stretch?"

"How much longer do we have?"

"Two more hours, at least."

I climbed off and picked through the food basket until I found a sandwich. "Want one?" I asked.

"Sure," she answered.

I handed her the second sandwich, and we watched the water flow as we ate in silence. "Nikita grows great tomatoes," I said after swallowing the last bite.

"There's not much she can't grow." River smiled. "Between the two of us, we will never go hungry."

The cry of an eagle filled the air, and we watched as the bird skimmed the river's surface, snagged a fish from the water, and sailed away.

"Ready?" River asked. She climbed on the ATV and offered me her hand. "Are you staying warm?"

"Yes, I am," I answered as I settled behind her.

†

River slowed, turned into the forest, followed a trail for several minutes before a small lake and a cabin came into view. It was a beautiful area, but River hadn't exaggerated the size of the cabin or outhouse. She parked close and walked to the door to open it to inspect for any unwanted visitors.

"Like I said. It's not huge but will keep us safe and warm for a few days. There is one spot that I'll need to repair, but otherwise, it's in good shape." River pointed to where the chinking between the logs had been destroyed. "It won't take me long."

"What can I do to help?"

"I brought some logs, but they must be split for the smaller stove."

"I can handle that," I said and walked inside to inspect the stove. I removed several logs and used a hatchet to split them into smaller sticks.

I watched River pull out a bucket and walk to the lake for water. Then she added dirt and ash from the firepit and several handfuls of dried grass to make a mixture to press between the logs to fill the gap. She walked around the building to make sure there were no other spots that needed reinforcement. River lifted the one window in the building to help circulate air through the musty cabin.

I carried an armful of wood inside and got an excellent inside view. There was a raised platform that I assumed would be our bed, getting us off the cold ground. It didn't look all that comfortable, but it was a clean surface.

"Do you want me to light a fire?" I called out to River.

"Not yet. Let's allow it to air out first. We can start carrying our stuff inside."

I placed the fly rod by the front door and carried our sleeping bags, blankets, and pillows inside. "I'll make up our bedroom." I grinned.

River placed the box and basket of food on the small counter. "When you're ready, you can light the fire and place a jar on the stove to heat for dinner."

"Any preference?" I asked.

"Let's do the soup tonight. I'm going to snack on a ham biscuit. Do you want one? There's probably enough coffee left for a cup."

"Sounds good," I replied. I followed River outside and sat on the sled while River grabbed the thermos.

"Tomorrow, we can run my traplines and bring more wood into camp. I'm sure there will be some trees we need to remove from the trail."

"How many miles of lines do you work?"

"Forty when I use all the traps and snares."

"I bet that takes forever in the winter."

"I run one half one day and finish the loop the second day."

"How long have you been trapping?"

"About fifteen years. I bring the pelts back to the village for use in clothing, and the women make goods to sell at the Depot. A raw fur may only be worth a few dollars at the fur market, but an item made from that same fur can be sold for ten times as much."

"What do you do with the animals?"

"Most are not edible, but I use them for bait in my traps."

"What are the most valuable pelts to harvest?"

"A lynx or wolverine can sell for hundreds of dollars, but they are the hardest to trap."

†

The cedar trees surrounding the cabin smelled terrific.

River saw me looking at them. "Not only do they smell nice, but they also help break the wind and repel pestering insects. I will cut a bough to place under the bed to make the cabin smell fresh."

A significant parcel of tundra surrounded the lake. "You've got a beautiful view of the mountains, and it seems like you can see for miles across the tundra."

"Over five miles. Sometimes, I can see large herds, such as the caribou, long before they arrive."

"Is this where you came to hunt them?"

River shook her head. "The herd's migration route was about two hours north of here. It's been years since they migrated this far south."

"I know Alaska is immense, but how much of it have you seen?"

"Maybe a third of it. I traveled to the ocean once, and the environment is so different than here. The seafood was wonderful, but I missed my forest."

"Do you get much seafood?"

"Sonya's husband and other men from the village bring some when they return for the holidays. It's a special treat and a great way to celebrate their homecoming."

"That sounds like a great celebration."

"One you will be a part of this year at Thanksgiving."

"I'm looking forward to that," I replied.

"Is there anything we need to do tonight?"

River shook her head. "Eat and relax. Tomorrow will be a long day."

†

A storm blew in during the night, and I could hear the wind howling around the cabin. The small stove took the edge off the cold but could not ward off the chill creeping into the cabin. I snuggled in closer to River, and our bodies were entwined when I woke hours later. There's no way we could have got closer.

"Are you warm enough?" River whispered in the dark.

"I'm cold, but it's not unbearable," I answered.

River surprised me when her lips brushed mine with a soft kiss. I felt the warmth surge through me and returned the kiss, deepening the exploration. When I offered no resistance, she rolled me onto my back, moved on top of me, and kissed me passionately. We were breathing heavily when she broke the kiss.

"Are you okay with this? Comfortable?" River asked.

"That's the best way to warm up yet," I answered, pulling her head down for another kiss.

†

A glowing green light shone against the walls of the cabin. "What the heck?"

When River realized what I was referring to, she chuckled. "Pull on your boots and coat. You've got to see this."

We scrambled out of bed and dressed as warmly as possible. River placed more wood in the stove and then reached for my hand.

I realized what made the walls glow when we stepped out into the cold dying night. The sky was filled with the northern lights. Green and purple rays moved in waves across the night sky.

River stepped behind me and hugged me. "Isn't it beautiful?"

"Yes. Do we not see these from home?"

"They appear during certain times of the year but are never this vivid."

I was so enthralled with the lights that I hadn't realized our footsteps crunched in the fresh snow or that it was actively snowing. When a snowflake landed on my cheek, I returned to reality. "It's snowing, and I didn't even know it." I turned in River's arms to face her. "Thank you for bringing me here." I kissed her sweetly and held her close.

"Thank you for being here with me. I don't think we will be able to return to sleep, so why don't we get an early start to the day? I could eat some of your warmed gravy over the leftover biscuits and coffee."

"Will you set up the coffee pot to get it started? I need to visit the outhouse," I told her.

River nodded and returned inside as I trudged toward the outhouse. Several inches of snow on the ground crunched beneath my weight. The outhouse was miserably cold, so I finished quickly and rushed back inside. I pulled off my gloves, held them near the stove to warm them, and placed the jar of gravy on top of it.

"That will take a while. Will you work the door while I bring in more wood?" River asked. "I'll carry in some fresh water too."

I nodded, and opened and shut the door behind her as she made two trips for wood. We would definitely need to harvest some today. The small supply we brought from home was dwindling quickly. While River walked to the lake for water, I peeled and seasoned four boiled eggs to hold us over until the gravy was warmed.

River smiled when she entered with the water and saw the eggs on the plate. "You must have been reading my mind."

"These should hold us over until breakfast is ready."

"I'm thinking it would be much faster to cook over the firepit," River said. "It has a spit to hang a pot or meat from, and shouldn't take near as long to heat over an open flame."

"Let's try it out tonight with some beans. I'll keep my eyes open for a grouse or some other fresh meat that will help keep us warm."

"We shouldn't have any problem getting enough wood for both fires," River said.

"If it keeps snowing, how will that impact your travel on your lines?"

"The ATV can pull through six to eight inches easily," River answered. "We don't have anywhere near that much yet."

†

I covered plates of biscuits with the thick gravy while River poured coffee. "It's not your coffee, but it's hot, and sugar will take the bite out of it." She grinned. "I hope," she added.

"I've got something even better," I answered and rummaged through the basket to remove a small bottle of honey. "A few drops of this will greatly improve the taste and give us energy."

River smiled. "You have learned so much in such a short time."

"I've had good teachers," I replied. "Let's eat. I'm starving."

†

I assembled a daypack while River fueled the ATV and inspected the chainsaw. We would travel too far to return for lunch, so I packed snacks and poured the rest of the coffee into the thermos. River had filled our water bottles as well.

I pulled on my thick gloves, slung the small rifle over my shoulder, and picked up the pack to walk outside to meet

River. The ATV was idling to warm up, and the supplies were loaded.

"Are we ready to ride?" I asked.

River held out her hand, and I climbed on behind her. "Hold on," she called out as we left camp.

The initial trail was much like home, but I could feel a slow incline growing the farther north we traveled. When River stopped to clear a fallen tree, I scouted the area for game, and I killed three grouse before midday.

"We will have meat tonight," I said when I returned with the last bird.

"Good job." River smiled as I dropped the bird in a bucket and helped her load wood.

We crested a hill, and River pulled to a stop. "This is a good place to have a meal break."

"The view is incredible." I stared across miles of tundra blanketed with pristine snow as I sat on the sled beside River and passed her snacks.

"We're making good progress. We should finish the loop today if we don't run into a blowdown."

I looked at the rapidly filling sled. "What will you do once the sled is full?"

"I'll make stacks beside the trail for use during the season and carry a load back each day."

"When will you begin trapping?"

"I have the best luck in late fall through the winter months. I think I will wait until after Thanksgiving this year. We've had a great hunting season, and the antler revenue is enough to get me through until spring."

"Only harvest what you need," I said.

"Exactly. Anything more endangers wildlife and is nothing but greed. I was not taught that way."

I fell silent for several minutes as I stared across the snow-covered tundra. River saw me staring across the vast expanse. "A penny for your thoughts?"

I lifted my hand and pointed across the open space. "That is like my life in Alaska."

"How so?" River asked.

"It's like a blank white page waiting for me to fill it with experiences and adventures," I answered.

"That's a unique perspective. What do you wish to fill your pages with?"

I turned to River and smiled. "Years of adventures with you by my side."

I saw River swallow hard. "I'd like that very much."

I leaned into River, and we kissed. It was as if the kiss sealed the bond we had just made, filled with the promise of adventures to come.

"Look," she said.

I followed her gaze across the snow and watched two animals trotting along in the distance.

River smiled at me. "Mated wolves. That is a perfect omen."

I linked my arm through River's, placed my head on her shoulder, and we watched until the pair disappeared from view.

With a deep sigh, she looked at me. "Are you ready to finish running the line?"

"Just waiting on you," I replied, hopping down from the sled.

CHAPTER SEVENTEEN

We were both famished by the time we returned to camp. The sled was filled with wood, and we had left significant piles along the trail. River cleaned the grouse, seasoned them, and placed them on the spit above the campfire to begin cooking. I emptied the beans into a pot to hang above the fire. I pulled out a package of cornbread wrapped in foil for the trip. It would go nicely with beans.

River was unloading the wood from the sled when I returned outside with water and several peanut butter bars.

"You need a break," I said, handing her the snack and sitting beside her on the sled.

"Thanks," she said and bit into the sweet treat. "I hope you never run out of peanut butter."

"There will always be peanut butter in my pantry."

"We've accomplished a lot today. What do you think about starting back tomorrow? I'd like to pick up those shed antlers and search the general area for more. Animals often shed in the same location each year. We can stop in the village, spend the night with Nikita and go home the following morning."

"That's a good plan. Do you want to leave the jars of food here for future trips?"

"We wouldn't have to transport them again if we do," River nodded. "Assuming you will return with me."

"I may not spend the entire season with you, but yes, I will return with you. Maybe I could visit and bring you some home-cooked meals?"

"That would be a godsend," River said. "You can see life here is extremely primitive."

"On my next trip to town, I want to get hot water bottles. That would warm your sleeping bag, especially if I'm not here."

"That's smart. I hadn't thought of that."

I stirred the beans and was pleased that they were warming nicely. "How much longer on the meat?"

"Just a few more minutes. It is faster warming food out here, isn't it?"

"Yeah, the campfire is nice, too. I'm sure the coffee will brew faster out here."

"We will test that theory in the morning, but I bet you're right. You can make coffee and breakfast while I get the sled loaded. I'll add more wood to the fire so we will have embers in the morning."

I nodded. "I'll get our plates and cups."

"I'll drop the rest of the wood. Dinner should be ready by then."

†

"The grouse is tasty over the fire, but I bet I could whip up some sauces for you to dip it in to flavor it up a bit. Ranch dressing would be easy, and I could make a honey mustard sauce, too."

"I do love your creativity in the kitchen. Those would store well, in small jars."

"I can't have you starving out here," I teased. "If I can teach you how to make a nice roux, you could bring a case of canned salmon and smother it in gravy. Hey, on second thought, I wouldn't have to teach you. I can jar some for you to bring along."

I was disappointed that the snow had slowly melted during the day, but I knew it would soon return with a vengeance.

Sleeping that night was more comfortable. The cabin stayed much warmer without the cold wind, and we slept through the night.

†

"Damn, I've got to pee," I groaned when I climbed out of bed and pulled my boots on.

"I'll get the fire started in the firepit and start loading the sled," River said.

I stopped long enough to kiss her before rushing out into the cold. "Damn," I squealed when my bare bottom touched the wooden seat. I returned to the cabin and prepared the coffee pot for the fire. "Please brew quicker," I told it as I placed it on the grill. I rummaged through the food basket and removed the last three biscuits and the boiled eggs. I laughed when I saw the wedge of cake in the basket. "Might as well add it to breakfast." I chuckled and split it between two plates with the eggs and biscuits.

River smiled when she saw the cake on the plate.

"Sorry, no milk, but we must eat this before it grows stale."

"You'll get no argument from me, even if there's no cold milk."

†

River parked beside the shed antlers next to the trail. "We won't venture far, but any sheds we find are bonus money. I didn't have to work or hunt for them."

As we entered the tree line, I moved away from River and searched for antlers. We didn't take long to locate another set and carry them back to the sled. I was about to give up the search when I spotted something significant in the bushes and called out to River.

"River, can you come here, please?"

River rushed to where I was kneeling down, inspecting a giant skull. "What is it?"

"A small fortune," she said. "It's a fully intact grizzly skull. You don't see these often, especially with perfect teeth. There are usually a few broken, so this is very rare. Erica will turn backflips for this piece."

"Why don't we plan a trip to town next week and drop these off to her?"

"We can pick up your heaters and a few other supplies," River said. "My treat, though."

"We'll see."

"I'll carry this to the sled and come back. There may be bear claws close that are also valuable," River said. "They are prized for jewelry."

I began searching and uncovered several while River was gone. "I've got four," I told her when she returned.

We recovered a total of ten before we decided to drive on to the village.

"That was quite a find," River said as she used the sleeping bags for padding.

†

Reba was the first to spot us as we entered the village. She ran beside us as we rode to Nikita's.

"I'm so happy to see you," Reba said when River stopped. "Nikita said you would come today."

"We promised. How are you doing in school?" River asked.

"Pretty good. I love recess." Reba grinned.

"That was my favorite, too," River replied.

"Have you been up north?" Reba asked, looking at the back of the sled.

"Yes, we found a few antler sheds, and you won't believe what Tatum found."

"What?"

"Do you want to show her?" River asked me.

"Sure," I replied and moved the sleeping bags. I watched Reba's eyes grow wide.

"A bear skull?" she said.

"Yes, with all its sharp teeth," River said with a growl as she picked Reba up and swirled her around.

Reba was laughing wildly when Nikita stepped onto the porch. "What on earth?"

"We found a bear skull," River said. "A perfect specimen."

"That is a big one," Nikita said as she approached.

"We're going to take it to Erica with a few sets of antler sheds we found up north." River smiled at her mother. "We also found these for you to turn into jewelry," she said, filling her hand with the bear claws. "Those should bring in some money."

"I would think so," Nikita said. "Are you sure you don't want to trade them with Erica?"

"You will make more if you turn them into jewelry, but if you don't want them." River reached for them.

"I did not say that," Nikita said and pulled her hand back. "Are you hungry?"

"We've worked up an appetite," River said as she covered the skull.

"Come on in. I'm just finishing your dinner. Will you stay the night?"

"We thought we might," River answered.

"Good. Reba, go ask your mom if you can eat dinner with us," Nikita said.

"Be right back," Reba said and raced home.

"She was so disappointed that she missed you the other day. I bet she stared out the window at school all day today looking for you."

"That's why we decided to stay. To see you and Reba. We miss not having you in camp," I said.

"We did have fun this summer, didn't we?" Nikita asked.

"Yes, we did. I think of you and Reba every time we have jelly," I replied.

"Come on in and relax. I think Hurricane Reba will be rushing in soon. I've already set the table for four."

"It smells heavenly in here," River said when we walked inside.

"I know how you love fried chicken, rice, and gravy. I even made some of Tatum's special corn," Nikita grinned.

"I hope Reba hurries. I'm suddenly starving," River said, hugging her mom.

"Mom said yes," Reba said as she skidded to a halt in the kitchen.

"Let's eat then," Nikita said.

We sat around the table for the feast, and River told them about our trip north.

"Your line trails were in good shape?"

"We removed quite a few trees, but otherwise, they looked good. I'm hopeful for a good season."

"Bring me as many rabbits as you can. They will taste good in your stew pot and make highly prized mittens."

"I'm going to load my traps in the morning, spend a few weeks prepping them, and make a bunch of snares for rabbits. There was quite a bit of activity in the willows. We will take the skull and antlers to Erica. Is there anything you need?"

"Not that I can think of," Nikita answered. "When will you go back north?"

"After Thanksgiving," River answered.

"Are you going too?" Reba asked.

"I will visit and take some meals to River, but I won't stay with her full time," I answered. "Maybe I can return a load of pelts when I pass through."

"Can I go?" Reba asked.

"We'll see. It's much colder there, and the cabin isn't big."

"Please?" Reba pleaded.

"I'll talk to your mom about it when we come for Thanksgiving, next month, but you must do good in school."

"I am doing good. My teacher says I'm the top of my class."

"Congratulations," I told her. "That means you still need to work hard, though."

"I will. Promise," Reba said.

†

"I'd like to get an early start in the morning," River announced as we sipped coffee. "I have a date with some beaver. If I'm successful, I'll bring you some pelts and meat for the elders before we go to town."

"That sounds good. I've got standing orders for clothes made from beaver hides," Nikita said.

"I'll bring as many as I can harvest without depleting the colony," River said.

"I'll pack these leftovers so you can take them for lunch tomorrow. I know you won't stop working once you get back." Nikita said. "I'll cook an easy breakfast of scrambled eggs and toast if that's good for you?"

"Perfect. Thanks, Mom." She looked at me. "Let's go grab our bags and guns," River said.

When we walked into the bedroom, there was only one bed. "Do you mind sharing?" Nikita asked.

"Not at all," I replied.

"Let me know if you need anything tonight," Nikita said.

"Thank you for a wonderful meal," I said.

"My pleasure," Nikita replied.

"I'll be right back," River said, following Nikita from the room.

I changed into bed clothes and climbed under the covers.

✝

I was beginning to doze when I felt River enter the bed. "Is everything okay?"

"Yeah, Mom was being nosy."

"Nosy?"

River chuckled softly. "She noticed you have a bit of a glow about you and wanted to know if things had changed between us."

"Really? So what did you tell her?"

"That it was none of her business. She pouted, which always works on me, so I told her the truth. We are working on it."

"Working on it?"

"I do not want our first time together to be on the platform at the trapper cabin in the freezing cold."

I snuggled into her. "I don't care where or when it occurs. When the time is right, it will happen."

"Yes, it will," River answered and kissed me. "Snuggle in, and let's get rested to go home."

†

"I hope to see you in a few days with some beavers," River told Nikita when we left.

"You are always welcome," Nikita told me. "Beavers or no." She winked.

"I've never known River not to get her prey," I said.

"Don't jinx me, you two." River climbed onto the ATV. "Love you, Mom."

†

Poe must have heard our approach. He flew next to us on the trail for several hundred yards and landed on the front porch railing. "Hello, my friend," I said. "I have something for you."

"I unwrapped a piece of the corn Nikita had cooked and placed it on the wood pile." I turned to River. "What is his natural food source, anyhow?"

"Besides whatever you feed him?" She laughed. "Ravens can't fish, but they are known as tricksters. They are incredibly intelligent and will scare off other small predators to take their catch or pick leftovers from a large kill."

"What do you think he eats when we're not here?"

273

"Small insects, berries, and seeds he can forage, I would imagine. He doesn't look malnourished at all. His coat is still glossy, and he's a handsome fellow."

"What could I get to feed him if we're gone for days?"

"You could hang dried corn ears or leave a pumpkin or squash. I'll ask Mom to dry some corn for him and keep any culls from her garden."

"Thank you. I worry about Poe when we're gone."

"I know you do. I see the joy on your face every time we return, and he's still here."

†

"I've got this if you want to set your beaver traps," I told River. "I know you're anxious to get them set, and I can finish unloading and start a fire for a bath. I don't know about you, but I'm past due for one."

"Will you wash my back again?" She grinned.

"Back, front, anything you need to be washed," I teased her.

"Keep that up, and those traps won't get set today." She chuckled.

"Take my ATV. It needs to be run, and my sled is empty," I suggested.

River picked up an armful of traps and an ax. "I'll see you soon."

"Be safe. Are you okay with eating the fried chicken leftovers?"

"Absolutely, especially if you add something sweet for dessert."

"I can handle that." I kissed River as she passed by.

†

I was happy to return to our bed, and it didn't take long to unload the sled and set up the house again. I lit the fire in the bathhouse and returned to make a cake for River. "I've got something sweet for you." I laughed as I mixed the batter. I brewed coffee after putting the cake in the oven and sighed. "Now, this is good coffee."

I picked up my notepad and began creating a list for the trip to town. I decided to get two small ceramic heaters instead of one. The stove did an admirable job supplying heat, but I feared it wouldn't be enough in the colder winter months. I surveyed the pantry and added several items to my list. I would add some smaller jars for sauces and cases to add cooked items for River that she could quickly reheat at the trapper cabin. If I could buy some ground beef, I could cook up a large batch of chili to send with River. We were barely home, and I was already planning her first trapping trip. I could relax. She wouldn't leave for several weeks, and I could work on food while she worked on her traps and built snares.

I added items to my list and then brought more wood inside for the stove. My heart raced when I heard the sound of an ATV returning. I had pulled out clean clothes for both of us and planned to do some laundry in the next few days. I looked at River's pants and how worn they had become and decided to add a few pairs for her when we went to town. Her boots were held together with some duct tape, but I would need her presence to try on a new pair. That might be a struggle, but she had more than gotten her money from that pair.

I grinned at the thought of buying clothes and other gifts for River. Not really gifts, as I would explain, but an investment in her safety. Even River couldn't argue that.

†

When I heard the sound of her boots on the porch, I tucked my list away and checked the cake. It was baking nicely and should be ready when we bathed and warmed food for dinner.

"It smells good in here," River said, placing her rifle by the door and removing her coat.

"I figured you could handle eating more cake."

"Most definitely," River answered. "What can I help with?"

"You can carry our clean clothes to the bathhouse and check on the water. The cake will take another hour, so we have time to bathe."

"I'll be right back then," River said, leaving the cabin.

A sudden case of nerves overwhelmed me when I realized we were advancing our physical relationship by bathing together. I felt like a teenager when the door opened, and River returned.

"It's nice and warm when you're ready." She smiled.

River must have seen some apprehension on my face. "Are you okay? Is this too much for you?"

"I'm fine, but I feel like a nervous teenager."

"I can bathe later if you'd feel more comfortable."

"No. I'm fine." I reached for River's hand. "Let's go. I have a back to wash."

It felt good to entwine our fingers as we walked across the yard. My nerves peaked and faded as we undressed and stepped into the tub. We sat facing each other for several minutes, allowing our bodies to adjust to the water.

"This feels good," I said as the water caressed my skin.

"Very relaxing," River said and reached for me.

I turned around and rested my body between her legs. She placed her chin on my shoulder. "Now, this is perfect," River said.

River soaped a cloth and bathed each arm, across my shoulders and chest. She was careful to not allow her hands to contact my breast, even though every inch of me ached for her touch. My nipples had grown hard, and I fought the urge to take her hands in mine to cover my breasts with her large hands.

Breathe, I reminded myself.

"If you lean forward for a minute, I'll wash your back," River said.

The sultry tone in her voice surprised me. I wasn't the only one battling emotions. I leaned forward and relished the feel of her hand on my back.

"Your hair has grown long," River said as she lifted it to wash my back and shoulders.

"My whole body has changed since I got here. I feel much healthier and am getting used to long hair."

"It looks lovely on you, especially at the end of the day when you untie it. I love the way it falls softly around your shoulders. If you lean forward and get it wet, I will wash it for you."

I never realized how sensual having someone wash my hair could feel, but my scalp tingled from the massage River's hands gave me. "That feels good," I moaned. I leaned forward, allowed River to rinse my hair, and then turned to her. "My turn."

River smiled and turned her back to me. I washed her hair, shoulders, and back. I leaned forward and kissed the base of her neck. "You have such beautiful skin."

"Nikita taught me that most people damage their skin by washing so frequently. Our people don't bathe as often as people living in the city, and our skin is enriched by the natural oils we produce."

"I've noticed that even though I perspire, I don't have body odor if I don't bathe for a few days."

"The diet you eat helps with that, and you've learned to bathe when your body gets soiled."

Our sensual bathing experiment had turned into a lesson in self-care, but I didn't mind. Everything River said made total sense. All the chemicals and scents we exposed our bodies to in civilization did more damage than good.

"I'll get Nikita to trim my hair when I'm home next time. It's been a while, and I feel shaggy."

"Would she trim mine as well when I'm ready?"

"You should realize by now that she has adopted you into our family. She will do anything she can for you."

"I feel much love from Nikita and Reba in particular."

"If you hadn't noticed, Reba worships the ground you walk on. She brags to everyone about you teaching her to make jelly and peanut butter bars. I bet there's not one person in the village that hasn't tried one yet."

"That's cute." I was washing my body as we talked. "The water is starting to cool, so we must finish bathing soon."

As we were dressing, River pulled on a sock with a hole in the heel. "There are new socks in your future. Those will need to go to the rag pile soon."

"They have traveled a few miles," River replied, and her eyes sparkled excitedly.

†

The smell of the cake filled the cabin, and I removed it from the oven to cool. "Good thing the water started cooling off, or this might have burned," I teased.

"I would eat it burned as good as it smells."

"I've added a few more cake mixes to my list. I'd like to make a cake and apple pie for our Thanksgiving meal. Is there anything else we can bring?"

River smiled. "There will be more meat than we could eat in one sitting. Prepare for leftovers. Don't forget David, Sonya's husband, will bring seafood home, and Nikita will cook at least one of the geese you shot for her."

"I'm looking forward to it. It's been a while since I've had seafood."

"It's not something we get often because of the cost."

"Another one of the luxuries I have taken for granted, but you know, I don't miss picking up the phone to order food or going to restaurants. There are a few dishes, like calzones, that I miss, but if I tried, I could make my own."

"You are very creative in the kitchen," River agreed. "I've heard of calzones but never had one."

"I will remedy that soon, then," I promised. I placed the food on the stove to warm it. "Would you grab us a beer?"

†

It was growing late when we finished dinner and ate cake for dessert. River patted her stomach. "I cannot eat another bite."

"Let me pick up the kitchen, and we can head off to bed. I know you'll want to check your beaver traps tomorrow."

"Yes, I was excited about all the activity I saw at the colony. I can harvest ten animals quickly and not impact the population. That was a good find."

"I'd like to do more exploring south before winter arrives. There may be other treasures to find."

"That's true," River said as she pulled off her boots and socks.

†

I undressed and prepared for bed. The baking and cooking had it warm inside the cabin, so I changed into a long shirt and panties. River was also sleeping in the bare minimum. We had slept in every piece of clothes we carried with us at the trapper cabin, and it had still been cold, but today we were comfortable.

"It feels great to be back in our bed," I said as I stretched out beside River.

"Yes, it does," River agreed. "It's so much easier to snuggle with you without having five layers of clothes on." She chuckled.

"One and only layer tonight," I said and pulled her in for a kiss,

River's hand rested on my hip, and my movement raised the shirt up my body. As we kissed, I felt her hand inching slowly up my bare skin, and my body thrummed excitedly.

"Wait," I said when I broke the kiss off. I pulled the shirt over my head and tossed it from the bed. I looked at River. "I want to feel your skin next to mine."

River swiftly pulled her shirt off with one quick motion. "Better?"

"Perfect," I replied, rolling onto my back and placing her hand on my chest. I pulled her head down for a kiss and felt the first caress of her hand. "Please," I whispered against her cheek.

†

River's hand played my body like a fine-tuned instrument, bringing me to the edge of release and backing off to build to a climax I was sure could be heard in the village. Her hands and mouth on my body felt like heaven, and I knew we were destined to be lovers. Everything felt so…perfect. Instinct took over as we pleasured one another for hours, slowly and tenderly ending with a primal passion that exhausted us.

I ran my fingertips down River's face. "I've waited all my life to feel this way."

"Which is what?" River asked.

281

"Totally committed and completely in love with someone. That someone I have waited for is you."

I felt a tear wet my fingertips, and I propped up on my elbow. "Why do you cry?"

River took my hand in hers and kissed it. "I've never felt so content in my life. It's overwhelming to surrender my heart to you, but I have no choice. I love you, Tatum."

I felt emotions swirling in my stomach when I heard her words. "I love you, too, River. Almost from the moment we met."

"I did too, but you terrified me. I was afraid I would fall in love with you, and then you would leave. I'm not sure I could handle that."

"I don't plan on leaving. I'm unsure of my future, but I'm positive it is here with you, and we will make the best of life together."

"I can't offer you the finer things in life," River said.

"All I need is you. The rest we will build together," I assured River.

†

The following morning, we woke entangled in one another's limbs. It was amazing to wake up next to the person I loved, and I felt like my life was beginning anew. "I enjoyed last night immensely, but my kidneys are about to explode," I said.

"Better hurry, then, because mine are right behind you."

We dressed hurriedly and rushed to the bathhouse.

"Dear Goddess, that's a relief." I grinned and moved quickly away from the toilet.

"Ah, you are so right," River replied.

"What do you want for breakfast?" I asked as we returned to the cabin.

"A big slice of cake and a glass of milk." River smiled.

"For breakfast? Don't you want something hot?"

"I'll be back from the beaver pond before lunch. We can have something hot then."

"Okay," I agreed and cut a huge portion of cake for her while River poured milk.

"What do you have planned this morning?" River asked between bites.

"I need to catch us up on laundry while you're gone."

"Please add two more bags of salt to our list. I'll need some for curing pelts."

"Anything else you can think of that we need or that you'd like to eat?"

"Not at this moment." River hadn't stopped smiling all morning.

"I think I know what Nikita meant when she said I was glowing. You are, too."

River reached across the table and covered my hand with hers. "You make me extremely happy."

†

I gathered the dirty clothes, built a fire under the washpot, and returned inside. My eyes landed on the iPad, and I realized it had been quite some time since I had made an entry. I turned on the power and chuckled when Poe tapped on the window. I had saved him some corn and took it to the woodpile.

"I haven't forgotten you, my friend."

†

I had to look at the calendar to remind me what day it was. Time was passing so quickly.

October 20th – Day 111

I can't begin to describe how gloriously happy I am. River and I made love for the first time last night, which was terrific. Better than anything I had imagined it would be. We've been working hard and spent a few days up north visiting her trap lines. The environment is so different than here, but I prefer home. The accommodations were rather primitive at the trapper cabin, but my first glimpse of the Northern Lights was a memory I shall have forever. Pictures and videos are nothing compared to the purple and green waves dancing across the sky. I saw my first wolves and a mother bear with her half-grown cub gorging themselves on the dying salmon as they prepped for their winter sleep.

The days are still long, and the work is hard, but I've never been happier.

CHAPTER EIGHTEEN

Three days later, River traveled to the village with five beavers while I stayed home to prepare for the trip to town. I loaded the shed antlers and the bear skull onto the boat and prepared snacks for our journey. I couldn't wait for a bison burger with River at the diner.

I had elk steaks that I would cook for dinner tonight marinating in the sink. We'd finish the cake, and I planned a pan of biscuits for breakfast and snacks.

I placed a bowl of vegetable trimmings on the woodpile for Poe, and then I whittled on the porch while I waited for River to return.

Poe squawked to alert me when he heard River returning. River was smiling as she drove into the yard. "Nikita sent you more veggies and some culls for Poe. She promised to have some dried corn for our next visit."

"Perfect," I replied and took the basket she offered. "Do you want me to add corn tonight?"

"I love your corn," River replied.

"Did you remember to ask her if she needed anything from town?"

"I did. Nikita needs a bag of flour and coffee."

"That's easy enough to add to my list."

†

"It's so good to see you," Erica said when we pulled up to the dock. "I haven't seen you in ages, River. You look well."

"Thank you. Life is good. How have you been?"

"I've been well. Business is good, and the weather kind so far."

"I have a list for you," I said and handed it to her.

"That's not all," River said. "You are going to love this." She pulled the tarp back to reveal the antlers and bear skull.

"Fully intact?" Erica asked.

"Down to every pointed tooth. This is a rare find," River said.

"I agree and will get you top dollar for it. Wow, this is beautiful," Erica said as River lifted the skull up to her. "I know a man in Anchorage who will go batshit crazy when he sees a photo of this. He has deep pockets, too." She grinned. "How long are you in town?"

"Just a day or two," River said. "We wanted to pick up supplies and visit you and Elizabeth."

"Does she know you're in town?" Erica asked.

"Not yet. I have a stop planned for the diner, and we'll walk to Elizabeth's after that," I told her.

Erica plucked out keys and handed them to me. "Take the truck and bring it back tonight for a few beers. I'll work on your order today."

†

"Oh, my word. Tatum and River," Elizabeth cried out when we entered the lobby. "I wasn't expecting you, but your room is open. I'll see if there's another."

"No need," I told Elizabeth with a wink. "We have become adept at sharing a bed."

"I see," Elizabeth said with a grin. "About damn time," she teased. "I've planned dinner for spaghetti, salad, and garlic bread. Is that good?"

"That's perfect. We have a run to make to the grocery store. Is there anything you need?" I asked.

"Not that I can think of unless you want to pick something up for dessert. Ice cream always works. Let me get you the truck keys."

"No need. Erica loaned us hers with an offer to stop by for a few beers later tonight," I said.

"Have you eaten? You know how dangerous it is to shop hungry."

I chuckled. "Yes, I do, so we had a bison burger at the diner."

"Smart move," Elizabeth said. "I'll see you when you get back from the store."

"Thanks, Elizabeth."

†

"It's been ages since I've been inside a grocery store," River said as we walked through the sliding doors.

"Don't worry. I'll protect you."

"Funny," she said as she grabbed a buggy. "Will one be enough?"

"If not, I'll send you back for another." I grinned.

I pulled out my list and guided River through the aisles; our cart filled quickly.

"Do I need to get another buggy?"

"That probably wouldn't hurt," I replied. "I'll be in the produce section."

I browsed the sparse selection of fruits and vegetables while River was gone.

"Hey, baby, can I squeeze your melons," River whispered in my ear when she returned.

"You are so bad," I replied. "Not much left in fruits. One bag of apples and some cherries. Maybe we can check the frozen section for strawberries and bananas. If not, you may be back to syrup crepes."

"It doesn't matter what's inside as long as you make them," River replied.

"That's sweet of you to say."

We entered the meat section, and River's eyes widened at the prices. "Good grief. This is highway robbery. I love my bacon, but damn."

"You're worth it," I said, placing several packs in the buggy. "Is there anyone in the village that raises animals?"

"Only chickens," River answered.

"Could someone raise some pigs and maybe a milk cow or two?"

"It's not for lack of desire, but the start-up cost of getting the animals here is outlandish."

"But it's possible."

"Yes, very much so," River answered.

"Grab two stick pepperonis and two pounds of the Italian sausage. Do you like chili?"

"I do. The spicier, the better," River answered.

"Two pounds of that hamburger meat, too, then."

There was little left in the way of frozen fruit, but I took the last bags of frozen strawberries, and we picked up various ice creams for Elizabeth. "Can you think of anything else we might need?"

"To rob a bank to pay for this?" River said.

"I got this." When we unloaded at checkout, the same familiar cashier checked me out. "Nice addition, *Cheechako*," she said, nodding toward River.

"Thanks. I think so, too."

River shook her head and loaded the boxes of goods into the cart. "What was that all about?" she asked when we loaded the items in the truck.

"She's waited on me every time I've come to the store. She was paying us a compliment for you being with me today."

"Oh, okay." River smiled and closed the door.

When I climbed inside the truck, I looked at River before starting the motor. "After we drop these at the B&B, would you ride back to the Depot with me?"

"Nope, but I'll follow you in Elizabeth's truck to return Erica's."

"There are a few things I want to get, but I need your opinion on them," I replied.

"Opinions are always free," River said.

†

I handed Erica her keys back. "Thanks for the use of your truck."

"Do you need it longer?"

"No, Elizabeth has loaned us hers. But thank you."

"I'm working on your order now," Erica said.

"I've got a few things I'd like to add to it, but I needed River here to make it happen," I said.

"What else do you need?" River asked.

"I need you to find four pair of new pants and socks, and try the pants on," I said.

"I don't…" River started to protest, but I stopped her.

"Stop right there. We've already witnessed your holey socks. We didn't buy nearly enough on our trip to town this past August. And some of your pants are nearly see-through, they are so thin. There's no way I'm sending you north to trap in those. You'll freeze to death."

River chuckled and held her hands up in surrender.

"I've got a new order of work pants that would suit you perfectly. Come with me, and you can try some on for fit," Erica said.

River followed Erica and then disappeared into the changing room. I motioned for Erica to join me. "She needs socks and a new pair of boots, which may be a tough sell. River will also insist on paying for this order, but that won't happen. Please tell her tomorrow that it automatically charged to my account or something. She works too hard for her money to pay for my supplies."

Erica nodded. "That bear skull alone would pay for this order five times over."

"I know, but just add it to her account. She may need to purchase something later."

Erica smiled. "She's lucky to have you."

I shook my head. "I'm the lucky one. What is the best type of boots for her?"

"With or without duct tape?" Erica teased.

"Without, please," I answered.

"I'll pick out a couple of pair. Size nine?"

"Yeah, I think so," I answered.

River walked out of the changing room and turned around slowly. "What do you think?"

"They look delicious on you, but how do they feel?" I asked.

"Very comfortable. These will definitely be warmer than what I have."

"How are you for shirts?"

"I think I'm good there. I grabbed two packs of socks."

"Just one more thing then," I said. "Change and bring those to the counter. Erica is searching for something else for me."

Erica returned from the backroom carrying four boxes of boots. "One of these should work."

River placed the clothes on the counter. "Boots?"

"Uh huh, something not held together by duct tape," I teased.

"I can't argue that."

"Size nine?" Erica asked.

"Yes," River answered. She tried on all four pair and couldn't decide between two. "What do you think? I can't decide."

"No need. Both, please," I told Erica.

"Do you want to wear one of these, and I will place the others in the dumpster for you?" Erica asked.

"Goodbye, old friends," River said as she surrendered her boots.

"They served you well, but it's time for new," I told her.

"I don't need two pair, though."

"Yeah, you need to alternate between these two," I said. "Just think. These will last twice as long."

"She has a point, my friend," Erica said.

"I have no chance of winning this argument, do I?" River asked.

I looked at Erica, and she shook her head. "Nope," we answered together.

"I'll add this to your load. Are you heading out tomorrow?" Erica asked.

River nodded. "Between this and the grocery store, we'd better. This was an expensive trip."

"We didn't buy anything we don't need," I reminded her.

"I've already gotten an offer on that bear skull, but I want to make him sweat a bit more," Erica said. "You've got a nice balance from the antlers you've already brought in. So, don't sweat it. You'll still have a nice credit for anything you need."

"All right," River replied. "I need a beer now."

"Head out to the deck, and I'll bring us some," Erica said.

After drinking two beers with her, we returned to the B&B for dinner.

†

"What have you heard from Troy lately?" I asked Elizabeth over dinner.

"He's still unhappy, but we've agreed he will finish the semester. When he comes home for Christmas, he must decide about a job."

"I don't think he will have a hard time finding something, do you?" I asked Elizabeth.

"It may not be what he wants right off the bat, but between Erica and I, we can keep him busy through the winter."

"Has he mentioned buying a boat and making deliveries or being a fishing guide for your clients?" I asked.

"He has, and those are undoubtedly options. Erica could use another delivery person. Fishing is hit and miss."

"Maybe you could advertise a personal guide on your website to bring more business for both?" I replied.

"That's an idea to ponder," Elizabeth agreed. "I just can't stand to see him so miserable."

"He worried he was letting you down," River said.

"His happiness is much more important to me than any piece of paper. I hope I made that clear to him when he was home. I think he has tried hard, but it's just not his cup of tea," Elizabeth said.

"I would pay extra for him to make deliveries for me," I said. "I'll still come to town every now and then."

"So, you're planning to stay?" Elizabeth said.

293

"Yes. I will ask Dad if he will sell me the cabin when my six months are up," I replied. "I honestly can't see myself anywhere else."

"How do you think Charles will react to that news?"

"I don't know, but that's my decision, even if I have to buy another property. I'll have a realtor liquidate all my assets in Chicago and make this home."

"Charles will understand that. I know how much he loves being here," Elizabeth said.

"I could build onto the cabin, and he can still come to fish," I said. "Mom will be the tough sell, but maybe she will stay here with you while Dad gets his fill of fishing."

†

The trip home was uneventful, but there were areas along the river where ice had begun to form. "Will it start to get colder now?" I asked.

Before River could answer, large flakes began to fall. "I think that's a yes from Mother Nature." She chuckled. "The days are growing shorter, and while it's not entirely dark, it significantly differs from what you've experienced."

When we reached home, we unloaded the goods onto the dock. "We may need to store the motor and boat for winter soon. The river will tell us when it's time."

†

The next few weeks passed quickly as Thanksgiving approached. While River made her snares and checked the beaver traps, I made meals she would take to the trapper cabin. I would ensure she had plenty of food to warm her belly after a long day on the trap lines. The route to the cabin was pretty straightforward, so I felt confident I could travel alone to visit. I planned to lay over with Nikita to split the distance I'd travel. I would bring baked goods and other items she couldn't prepare herself. I would stay a few days before returning home to start the cycle again.

River planned a season of four to six weeks. If the production was good, she would be home sooner. She trapped five more beavers before pulling her sets. When she took them to the village, Nikita asked if we would stay a day or so for Thanksgiving. River assured her we would.

I baked a cake and two apple pies to take for the feast. When the morning came for us to travel, I was excited to participate in the celebration with my new family. Thanksgiving dinners in Chicago had been formal, with meals prepared by my parents' cook and rarely anything ever made by our hands. Here it would be the complete opposite, and I was proud to be able to contribute.

I left an ear of the dried corn for Poe. "We'll be back soon," I promised.

CHAPTER NINETEEN

The village kitchens, grills, and fryers worked overtime to prepare for the feast. The meal would be held at the council hall of the elders to accommodate everyone in the feast. David and some other men had returned home with halibut, shrimp, and clams from the coast. The aromas that filled the air made my mouth water, and when it was time for us to meet at the hall, Reba walked between River and me holding our hands.

Thanks were given to all those who had contributed to the meal, and I was welcomed not as a guest but as the newest member of the community. Many families thanked River and me for providing the food to help them survive the winter, and I felt a genuine appreciation from the village.

Everyone was enjoying the meal when the hall door opened. I felt my mouth open in shock when Troy and my father entered the room. He was the last person I expected to see today.

I stood and walked over to him and wrapped him in a huge hug. "What are you doing here?"

"I've been trying to call my daughter for weeks without success, so I figured you had either gone batshit crazy, been eaten by a bear, or were thriving here. Your mother was not pleased when I mentioned you being eaten by a bear, so she sent me here to check on you. Troy told me you would be here for Thanksgiving, and promised to give me a lift, so we decided to crash the party."

A village elder spoke. "You are more than welcome, Charles. Please make yourself a plate and join us."

River cleared two spots at our table, and I brought glasses of tea for Troy and Dad.

When he sat down, I smiled at him. "I'm sorry, but I haven't checked the sat phone in weeks."

"No kidding," he teased. "Troy has been filling me in on all the work you've been doing. We didn't stop at the cabin, but I saw you significantly improved the camp. Did you cut all that firewood?"

"I did." I smiled. "I feared being caught without enough."

Charles smiled at me. "I'm so proud of you, and you look great."

"I feel great. How are Mom and Charlie?"

"Your mom is okay. Worried when we couldn't reach you, but she's good."

"Charlie?"

"Let's just say he didn't do as well in the wild as you have. He tucked his tail and returned home in three weeks after burning through all the basic food supplies. I wasn't surprised, but you have amazed me."

"You've raised a remarkable woman. The goose you're eating, she provided," Nikita said. "Not only has she added to her food stores, but she has aided many in this community. She and my daughter, River, have hunted all season, and this is the first time in years the village meat locker has swelled with meat, fish, and fowl."

"She's a great cook, too," Reba said as she bit into a slice of cake.

"That, too," Nikita said. "She's even taught this little one and me a few things in the kitchen."

"We made tons of jelly," Reba said.

"Tons, huh? That's a lot of jelly," Charles stated.

"More like ten cases, but it was fun, and many in this village enjoy the jelly," Nikita added.

"You two did a lot of the work," I said. "We wouldn't have half of what we made if you hadn't helped."

"This is a fantastic meal," Charles said. "So much better than our traditional Thanksgiving meal, but I will deny it if you ever tell your mother I said that."

"No problem." I grinned. "I had the same thought earlier. Everything here was grown, caught, harvested, and cooked by our hands. There's little, if anything, store-bought in this meal."

"It looks like the village has grown a bit from my last visit," he said to Nikita.

She nodded. "We've added a few new homes when youngsters return after trying their hand at city life."

"I know that feeling," Troy said. "I've never been more miserable in my life. I'm glad my mother is allowing me to return home."

"How long can you stay?" I asked my father.

"If you're okay with it, I'll stay for a few days. Troy says he'll drop me off and return to pick me up. My flight is open-ended, so there's no set time for me to return."

"You can stay as long as you wish. It's your cabin." I grinned.

River stood to get some dessert and nodded for me to join her. "Why don't you ride back with Troy and Charles, and I'll see you in a day or so. I know you both have a lot to catch up on."

"Promise you'll be home in two days? I know you need to pack for the trapping trip."

"No more than two days." River smiled. "I'll miss you, but you need time to discuss the future with Charles."

"Thank you," I said and selected a small slice of pie and some banana pudding.

"Your pie is fantastic," Troy said. "I keep eyeing that cake Reba has, too."

"You'd better hurry then. It's going fast," River told him.

"Do you want some dessert?" I asked Dad.

"That cake does look good."

"Sit tight, and I'll get him a slice. You're on your own," River teased Troy.

When Troy returned, I looked at him. "Can I ride back with you and Dad?"

"Sure, that's not a problem. The more, the merrier. We will need to leave soon, though. It will already be dark before I get home."

"You could stay the night?" I offered.

"No can do. Erica's got a colossal delivery planned for me tomorrow. She will use me for deliveries when I'm home."

I looked at Nikita. "I'll see you when I take supplies to the trapper cabin in a few weeks."

"Just don't be a stranger. I'll send more corn with River."

"Thank you. Poe has been enjoying it, so I don't feel as guilty leaving him for a few days."

"Poe?" Charles asked.

"A handsome raven that showed up right after I arrived. I named him Poe, and he's stayed ever since," I explained.

"Her protector," Reba said.

"He's been that and a source of entertainment. If I'm later leaving food out for him than he thinks is allowable, he taps on the window until I feed him."

Charles laughed, and I could see the delight in his eyes. "I can't wait to meet him."

†

River and Reba walked with us to the boat carrying plates of leftovers for the trip. River hugged me. "I'll see you in a couple of days."

I nodded and handed the food to Troy to store. I turned to Reba. "Keep her out of trouble for me, will ya?"

"You got it, Tatum." Reba giggled and took River's hand.

"See you soon," Troy called to River and pulled away from the dock.

300

As we pulled away, I turned to find River watching, smiling, and I waved to her. Leaving her behind felt odd, but I knew I'd see her again soon.

I chatted with Dad and Troy as we drove to the cabin. "Have you started looking for a boat?" I asked Troy.

"Nothing serious yet. I'm still thinking about other options," Troy replied.

"A boat?" Dad asked.

"I've been thinking about buying a boat and making deliveries for Erica, and maybe do some tour guide fishing in the summer and fall," Troy explained. He looked at me. "Mom said you had suggested she list it on the website to see if it would help business at the B&B."

"I did. That seems a big draw for this region, so it may work well. You sure can't beat the fishing."

"That's true," he answered. "You should have seen the fish Tatum caught with her gill net. She found a honey hole on her first try. Make sure she cooks some filets for you. I've never tasted anything so delicious. She was damned good with the smokehouse, too. I was lucky enough to have several meals of those. Do you have any moose steaks left?"

"I think so," I answered.

"Wait until you taste her moose. It melts in your mouth it's so tender."

"I didn't think tender and moose belonged in the same sentence," Charles teased.

"The way Tatum cooks, it does. Tatum makes a compote that she covers the meat with that is out of this world."

"Are we sure we are talking about my daughter? I wasn't sure if she knew how to cook."

"Definitely your daughter. Prepare to have your taste buds rocked," Troy said.

"I hope you don't jinx me," I said.

"He is setting the bar pretty high." Charles chuckled.

"Just wait. You'll see," Troy promised.

†

When we arrived at the cabin, I hugged Troy. "Be careful going home, and we'll see you in a few days."

"Have fun showing your dad around. You're gonna be impressed with all her progress."

"I already am," Charles answered and picked up his bag.

"Let's drop that on the porch, and I'll show you around," I suggested.

Poe was preening atop the smokehouse. "This is Charles. He's going to be with us for a few days," I told Poe.

Poe stopped temporarily, eyed Charles, and resumed preening.

"He can be quite the diva at times." I laughed.

I showed Dad the new water storage system and the bush coolers. When he saw all the food inside, he looked at me. "You have been busy. That was genius."

"Troy helped me install both. He's been a good friend and helper on some projects."

We walked to the bathhouse, where I showed him the new power banks. "I wasn't sure I would have enough sunlight to keep my batteries charged, so I added a dozen power banks. It has a tendency to get a bit chilly in here, so I was able to add a small ceramic heater. It puts off enough heat to make it pleasant."

302

"A Blackstone was a smart addition," Charles said when we reached the porch.

"I do a lot of my cooking on it. The two-burner stove takes forever to cook, but I'm managing."

"It sounds like you're doing much more than managing, according to your fan club. I haven't heard the first negative word about you. I have to ask, though, what's that?" He pointed to Poe's bed.

"Poe's condo," I replied with a grin.

He smiled at the small refrigerator/freezer unit when we walked inside. "Another smart move."

"I freeze items and place them in the bush cooler, and they stay cold forever." I removed a large package of salmon and moose steaks and placed them in the sink to thaw.

Charles whistled when he saw the pantry loaded with canned foods. "You learned to can?"

I nodded. "I jar leftovers, too, for an easy meal to reheat."

The menagerie of carvings on the windowsill caught his eye. "Did you do these?"

"All except for the beaver. River did that. I found a knife in one of the drawers and used it. I whittle to pass the time after chores are done."

"An old Case knife?" Charles asked.

"Yes." I pulled it out of my pocket.

"I wondered where I had left that. Your grandfather gave that to me."

"You should take it back then."

"No, you keep using it to carve. These are beautiful." He picked up one of the bears. "Are these animals you've seen or hunted?"

"Most of them are. I started with the salmon and then Poe. That's Brother Bear. We shared a blueberry patch this year."

"Seriously?"

"Yeah, it was a big patch. Brother Bear stayed on his side, and I stayed on mine."

"Were you not scared?"

"I was at first until I realized he was more interested in the sweet berries than me, and we learned to share the space."

"Please don't tell your mother that story. I will never get out of the doghouse for sending her baby girl to live with bears. She's finally forgiven me for challenging you and Charlie."

"That was probably the best thing you could have done for me," I said.

He walked over to the gun rack and studied the necklace. "Your first kill?"

"A moose. I was shaking so bad I didn't think I could aim, but I took it down with one shot."

Charles shook his head. "Incredible. To think, six months ago, you were getting manicures and spa days. Now look at you."

"Do you want a beer?" I asked.

"Sure, that sounds good."

"I'll light a fire, and we can have a few until you get hungry again. Have a seat," I directed and walked to the dock to pull out two beers from the crate.

Charles laughed. "That was genius."

"I devised that before I got the fridge. It keeps beer and food ice cold, and it's convenient."

Charles took a sip of the beer. "Damn, you aren't kidding. I got brain freeze."

I settled into a chair next to him as the fire grew. I looked over at him and smiled.

"I'm jealous," he said.

"Jealous of what?"

"Of how well you have thrived here. I would have never guessed you would make it this far, and you have blown my mind."

"What you presented was the perfect challenge, and it pushed me down a road of self-discovery that I needed to travel."

"So, you don't hate me for sending you here?"

"Hell, no. This has been great."

Charles shook his head. "Charlie still grumbles about the bug bites and starving to death."

"Charlie has always been a wuss," I teased.

"You seem happy. I don't think I've ever seen you smile this much."

"This is a good place for me." I wasn't sure I was ready to broach the subject of staying here yet. "How's the business?"

"Things are good. We landed several projects you did the legwork on before coming here."

"That's great to hear." I took a sip of beer.

A group of geese honked as they flew down the river.

"I've never been here this time of year. It's beautiful and peaceful. Does the solitude ever become too much?"

"Never. It took some getting used to all the quiet at first, but I fell in love with the sounds and smells here. It's so different from the city's noisy, polluted air."

"That's for sure."

"What about companions other than Poe?" He grinned.

"I met River while she was hunting in the area, and she has taught me so much about hunting and harvesting animals. I've been to Glennallen a few times to barter and resupply, and I enjoy visiting with Elizabeth, Erica, and Troy. I've spent some time in the village with Nikita and recently traveled north with River to stay at a trapper cabin and perform maintenance on her trapping lines.

"River sounds like she's important to you. The love you share is obvious, watching you together."

I was shocked by Dad's keen observation. "We have recently become more than friends," I admitted.

"So, tell me about her. I know she's Nikita's daughter, but not much more."

"She is the designated hunter for the village. River supplies all the red meat for the entire population." I took a sip of beer. "Most village men work offshore on fishing boats, so they miss out on the hunting season. River has taken on the burden of hunting and will spend weeks deep in the woods. The other women in the village grow vegetables, forage what they can, and fish."

I paused and took another sip of beer. "I had so many fish, I couldn't store them all, so I began bartering for fresh vegetables in exchange for smoked fish or filets. Once I filled my stores for winter, I started hunting geese and grouse to send to the village." I smiled. "I rarely left the village without a sled full of vegetables or other goods."

"You mentioned trapping. Is that what River does after hunting?"

"Yes, the pelts from the animals she hunts are used for clothing in the village or native goods. The women sell items to raise money to survive the winter. River uses the antlers and the pelts she traps to supplement her income. We've delivered several loads to Glennallen, and Erica brokers the sales for her. When we were up north, we found a grizzly skull that was perfectly preserved. When we delivered it to Erica, I could almost see her salivating. She had an offer for the skull within twenty-four hours but held out for more money for River."

"She sounds like an amazing woman," Charles said.

"She's got an enormous heart and love for her village. Their needs always come first. They were awarded nine permits for caribou this year, and she was gone for weeks searching for the migrating herd. She finally collected the permits, but she was exhausted and had lost weight during the pursuit." I smiled. "She told me she had to chase them to the Arctic Circle. Nikita had to pull the mother's card to convince her to rest for a few days. She was ready to get active after a few days of rest and hot meals."

"Your eyes light up when you talk about her. Do you think it's love? I know I'm being blunt here."

"That's okay, Dad. I am in love with her. I felt empty the few times we've been apart, and since we've become lovers, that's only gotten worse."

I gave him time for that to sink in. "Ready for another beer, and then I'll put dinner on to warm?"

Charles nodded. "I'll try to not get brain freeze this time."

"Amazing how cold it gets, isn't it? I rinse the aluminum bottles and freeze water in them for ice packs when transporting food that needs to stay cold. Works like a charm, and I've always got cold water to drink."

"I love that you have adopted the 'waste nothing' approach."

"There is always a use for items. Sometimes you just need some creativity to come up with an idea."

"What is your plan for tomorrow?" Charles asked.

"To spend it with you. I'd like to show you some of the great locations around here, and maybe we can rustle up a few grouse to add to our menu while you're here. Are you up for that?"

"Sure, but you better do the hunting if you want something to eat." He laughed. "I'm great at fishing but not so much at hunting."

†

After dinner, I noticed Charles was fading fast. "Are you ready to call it a night?"

He didn't hide his yawn. "I do believe I am."

"I want you to take the bed and let me sleep on the cot," I suggested.

"Absolutely not. The cot is fine with me. I will be gone in sixty seconds," Charles teased.

"I need to hit the bathroom, and I'll be ready to turn out the lights," I said. "Do you need anything? More blankets or pillows?"

"No, Tatum. This is perfect."

When I returned, he was already fast asleep. I turned out the lamp, slipped into sleep clothes, and crawled into bed.

†

I woke the next morning surprised to find the cot and cabin empty. Charles had gotten up earlier than I expected. I opened the door, and he sat on the steps, talking with Poe as he broke off bits of cornbread to toss to him for breakfast.

"Good morning," I said.

"Good morning. I hope I didn't wake you laughing at this clown," Charles said with a smile. "He was tapping on the window, and cornbread was all I could find."

"It looks to be working out well for both of you. Ready for some coffee?"

"I would love a cup."

I brewed coffee, carried them to the porch, and sat beside my father. "How did you sleep?"

"I haven't slept that great in years. I woke with energy and excitement to start the day."

"Well, let's enjoy coffee and breakfast, and then we can hit the trail."

†

Charles sliced the remaining strawberries while I whipped up batter for crepes and began cooking on the Blackstone. After cooking a dozen, I returned inside with them and placed bottles of maple, chocolate syrup, and fresh blueberries on the table.

"This looks delicious," Charles said as he began building a crepe.

"I normally use banana slices with the strawberries, but the fruit was wiped out on my last trip to town."

"I don't think either of us will go hungry." Charles smiled and took a bite. "Damn, these are good."

"What would you like for dinner tonight? We have salmon filets and moose steaks, and I can pull out more geese. I hope we get some grouse today, too."

"When do you expect River to come home?"

"Probably tomorrow," I answered.

"Let's do the salmon tonight and save the steaks for when she's home," he suggested.

I smiled, pleased with his acceptance of River as essential to my life.

"That works for me," I replied. "One more cup of coffee, and I'll be ready to roll."

When we finished coffee, I pulled on my shoulder rig and then my coat.

"I'm happy to see you wearing protection," Charles said.

"It's become a part of my wardrobe." I grinned and pulled down the twenty-two, checking to ensure it was loaded and slipping a box of shells into my coat pocket.

†

I placed the rifle in the gun rack across my handlebars, and after giving the motor time to warm up, I mounted the ATV and offered a hand to Charles to climb on board. We drove to the larger lake first, and I explained this was where we hunted most of the larger animals.

"I use the smaller lake for geese and waterfowl because it's more shallow and easier to retrieve downed birds with the cast net."

"I could see where a canoe might come in handy here," he replied.

"Possibly, but I've managed without one."

When we reached the blueberry patch, I was surprised that there were still berries in the bushes. "This is where the berries from breakfast came from."

Charles picked a handful and popped them in his mouth. "So sweet and juicy," he said. "I know you mentioned berries. What else have you found?"

"Cranberries and cloudberries," I replied.

"I've never heard of cloudberries," Charles said.

"Let's ride, and we can check to see if some are still available."

I drove the ATV to the place where we had picked the cloudberries. It wasn't as large as the blueberry patch, but there were still a few ripe berries.

"Let me warn you before you pop those in your mouth. These are not as sweet as the blueberries. I usually have to add sugar to them, but they made great jelly."

He tentatively placed three berries in his mouth and chewed. "Even these are not bad."

"I can send a few jars back with you if you'd like. Troy could get Erica to package them for travel for you."

"I'd like that. Your mother would probably never believe you were making jelly without some evidence," he said and then frowned. "I'm sorry the way that came out."

"I know what you meant. I have changed so much since arriving. I've done things that were never in my wildest dreams before."

As we talked, several grouse landed in trees around the berry patch. I motioned for Charles to be quiet and lifted the rifle to my shoulder. Two birds were down before the rest were startled and flew away to other trees. "Let's collect those and see if we can find a couple more."

Charles nodded and walked with me to collect the birds. We placed them in the rear storage rack and drove deeper until we found more birds. When we stepped off the ATV, I grinned at Charles and handed him the rifle. "You try. Aim for the chest."

Charles smiled, and after steadying his aim, he pulled the trigger. Feathers began fluttering to the ground.

"There is another ten feet to the right," I instructed.

Charles shot another bird, and I could see the sparkle of excitement in his eyes. "That was great shooting," I praised.

"Thanks. Wasn't as hard as I feared, but they were sitting still," Charles grinned.

"Geese and ducks are a bit more challenging."

"I can only imagine," he replied as we walked to pick up the birds.

"This should make for a decent meal for two. Are you up for more exploring tomorrow?"

"Absolutely," Charles answered.

"I'd like to show you the eagles and the beaver colony, but they are farther south."

"Sounds perfect to me."

As we drove by the blueberry patch, I sensed movement and slowed. Looking across the field, we saw Brother Bear stand on his hind legs to check us out.

"Dad, meet Brother Bear."

"Even from this distance, he looks huge," Charles said.

"He's a big boy." I chuckled and drove home.

†

After processing the grouse, I placed them in the sink to brine. "I'll cook these for lunch if you're okay with dinner being a bit later."

"I'm perfectly fine with that. You haven't disappointed me yet. Could we have a cup of coffee and chat for a few minutes? I'd like to run something by you."

"Sure, sit, and I'll make some coffee."

Charles walked to his bag and returned with a large envelope.

When I finished the coffee, I sat across from him. "What's up?"

"I had an inkling of your success when I hadn't heard from you in ages, but I needed to come to see for myself. I've got a couple things I would like to discuss."

I nodded. "I'm listening."

"The first is your desire to return to Chicago. I thought at first you may have become enchanted with the fairy tale quality of the assignment, but watching you today and listening to you talk, it's more than enchantment. Unless I am horribly misreading you, this is where you wish to be." He paused and looked at me.

"I have fallen in love with everything here and never felt so happy or healthy. I thought I would miss the hustle and bustle of the city and the challenges of long hours in the corporate world, but I don't. I work much harder for extended hours here but feel at peace. Does that make sense?"

"I agree completely with that statement," Charles answered. "I would like to propose something to you. Rightfully, the CEO position should be yours after Charlie failed miserably in his assignment, but I don't feel that's your dream anymore. I propose that you are a third business owner and sit on the Board of Directors in absentia. Charlie will do a fine job of maintaining the business, but I don't think he has what it takes to grow it further, and I'm good with that." He paused. "You and I will step back from the business and still draw quarterly checks from the company as income."

"I wouldn't be working locally, but still draw a check?"

"That's correct. You have more than paid your dues in building this company into what it is today, and now it's Charlie's turn to step up to the plate."

"Have you discussed this with Charlie, and he's okay with it?" I asked.

Charles' face turned stern. "I don't need his permission to make decisions on behalf of my company. Charlie will be delighted to no longer feel a need to compete with you because he knows deep down that you run circles around his performance. I will allow him the control, but I won't hesitate a heartbeat to shut him down if he starts making unwise moves."

He pushed a few pages across the table for me to review. "Look at those while I nap today. Your signature will seal the partnership as I have discussed with you."

He took a sip of coffee. "The other discussion we need to have is your life here. I have had the legal boys draw up a transfer of deeds to this cabin to you under one condition."

"What's that?"

"That I can come for a visit and fish anytime I wish." He grinned.

"I only have one problem with that," I replied. "You need a new fly rod. I have taken possession of yours and made her my magic stick."

Charles broke into laughter. "I can certainly handle that. I see how much you love this place, and what you've done to upgrade it is marvelous. I hope you accept my offer and make it a permanent home for you and River. Add onto it, grow a garden, whatever you need to do."

I couldn't hold back the tears that slid down my face.

"Why are you crying?"

"Because I'm delighted by your offers and relieved. I've been figuring out how to have this conversation for weeks. The last thing I've ever wanted to do was disappoint you or let you down."

"You've done neither. I am so proud of you and all you have accomplished here and in Chicago. The change I've seen in you is remarkable, and I can't imagine you ever being this happy in Chicago running the business. You would work yourself to an early grave and have no family or life to show for all your sacrifice. I don't want that for you."

I walked to him and pulled him into a hug. "Thank you for everything. I will read through the documents, but my answer is a resounding yes."

"I'm not sure I could convince your mother to visit, so you must come to visit occasionally. I hope to return for a lot more fishing."

"Speaking of which. If you want to wet a fly, I haven't fished from the dock for a few days. The salmon are gone for the season, but the trout and white fish are both tasty. You could fish while I prepare lunch, and we'll add anything you catch to dinner."

"I guess I really don't need a nap." He grinned.

"The rod and tackle box is at the end of the porch. I'll read over these, sign, and prepare lunch."

Charles left the cabin wearing a smile that I was sure would match the one on my face. Life was good. Life was very, very good.

†

I skimmed over the papers and signed them before slipping them inside the envelope. I couldn't wait to share the news with River when she returned home. We had planning to do.

I prepped the grouse for frying on the stove and put rice on to cook. I used the drippings to make a rich flour gravy, and when everything was ready, I stepped outside to call for Dad.

He turned toward me and lifted the stringer with three fish. "Just one more," he said.

I laughed, nodded, and plucked two beers from the crate as I joined him on the dock. "Addicting, isn't it?"

"Yeah, to walk out your front door and catch a meal is something else."

When he landed the next fish, I looked at him. "Put it on the stringer, and we can clean them after lunch. Then if you feel tired, you can nap," I teased. "Or do more fishing."

"I'd like to fish more if that's okay. Replenish the food we'll be eating the next two days."

"That's fine with me. I will kick back at the firepit and carve while you fish."

†

Lunch was delicious, and while Charles fished, I began carving. Soon Brother Bear appeared in the wood, standing on his rear legs. Just as we had seen him earlier. When I finished, I held him over the fire with tongs until the wood became scorched. Then once it cooled, I used some oil to make the grains shine through. *Handsome bear, even if I do say so myself.* I placed him on the table where Charles would sit for dinner.

Charles was in heaven fishing from the dock, so I returned inside to prep the filets for cooking and preboiled corn for grilling. I diced potatoes and onions to fry on the grill and made a compote to spread over the cooked fish. I decided to cook a trout and a white fish Charles had caught to provide a sampling of fish for him. The rest I sealed in a bag and stuck in the freezer.

†

Charles cleaned up from fishing and joined me in the kitchen. "What can I do to help?"

"Have some coffee with me for starters, then you can replenish the wood bucket next to the stove while I prep the grill for cooking. Then you can grab a seat on a bucket while I cook."

"Those all sound doable." He smiled.

I placed a cup in front of him and pointed to the carving.

"You made Brother Bear for me?"

"Yes. I never know what to make until the animal appears in the wood, so Brother Bear is today."

"He's beautiful. You really have a talent with a knife."

I chuckled. "I haven't tried a moose yet, but the smaller animals seem to come easily. I figured I would have all winter to experiment with a moose."

I pushed the envelope toward him. "All signed and with great thanks."

He placed the package back in his bag. "I'm happy to see how much you love it here. I've only gotten a small taste when I've come to fish, but you've made this a home. What other plans do you have now that it's yours?"

"I'd like to add another bedroom to the cabin and maybe a small sleeping space in the bathhouse now that we have heating sorted out. Troy usually sleeps on the boat when he visits, so extra space would be convenient."

"He may never go home." Charles chuckled.

"I would like to start a garden plot and maybe a greenhouse. The soil is good, but Nikita said it takes years of amendments and care to make it produce well."

"Maybe add a compost bin to use in building up your soil. Food scraps and fish would add many nutrients and provide another use for the scraps," Charles suggested. "If you had a larger smokehouse, you could smoke more fish and meats to barter in Glennallen once you have enough stored and share with the village."

"If the salmon run was typical this year, I will have plenty of fish to barter next year. I can experiment with smoking more meats for jerky. I bet that would be a good seller."

"What will you do with your home and vehicle in Chicago?"

"I'll get my realtor to liquidate everything and donate clothing and other items I won't need. Will you ask Mom if she will store personal items like photographs and anything else she would think I'd want?"

"I bet she would offer to buy your car. She's been hinting about an electric car for months."

"Sold," I said. "Let's keep her in the family."

"I'll have a check transferred to your account when I return. Just tell me how much you want."

"Whatever the trade-in value would be. That should be a fair figure."

"Done," Charles said. "I know you probably won't need money, but if you ever do, please don't hesitate to ask."

"Thanks, Dad. After a few additions here, I won't need much money to survive. I'll try to fly home a couple times a year, but other than occasional groceries, I won't need as much."

"Speaking of groceries, I think I worked up an appetite."

"I'll start cooking while you bring in some wood."

†

Charles watched in amazement as I cooked dinner on the Blackstone. "That is a handy piece of equipment."

"I can cook almost everything on it and do," I replied. "Breakfast, lunch, and dinner."

I turned the corn, potato, and onion mix while the fish cooked slower. I added two fish Charles had caught and experimented with various spices and sauces.

Each time I lifted the lid, he moaned loudly.

"Damn, that smells good."

"Wait until you taste it," I said and walked inside to rinse the pan to carry the cooked food inside. I picked up the syrup bottle and added some to the salmon and trout pieces. I sprinkled two ears of corn with ranch and two with Parmesan cheese. "I think we're ready. Will you hold the pan for me?"

I carefully removed the fish, which threatened to crumble, then the vegetables. "Put that in the middle of the table, and I'll grab the compote and some water unless you want another beer."

"Another cold beer sounds good. I'll come back for them in a minute," Charles said, following me inside.

I placed the bowl of compote on the table. Charles handed me a beer and sat. "Where do we even start?"

I explained the different flavorings of the fish. "Try a portion of each and help yourself to more if you like it. We've got plenty."

I broke a piece of corn in half and took it out for Poe. "Maybe we can eat in peace."

I served myself and watched Charles sample each fish, his smile growing with every bite.

"I can't say I have a favorite. They all taste good and are different. What's your favorite?"

"I'm partial to the salmon with maple syrup or brown sugar," I answered. "However, the trout with the blueberry compote comes in a close third."

"I love this corn, too," Charles said, taking a bite. "You are a creative cook."

"I've enjoyed experimenting with different spices and sauces. Eating the same fish, fowl, or game can get dull quickly if it's always the same."

"I would have never dreamed of some of these combinations, but they are wonderful."

"The compote is another way to use up the berry pulp from the jelly."

"Waste nothing." Charles grinned.

"Exactly."

†

"Damn, I forgot a dessert. I can whip up some pudding or peanut butter bars quickly."

"After that meal, I couldn't dream of eating another bite," Charles said with a groan. "That was one of the best meals I've ever eaten."

"Maybe it will hold you until breakfast."

"No doubt it will. I think I went up a pant size today."

"Careful, or I'll put you to work splitting wood or something," I teased.

"I'll do anything you need," Charles answered.

321

"I was kidding. Tomorrow, we will explore the south. We might push a little farther to see what we can find. I'll fix a hearty breakfast, and we can pack some of the biscuits I've got cooking with some meat for lunch."

"Oh, lord, don't make me think of food right now," he groaned. "You've got to promise me something before I leave."

"What's that?"

"You will give me a few days with your mother to soften the blow that you're not returning, and then you should call her. I've already prepaid the satellite phone, so you can call as often as you like."

I nodded, walked to the counter where it sat, and plugged it in. "You did call a few times." I hung my head. "After a while, I forgot I had it. No excuse, but it's the truth."

"Just don't forget again. I'd like to hear from you at least every two weeks, weekly preferred." Charles grinned.

"I promise to check for missed calls more often, too. I didn't mean for you to worry needlessly."

"I don't have to worry anymore. You are doing so well here."

"Thank you for sending me here. It's the best thing to ever happen to me."

"I know you don't have internet service, but I want to snap pictures of you and River tomorrow."

"Proof of life?" I teased.

"That and to show your mother how happy you are and how good you look."

"I think that can be arranged. I expect River tomorrow afternoon. I wish you could stay longer and we could take you to see the northern lights at the trapper cabin. They are so beautiful."

"I have an idea," Charles said. "I'll get a digital camera shipped to Erica, and you can take photos to send me of what you and River are doing. Snail mail is better than nothing. I bet Elizabeth in Glennallen has internet service."

"That would be great," I answered. "I could email photos to you when we go to town."

"You know, I was thinking about something else while fishing."

"Should I be afraid?"

"It's about Troy."

"He's a fine young man," I said.

"I was chatting with the bush pilot, Tom, who flew me here from Anchorage. He told me the area desperately needed more pilots, but few were willing to be bush pilots. Do you think he could get his pilot's license?"

"I think Troy could do anything he sets his mind on."

"I think it would expand Erica's ability to make deliveries, bring in a flight and stay package for the B&B, and be good for the town in general."

"I don't argue that at all. The school will be expensive but Troy has college money. What do you suggest for a plane?"

"A personal loan between Troy and me that he can pay back with interest when he starts his business."

"Wow, that's a generous offer. Troy would probably jump all over that prospect."

"I want to meet with him, Erica, and Elizabeth before I head home to hammer out the details."

"Properly equipped, there are very few areas he couldn't travel to," I said. "He could hook up with hunting guides and transport their customers. There's a world of possibilities other than just delivering goods. I like the idea."

"It gets him home and working with the people he loves," Charles said.

"Yes, it does. It's no wonder people think so highly of you here," I replied.

"I fell in love with this place and its people the first time I visited. I have money to invest and can't think of a more worthwhile investment."

"Just make sure everyone is sitting down when you make the offer. We don't need anyone passing out and going to the hospital for a head wound."

"Noted," Charles said with a chuckle.

"Will you share your idea with River? She may have some additional suggestions."

"I planned to, but I wanted to run it by you first."

†

I had difficulty sleeping. My mind whirled with all the excellent ideas Charles shared, and I was excited to begin new projects. I thought about David and some of the other men in the village being home for several weeks and wondered if I could hire them to build the addition to the cabin and bathhouse. River would soon be gone trapping, and I had no construction experience. Paying them would also assist their families during the winter. The cabin addition could be a large bedroom, and we could add a fireplace to help keep it warm. Yeah, I liked this idea. I couldn't wait for River to return so we could get some projects off the ground.

†

Charles was outside having a conversation with Poe when I stepped outside. He had snagged a biscuit off the counter and was tossing bits to him in a game of catch. "He's very talented," he said when I emerged.

"Yes, he is. I'll use the bathroom and start on breakfast. It feels like snow is in the air this morning."

After we ate omelets, I packed some biscuits with meat into my daypack. "Are you ready to explore?"

"I am," Charles answered and pulled his coat on. "Let's roll."

We had barely left the yard when the snow began to fall in large, spiraling flakes. The deeper we traveled, the more the snow started sticking to the ground and trees. Limbs quickly became covered, adding more beauty to the landscape. We slowed as I neared the eagle's nest. I held my breath, hoping the pair were home. I was pleased when the two adults popped up in the nest, and an eaglet appeared between them. "That's a relief. I didn't see the baby the last time I came through, which worried me."

"They are such majestic creatures," Charles said as we watched one bird, which we presumed was hunting for breakfast, leave the nest.

"The farther north you go, the more you see. We saw many on the trip to the trapper cabin, with nests along the river and around the lake." I was surprised when we watched the bird dive suddenly and reappear a moment later with a rabbit in its talons.

"Breakfast is served," Charles said.

I waited for the eagle to return to the nest before driving on. The pond was filled with activity as beavers swam everywhere, adding sticks and limbs to bolster the lodge. "Didn't you say River harvested ten from this pond?"

"Yes, and you can see quite a few still left."

"She probably kept some of them from starving this winter," Charles said.

"I hadn't thought of it like that, but you're right."

I turned to look at him. "Beyond this point is virgin territory for me. Are you game to explore a little farther?"

"I would be disappointed if we didn't," Charles said. "You can see the ice forming around the pond's edge. I wonder how long it will be before it is completely iced over?"

"It's difficult to tell. This isn't the first snow, but the first one to stick like this. Maybe we have turned a corner heading into winter?"

I followed a game trail for thirty minutes until it opened into the biggest lake I had seen.

"I bet this place is full of geese and ducks in the fall. By the looks of the game trails heading to the lake, I'd say there are some bigger animals, too."

We drove by grouse that perched on branches, with snow covering their feathers. I knew we had food for dinner, so I did not shoot them. I circled the lake and saw the skeleton of an old cabin hidden in the trees. I stopped, and we walked to inspect it. From the charred timbers partially buried in the ground, it was evident at some point the place had burned.

Dad circled the building and called out to me. He knelt by a stack of rocks and pointed out a prominent cornerstone. The number 1931 was chiseled into the stone.

"I guess that answers one question," Charles said.

I rummaged through a pile of debris and pulled out two traps. I held them up to inspect them. "Similar to some that River uses, but these must be very old. I'll take them to show her and see if she can salvage them."

Further inspection of the building revealed a gravesite with a worn wooden cross. Reading anything inscribed in the wood was impossible. "At least one person never returned," I said.

"If I had to guess, I would say trappers stayed here to hunt otter, beaver, and other fur-bearing animals. It was a big trade back in those days. It's impossible to tell if the cabin was set on fire or burnt in a wildfire. The trees in the area don't appear scorched, but after nearly a hundred years, any damage would be long gone."

"We'll probably never know," I said.

After eating biscuits, we climbed onto the ATV and checked the time. River would be on her way soon. The snow fell in earnest as we reached the main trail back to the cabin. I pulled the ATV into the shed and smiled to see River's was already in place. The engine still ticked from cooling down, so I knew she hadn't been home long.

"Thanks for exploring with me," I told Charles as we walked across the yard.

"I had a great time. Thanks for sharing that with me."

River had heard us arriving and was making coffee when we entered the cabin. I removed my jacket and walked over to her to kiss her.

"Welcome home."

She looked surprised when I kissed her and glanced quickly at Charles for his reaction. I smiled at her startled look. "We have a lot to discuss."

We sat around the table sipping coffee while Dad and I discussed the agreements we had made.

"I love that Tatum has you in her life, and it's apparent you two belong together. I'll miss not having her in Chicago, but now I will have two reasons to come to Alaska," he told River.

"You are welcome anytime." She smiled.

"Dad also has an idea for Troy he wants to share with you and get your opinion."

She listened to his proposal, her smile growing with each passing moment.

"He would be a fool to pass on that offer, and Troy is no fool. I can easily see him doing great business as a bush pilot. Erica can significantly expand the territory where she can offer deliveries, too, and the human transport to hunting or fishing camps alone could be profitable. It could benefit Elizabeth's business, too, to make a flight and stay package for the B&B. I love the idea, and I'm positive he will, too." She smiled. "Another option is delivering goods and replacement staff to some of the remote ranger stations, which would pull in federal and state revenue."

"That's good thinking," Charles said. "I'll add that to my list of discussion items."

"You two have been busy since you got home."

"Dad and I did some exploring, and he met Brother Bear. We ventured south today and found a burned-out trapper

328

cabin from 1931. We found a couple of old traps and a gravesite, but we couldn't determine who was buried there."

"There's another vast lake, too, with all kinds of game trails leading to it. Tatum also forgot to tell you I shot my first grouse yesterday, which we had for lunch."

"He also caught fish from the dock, which we added to dinner last night."

"Which was one of the best meals I've ever eaten."

"You two have been busy," River said. "I feel like I've been slacking compared to you."

"I'm surprised Reba didn't return with you," I said.

"Oh, she tried, so I promised her I'd return for her in a few days," River said.

"She's an adorable child and worships you both as her heroes," Charles said.

"Reba is a fantastic kid," I agreed.

"I hope you didn't mind me agreeing to a visit," River said.

"Not at all. I want to discuss a proposal with David to build an addition here and add a small room to the bathhouse. I don't have construction skills, and you will be trapping, but I'm sure he can lead us in the right direction and generate some income for the families."

"David is a skilled carpenter and would enjoy a project like that."

†

"I'm going to get started on supper," I said as I put a pot of water on to boil pasta. "You can stay in here or join me outside."

"Beer?" Charles asked River.

"That sounds good to me," River answered. "Make it three?"

"Sure. I'll be out in a few minutes."

"Do you want me to start the grill?" River asked.

"Yes, please."

†

I watched them leave and then made a bowl of pudding to chill for dessert. There was corn left from last night to grill, so as soon as the water started to boil, I dropped the pasta inside and mixed up Parmesan cheese and some spices to add to the cooked pasta with a dash of olive oil. *I really am getting good in the kitchen.* I smiled and walked out to join Charles and River.

"Thanks," I said when River offered me a beer. I checked the grill and sat beside her. "A few more minutes, and I can start the steaks."

"Man, you have a treat coming your way," River told Charles. "You can cut her moose steaks with a fork."

"Maybe, but use a knife to make it easier to eat," I replied. I was happy to share a beer and a meal with my two favorite people.

†

"Last night was fantastic, but I think you've outdone yourself tonight," Charles said. "I always thought moose was

330

tough and stringy, but that cut like the best filets in the world."

"I told ya." River chuckled.

"I can't believe how quickly this visit has gone," Charles said when he sipped coffee after dessert.

"You can come back anytime," I said. "It's been great to share this experience with you."

"What time do you think Troy will be here?" he asked.

"He's an early riser, so I'd bet by noon," River said.

"One last meal with Troy here?" Charles asked.

"What would you like?" I asked.

"More fish?" Charles asked.

"Crap, I forgot to tell you David sent a large halibut filet. I put it in the bush cooler."

"Fish it is, then," I said.

"Will you halve some of the Brussels sprouts for me in the morning?" I asked River.

"No problem."

"What can I do?" Charles asked.

"You can help us measure for the additions," I said. "I'd like to talk to David about dimensions and get a supply list developed and ordered as soon as possible."

"That's painless."

"You're welcome to do a bit more fishing if you want."

"We'll see what the weather is like in the morning. I may be hovering around the heater if it continues to drop and snow tonight," Charles answered.

"Good point. There's ice forming along the banks already. I saw quite a bit driving home today."

"How do you travel in the winter?" Charles asked. "Do you have snow machines or use the ATVs?"

"The village owns a snow machine I use for trapping once the snow gets deep. We will travel between here and the village to keep the trail open for most of the winter."

"I need to make a visit to the bathhouse. Would you mind if I use the sat phone to confirm when Troy will be here?"

"Knock yourself out. Turn the heater on if you will be there long," I teased.

"Got it. Should I leave it on for you?"

"Yes, please. I'll pick up the kitchen and relax until you return. Then we can get ready for bed," I replied.

"I won't be long," he said, walking to the door.

†

"Can you believe how well things are turning out for us?" I asked River.

She laughed. "I nearly had a heart attack when you kissed me in front of Charles."

"He's very cool with our relationship if you haven't figured that out," I told her.

"That's a big relief." She pulled me into her arms for a deep kiss. "I've been thinking about kissing you all day."

"I will be all yours again tomorrow," I said.

†

"We have plenty of biscuits left over. How about I make some gravy to cover them, and you can also try some of the jellies," I suggested.

"Don't let me leave here today without some to take home," Charles said.

"I have one request. Will you make a cake?" River asked. "I felt shorted when I only got one piece of the last one." She pouted.

"No problem. I'll put it in to bake while breakfast is cooking," I said. I finished my coffee and mixed the cake batter before heating the biscuits and making a thick gravy.

"I love the smell in here when you cook," River said as she hugged me from behind.

I turned in her arms. "Will you box some jelly for Dad before we forget?"

River nodded. "Do you want to send a jar or two of the canned fish since you have plenty?"

"That works for me," I said as I resumed stirring the gravy. "Where's Charles?"

"He wanted to walk out to the dock to check for fish. It's pretty cold out, so I think he'll want to stay inside where it's warm until Troy gets here. It will be a cold ride, but the console on the boat will offer some protection from the wind."

Seconds later, Charles walked through the door. "I can't believe how much colder it is this morning."

"We'll keep the stove and heater going and stay inside after we take some quick measurements," I said.

†

We used wood rounds to mark the two additions, and I wrote down the dimensions. It was exciting to see them in place, and I couldn't wait to get them built. We talked for hours, and when noon approached, I started cooking lunch. Troy would need to quickly turn around to arrive home before it got too dark to travel safely. I was surprised when Poe announced Troy's arrival.

"Someone's early," I said. We walked onto the porch, and I got the grill warming. I was surprised to see Troy backing the boat next to the dock.

We walked out to meet him, and I was curious about large items stored under tarps.

"Ho, ho, ho," Troy said, slipping a red Santa hat on his head.

"What's up with the Santa hat?" River asked.

"I'm delivering an early Christmas gift for you two," Troy said, pulling back the tarp to reveal two new Arctic Cat snow machines.

"What the hell?" I asked.

Troy laughed. "Santa called in an order, and I loaded up my floating sleigh and brought them."

I looked at Charles. "This was the call you made last night?" I asked. "I thought you were calling Troy."

"Oh, I did call Troy. After I called Erica to see if she could get her hands on these babies," Charles replied. "I can't wait to come out and ride them once you've got them broken in."

"You can't do this, Dad. It's too much," I told him.

"Too late. There is a no-return policy." Charles laughed. "I can't have you two getting stranded in thick snow, now can I?"

River looked at me in shock. "Are you serious?"

"Deadly," Charles replied. "Merry Christmas."

"I get the black one," River said and jumped onto the boat. Did you bring ramps?"

"Do I look like a rookie? Wait, don't answer that. Yes, I have ramps. Let's get these babies offloaded. I hear there's a big lunch planned."

"I better get to cooking," I said, returning inside with tears running down my cheeks.

"These are beauties, Charles," River said as she inspected the vehicles. "I brought more gas and oil, too," Troy said.

"I'll take those to the shed while you two youngins unload these," Charles said, carrying gas cans and a case of oil to the shed.

River carefully drove the machine down the ramp onto solid land and parked it in front of the porch while Troy unloaded the second.

"I dunno," River said. "The red one is pretty, too."

"I'm with you, though. I like the black one better," Charles said.

River nearly snapped Charles in two when she gave him a bear hug. "I could ride to the north pole on this bad boy."

"I hope it will help you during trapping season and give Tatum a reliable means of visiting you at the trapper cabin."

"Thank you so much. It is a lot, and I could never repay you," River said.

"All I can ask is that you take good care of my baby girl," Charles said.

"I will do my very best," River promised and wiped away tears.

†

When I emerged from the cabin with the pan of fish to cook, River, Charles, and Troy were busy admiring the snow machines.

"I had no idea about helmet size, but Erica says she will fit each of you on your next visit," Charles told River. "I've picked out ones with a heating unit to keep your head warm." He grinned.

"This is incredible," River said as she hugged Charles again.

The snow continued to fall as we moved inside to eat lunch. "You may get enough snow today to test the machines," Charles told River.

"We may just ride one to the village to pick up Reba. There looks to be plenty of room for three to ride safely," River said.

†

"I hate to break up the party, but we need to leave soon," Troy said. "I wish we could stay longer, but you have a plane to catch in the morning."

"I know," Charles said. "It's been a great visit, and I'll be back soon."

"Will you call me tonight to let us know how tonight goes?"

"I'll call from the airport," Charles smiled, "with good news, I'm sure."

River handed Troy a box of jelly and canned fish. "Will you get Erica to package these for travel?"

"Absolutely," Troy answered and reached for Charles' bag.

Charles waved him off. "You go ahead. I've got this."

"I'll see you soon," Troy said, leaving to warm up the boat.

"Thanks, Troy," I called out.

Charles turned to us. "I had a fantastic time and am excited to return. Would it be okay to visit at Christmas?"

"Absolutely," River said. "We will spend Christmas Eve day in the village and Christmas day here. If the weather is suitable, we plan to go to Glennallen the day after."

"I'm sure we can coordinate a visit," I said. "Hopefully for longer next time. A week at least?"

"I don't see a problem with that," Charles replied. He hugged us and had tears in his eyes when he said, "I love you both and hope you will always be happy together."

I reached for River's hand. "We are going to give it our best shot."

We walked to the boat together, and Troy stored Charles' bag.

"Don't forget to call," I said.

"Don't forget to answer," Charles teased.

"I won't. I'll start carrying the phone so I don't miss your calls."

We stood hand in hand on the dock, waving until the boat moved out of sight.

†

I looked at River, and tears were flowing down her cheeks. I wiped them away and kissed her as the snow landed in her hair. "You are so magnificent."

"Even when I'm ugly crying?"

"Yes, because I know those are tears of happiness," I replied. "So what do you think? Is there enough snow on the trail for the snow machine?"

"Probably, but I would prefer to wait until I'm sure. The machines are such a special gift. I don't want to damage one right off the bat."

"I agree. Will you pull these under the shed and bring out an ATV to drive to the village while I pick up from lunch?"

"Yeah." River smiled. "I think our building projects just grew. We need storage for these babies, but that should be an easy extension to build."

†

I watched River through the kitchen window as I washed dishes and relived the events of the past few days. My heart swelled when she looked to see me watching her, and she waved at me. I had never felt so loved in my life. I waved and finished in the kitchen before grabbing my coat and walking outside.

River sat atop her ATV and reached out her hand to help me onto the back of her machine. My body melted into hers as I snuggled close and wrapped my arms around her middle. I never wanted to let go of the beautiful woman who had changed my life.

†

When we returned home with Reba, we ate and prepared to retire. When I returned from the bathhouse, River had already placed a sleeping Reba under the covers and sat on the edge of the bed waiting for me.

"I have one more thing I need to do tonight," I said, picking up the iPad. "Go ahead and stretch out, and I'll be there soon."

I sat at the table and waited for the unit to power up. For a minute, I watched the cursor blink, then took a deep breath and began typing.

November 28th – Day 151? It's been so long since I made an entry.

This will be my last entry on this thread. What began as a challenge has become a brand new life for me. Never in my wildest dreams did I believe I could fall so deeply in love with a woman, a wilderness, and a village of people, but that dream has been realized here. The test Charles assigned me to gauge my ability to run the family business was passed with flying colors. Still, I realized my future was not in Chicago running Chastain International. It is here in the bush of Alaska, living a life of freedom and independence like I have never experienced.

Today marks the beginning of my new life with the woman I love beside me. Our path will have challenges, but I am confident our love will bring us through any obstacle. So, today, I say goodbye to my old life and immerse myself in a new journey. The end of one leads to the beginning of the next, and I look forward to filling these pages with adventures and life with River.

I smiled and powered down the iPad, then entered the bed to snuggle into River's warm body.

"Is everything okay?" she whispered.

"It couldn't be more perfect. I love you, and that's all that matters." I kissed her cheek and surrendered to dreams of our future together.

Epilogue

Six months later, as the spring turned into early summer, Tatum called home on one of her weekly calls. She was delighted to hear that Charlie was doing a remarkable job running the company, and her father only visited once a week. Her mother had also come to terms with Tatum living in Alaska and even agreed to a short visit when her father came to fish. Tatum ended the call with a deep sigh as she and Poe watched River chop wood. Life was good. Life was very, very good.

About the Author

Ali Spooner

Ali Spooner lives in beautiful northwest Florida with several fur babies. Ali's writing began as a hobby, and with the assistance of the Affinity Rainbow Publishing team, her love of storytelling has advanced to a new level.

Ali's characters are primarily everyday people, from cowgirls to psychics. Ali also has created a few supernatural characters in her paranormal series. Several of her thirty-plus books have been Amazon-rated number one choices and always include a happily ever after. Ali's hobbies include photography, reading, travel, college sports, and spending time with family and friends.

OTHER AFFINITY BOOKS

<u>Love Hacks by Annette Mori</u>

Joy Stiles is adrift. Having finally finished her graduate degree at the National Defense University, the only thing keeping her interest is an ongoing feud with a fellow hacker to gain access to sensitive information. Against all odds, the person snuck their way into her tech and kept leaving taunting messages. It's driving Joy crazy. She doesn't have time for this. Operation Elephant Bites isn't working as The Organization thought it would when they started down that path two years ago. Now they have a new worry. Someone is desperately trying to find out more about The Organization, believing they are behind the attacks on the mines. Whoever that person is has not only ties to the Chinese and Russian governments but also members of the US Government. Top secret files at the NSA call their unknown group The Crusaders. Joy's efforts to uncover the identity of the enemy lead The Organization to a lot more than evil plans, and it's up to The Next Generation, with support from senior members of The Organization, to thwart the inevitable trajectory, perhaps with the assistance of Joy's irritating foe.

Strength Within by Mia Barnes

Samantha Wilson is an award-winning freelance writer with a passion for being the voice of others. Despite vowing never to go back, she returns to Milwaukee, Wisconsin, for an assignment. Her return awakens memories that force her to confront her sad and lonely childhood, including the violent attack she'd rather forget. Moving away and making a quiet, successful solo life for herself, leaving the life she knew behind cannot keep Sammie from facing her past.

Fortunately, her best friend, Zoë, flies in from New Mexico to be by her side while she confronts the demons of her past. Sammie has a knack for helping others find their happy endings. Will she finally let Zoe help her become whole again and maybe discover her happy ending in the process?

Mom's Last Wish by Charlene Neil

After fifteen years away from home, Lucy Donald receives an email from her mother's personal assistant, Cameron Bishop, compelling her to return. Soon after Lucy's arrival, threatening letters start to appear, and Lucy realizes her life is in actual danger. She seeks comfort in the arms of the alluring Cameron Bishop, but can Cameron really be trusted?

Lucy's return home and the events that unfold lead to an intense and suspenseful atmosphere.
Left to uncover the mysteries by herself, she finds herself grappling with the dilemma of not knowing whom to trust.

The Next Generation by Annette Mori

Despite Toni's legendary brilliance, even she could not stop the march of time. After learning her daughter, Joy, and Joy's two best friends, Pepper and Alina, attempted to deceive the senior agents in The Organization with a bogus Spring Break cover story, she convinces her wife it's time to let the Next Generation take over.

The last thing Pepper Maggio expects after agreeing to lead a mission is literally running into the woman she's followed for years. Not only is Grace Turner beautiful, but she's a passionate crusader for the same innocents that The Organization vows to protect. Along with her two best friends, the three young women embark on an adventure to save the day. But the mission quickly gets out of hand as the human traffickers target not only Grace and her film crew, but also the young Mexican woman who managed to catch Alina's eye. Maria might be the bravest of the bunch as a survivor of one of the Mexican mines, but she's a sitting duck if they don't intervene. They might be the Next Generation, but they'll need the full support of The Organization, including Pepper's lethal mother, Val, to get out of Mexico alive.

Turn the Page by Ali Spooner

Continue the journey with Whit and Eli in this final installment of the Cast Iron Farm series. The brilliance of their twins, Mack and Zack, rapidly develops, challenging Whit and Eli to keep up with their education. Their sensitivity to others and kindness are far beyond their youth and a testament to the family's efforts to help them grow into young adults. In addition to more adventures, a budding romance, and wedding bells ring for the Fortner family once more as a new generation begins life on Cast Iron Farm.

A Breath of Scandal by S Anne Gardner

Adele Visconti, Contessa de Caravagio, is passionate and wild and doesn't know the meaning of the word no. One day by chance she turns her head and in a very old cliché fashion she sees a face across the expanse of a Polo field and goes to meet it. Unknowingly this would change her life forever.

When Gillian meets Adele, she is in a committed relationship. The last thing she wanted was to be sucked into the maelstrom that is Adele. However, Adele was something that she could not fight against and her world was turned upside down from the moment they met.

Will their relationship survive against a tide of intrigue, manipulations, passion, family, and most importantly reconnecting the magic of their love for each other.

The Sky People by Ali Spooner

After a beautiful wedding, Eli and Whit return to plan the next phase of their relationship. Whit discovers the identity of her father, and he shares a future with her that will change life on Cast Iron Farm forever. Twins bless the Fortner family, and Eli shares a special secret with Mitch, who bonds with the children in a unique way. Ride along as the Fortners begin a new chapter of their story.

Love Bonds by Annette Mori

When Mila Thompson, a rookie police officer, discovers her mother is missing, she engages the assistance of San Diego's number one detective, who is more than a little reluctant to enter the fray, noting she works in homicide, not missing persons.

Bernie doesn't play well with others, which is why she doesn't have a partner at work or in her personal life. When Mila approaches her, she tries hard to refuse the request, but Mila will not accept no for an answer. For reasons she does not understand, Bernie doesn't want to say no to Mila, who can charm her way into anything, including smoothing the rough edges of Bernie's crusty heart.

Things get complicated when the women in The Organization have an unusual tie to Mila's mother. This sets up an action-packed adventure with twists and turns and a healthy dose of love. Find out the future of The Organization and whether an unlikely pair can find their way to love.

Holy Water and Whiskey Scars by Ali Spooner

Faith Wilson and Logan Bronson have family secrets to protect and a legacy to uphold to support their small rural Appalachian community. Their commitment to each other is strong, and their desire to aid the struggling families however they can, lead them both down an exciting but dangerous path. Will their love continue to grow and be the glue that binds the community together, or will they flee the withering community?

Affinity
Rainbow Publications

eBooks, Print, Free eBooks

Visit our website for more publications available online.

https://affinityebooks.com/

Published by Affinity Rainbow Publications
A Division of Affinity eBook Press NZ LTD
Canterbury, New Zealand

Registered Company 2517228